THE BEST MISTAKE

COOKIE O'GORMAN

Southern U O'Brien Brothers Series

Ordering Information:
For details on quantity orders for educational or business purposes, please visit the author's website at http://cookieogorman.com.

The Best Mistake / Cookie O'Gorman. -- 1st ed.
ISBN 978-0-9978174-4-7

To Susan Elizabeth Phillips, Julia Quinn,
Mom, Pat, and Colleen

&

To anyone who brings a paperback to a
party

This one's for you

1

Honor

Did all frat houses smell like beer, sweat and regret?

Tonight was my first—and hopefully last—college party, so I didn't know. Could've been that guys of Omega Beta thought everyone in the room was just too drunk to notice. And maybe they were. Earsplitting bass pumped through the walls, rattling my bones, as I took in the room. I was pretty sure that guy in the corner was peeing in a potted plant, two girls were grinding on a human banana (no lie, someone came dressed like a banana), and one girl just nearly puked on my (borrowed) red shoes as she made a mad dash to the bathroom.

I shook my head. This was *so* not my scene.

"Honor, you've gotta relax."

I raised a brow. "Who says I'm not?"

Charlie, my roommate and best friend since birth, rolled her ice blue eyes. "First, you've been hugging that stretch of wall since the moment we got here. Second, you've got this deer-in-headlights look that I recognize from grade school. It means you're about to bolt."

"I'm not," I lied.

"Yeah, right," Charlie said. "I see you gripping your copy of *Jane Eyre*."

I instantly eased my grip on the paperback.

"Chill out, girl. As far as college parties go, this one's pretty tame."

I looked over to the makeshift dance floor and the writhing mass of bodies. The level of grinding was escalating by the second. *Where did girls learn to move like that?* I wondered. Had I missed some required course called *Pole Dancing 101*?

"Tame?" I asked. "Really?"

"Yeah," she said, "which you'd know if you hadn't waited until now to break out of your hermit's cave."

"That's not fair. I go out sometimes."

She gave me a look. "The library doesn't count."

"How could it not count?" I asked. "It's one of my favorite places, and I get to spend time with all of my favorite people. Besides you and Rose, of course."

"*Fictional* friends." Charlie shook her head. "Don't lump us in with them."

"And?" I said back. "Fictional people are awesome. Real people often suck. It's an indisputable fact."

Charlie's sigh seemed to rise up from her feet. "And that right there is proof you have no social life."

I frowned, looking down. My eyelids felt heavy with all the mascara I was sporting, my lips slick with gloss. Charlie had straightened my hair to within an inch of its life. The glossy dark brown strands falling against my face looked like they belonged to someone else. I felt like an impostor in my own body.

"Honor, I thought tonight was supposed to be about busting out, taking chances."

"It was," I said. This night had a lot riding on it. "It *is*...but you know how I get nervous in strange, new places."

Charlie nodded, fluttering her lashes at a rocker-type who'd been surreptitiously eyeing her since we'd arrived almost an hour ago. Jet black hair, brooding expression, beer in one hand, acoustic guitar in the other, he was staring at Charlie like he was starving. For her. But he hadn't come over yet, which was enough to pique her interest.

"Seriously, Charlie? Not another musician," I said.

"See how he's pretending like he hasn't noticed me?" She tilted her head. "That's so cute."

"Didn't you get enough self-absorbed, gloomy poetry from the last guy?"

She smiled as Rocker Guy finally rose to cross the room. "The last one was lead singer," she said. "This one might actually be good with his hands."

I groaned.

"And what do you care anyway? I thought you were here for one reason and one reason only. You should be over there getting cozy with Baylor O'Brien, not here salting my game."

True enough. O'Brien was the sole reason I had come tonight. After hearing so many stories about the legendary playboy—and his many, *many* conquests—I figured he was the one guy guaranteed to solve my little issue.

If only I could work up the lady balls to approach him.

As if she'd read my mind, Charlie said, "Just take him by the hand, lead him upstairs, and say: I'm a twenty-one-year-old virgin, and I need you to have sex with me. Immediately."

Good grief.

Eyes wide, voice low, I said, "Charlie, not everyone here needs to know about The Plan. Try to keep it down, okay?"

Pushing her long dirty blonde hair over one shoulder, Charlie laughed. "He's a sure thing, honey. Baylor O'Brien is God's walking, talking gift to women. Far as I know, he never says no and always leaves his partners more than satisfied."

This wasn't news. It was exactly why I'd chosen him. "That's what Anna in my Stats class said. And Clara in Business Accounting...and Jeanette."

"Then what's the problem?" she said. "He's hot, easy, and I know you're packing protection. You've still got the condom I gave you, right?"

I nodded, very aware of the little foil packet currently in the confines of my modest B cup. The edges bit into my skin. Like Hester Prynne and her scarlet letter, I had a Trojan horse stamped on my left breast. With the ridiculously tiny dress, there was no other place for it.

"And for God's sake, are you ever going to take that coat off? It's like a hundred degrees in here."

"I will in a minute," I mumbled.

"You said that forty minutes ago."

I had. "Well, I'm working up to it."

"You said that, too." Charlie sighed—then shot a smile at Rocker Guy who'd finally reached us.

"Hey," he said in a gravelly smoker's voice. "I'm Vayne."

Figures, I thought.

"Hey yourself," Charlie said, "I thought you were just gonna stare at me all night and never come over."

"Well, you're so beautiful for a second I thought this might be a dream."

"Cute," she said, reaching for his beer. "May I?"

"Sure thing, sugar." Vayne grinned. "What's mine is yours."

She smiled at him, slowly running the edge of the bottle against her lips. "Thanks."

Vayne followed the movement, eyes entranced as she took a small sip.

"And it's Charlie, not sugar."

He was so awestruck he didn't notice her slight frown, how her eyes suddenly lost interest. But I did. I'd seen it too many times to count. Vayne/Rocker Guy didn't have a chance with my best friend now. He'd made it too easy. Shaking my head, I had to give it to her. Charlie was a master at this whole seduction thing. Too bad I wasn't more like her. If so, I might never have been in this situation.

Shifting her eyes to me, she said, "Honor, are you sure you still want to do this?"

"Do what?" Vayne said, but we both ignored him.

"Because if not, that's totally cool," she added.

"I'm sure," I said, hoping I sounded more confident than I felt. The Plan had been my idea, after all, and I did want this.

"Then take off the coat. I'm not going to ask you

again."

"It's actually kind of cold in here," I said, faking a shiver. "I think I'll just wait another—"

"21 years?" she finished. "Sorry, don't think so."

"Charlie!" I shrieked as she directed a small spray of beer my way. I scrambled out of the coat, holding my book out, checking it frantically for damage. "What the heck was that for?"

"Just giving you a jump start."

The book was safe, thank God, but the coat was a lost cause. Did beer stain? I wondered, watching the liquid drip to the floor, glad it hadn't gotten on my skin. It was only a small amount. I'd admittedly over-reacted because of my beloved book. But the smell was awful, and I still didn't understand why people drank it. "What do you mean jump start?"

Charlie shrugged as I shot her a glare. "You now have the attention of every guy in here, including the O'Briens."

"Huh?"

It wasn't until that moment I realized two things: Charlie was right. Everyone in the living room had stopped what they were doing to stare at the crazy, flailing girl in the corner. And if that wasn't horrifying enough, without the protection of my outer layer, I was now completely exposed. The red mini dress Charlie had convinced me to wear wouldn't quite reach mid-thigh no matter how much I tugged. The V in front seemed a lot more risqué than it had in my bedroom, and I still wasn't convinced that high heels weren't torture devices. I tucked my hair behind my ear. Why couldn't they just look away already?

"Smile, dammit," Charlie muttered.

I forced a smile while adjusting the much-too-short dress.

"And stop fidgeting. They're staring because they like what they see."

"Really?" I asked, taking in the faces again.

Even if their last name hadn't been written across the back of their jerseys, Charlie had taught me how to spot an O'Brien. Broad shoulders, sharp jaw, dark-golden-brown hair and the most unusual, piercing gray eyes. They were all man, and their pure masculinity made any female glad to be a woman.

Actually Charlie's exact words were, "They're hot as hell. One look and you'll go up in flames."

Having four pairs of those gray eyes on me was unsettling.

I didn't know which one of these guys was Baylor—and that was a problem. I mean, how was I supposed to offer up my V-card if I couldn't tell one O'Brien from another? They were all "hot as hell" in their own way.

The first brother I noticed was leaned back against the fireplace, flicking his lighter open then closed, a curl to his lips as he watched me. Or actually, that could've been from the scar. As I watched, he flipped that lighter again, the flame highlighting a scar that ran from his temple to the corner of his lower lip, pulling it up just slightly. I knew in my head the imperfection should make him less attractive.

It didn't.

Hair close-cropped to his scalp, silver earrings and a tattoo peeking out from the collar of his jersey completed the whole bad boy image. He lifted a brow, his grin turning a bit wicked, and I swallowed. Nope. I was so not ready for that. Unable to hold his gaze a second longer, I looked away...

...and immediately caught sight of another O'Brien.

This one was sitting in a recliner off to the side. He wasn't any less attractive, but he was a whole heck of a lot less intimidating. Maybe it was the clean-cut, all-American look—fresh face and windblown hair—that contrasted so greatly with his brother's. It could've been the small smile he flashed me, as if to say, "Hey, it's alright. Everyone gets a beer to the chest at some point." It was probably the book resting in his lap. Yeah, I thought, definitely the book. I returned his smile instantly recognizing a kindred spirit, a fellow bookworm.

God, I hoped this was Baylor.

A flush stained his cheeks, and he quickly

lowered his gaze. I frowned. Nothing I'd heard about Baylor "Take-Me-to-the-Bedroom" O'Brien made me think he'd blush at...well anything let alone a little smile. Come to think of it, no one had mentioned a scar either.

A sudden feeling drew my attention to the other side of the room. I couldn't really explain it. It was hot like electricity, something magnetic. My eyes searched for the source of that strange pull—and clashed with gray.

My breath caught.

It was like looking into the heart of a storm, intense, powerful. I hadn't gone up in flames for any of the others, but this guy... Well, this O'Brien who was staring at me—devouring me—with those unusual gray eyes, wearing a frown like he never smiled, a stare so focused I thought he might be memorizing every move I made? Or reading my mind?

"Wow," I said, voice nothing but a shaky exhale.

This guy caused a slow burn inside me. I wanted to run. Either to him or away, I wasn't sure. But as his eyes traveled the length of my body, all the way down to my shoes, and back up again to meet my gaze, everything inside me turned to wildfire. I licked my lips, thighs clenching together instinctively.

His frown deepened, jaw tight.

And that made him seem even sexier.

Dangerous, my mind whispered, ignoring my tingling girly bits.

This brother could *not* be the one, I decided, hoped really. Anyone who made me feel this out of control was out of the question. I wanted one wild night. I wanted passion and heat, something to remember. What I didn't want was someone who would ruin me for all other men.

And this guy could.

I knew it just by looking at him.

That was why I broke the connection, looked away, as a hand landed on his broad shoulder. Following that arm up to its owner, the first thing I saw was a playful grin. I remembered this O'Brien because he'd done a keg stand minutes ago that had everyone cheering. He was a dead ringer for the bookworm. They could've been twins, probably were, one good and one devious. Two girls were plastered to his sides, but I couldn't care less. I was trying too hard not to look at his scowling brother. Shooting me a wink, he leaned down to whisper something—which made the other man stiffen, ripping his eyes off of me.

"Looks like you're approved."

Glancing at Charlie, I said, "Approved?"

She smiled. "At this point, you could have your pick of the O'Briens in the house. Told you that dress was a knockout."

"You did."

"Well?"

I gulped. "Well what?"

Charlie rolled her eyes as Vayne tried to put an arm around her. "We didn't come here just to look at the scenery, Honor. You remember the plan?"

I nodded, but my head would not shut up. Was I really ready for this?

"You remember everything we practiced?"

Another nod, but Charlie seemed to pick up on my mood. Shaking Vayne off, she stood in front of me, looking straight into my eyes, hands on hips.

"Tell me the three S's."

"Charlie—"

"Come on, Honor, I gave you all my best tips," she said. "Now let's go: What are you?"

"Sexy, smoldering, seductive," I muttered.

"Damn right." Charlie nodded. "And what's our mantra?"

I repeated the words she'd said to me tonight as we were getting ready. "All good girls need to experience a bad boy once in their lives."

"And do you want that experience?"

"Yes," I said with more conviction.

"Do you want it with a guy who we have on good authority is a great lover? One who never gets attached? One who is sure to leave you more than satisfied?"

"Hell yes," I breathed.

She gestured to the two brothers standing by the

staircase. "Then get your butt over there and introduce yourself to Baylor."

The thought had me shaking in my high heels. So, it wasn't the scarred one or the bookworm. *Don't let it be the one with the sexy frown. Don't let it be him. Not him, not him, not him.* I crossed my fingers before asking the question I feared but knew had to be asked.

"Which one is he?" I said.

Charlie gave me a vaguely pitying look. "The hot one, honey."

I shook my head. "They're all hot."

"True, true," she said then glanced back over to the brothers. "He's the one with the vodka. Now go have some fun, Honor. That's what this is, wild, sexy, impulsive." She lowered her voice. "And make sure he gives you at least one absolutely mind-blowing orgasm."

"That's just wrong." I shook my head.

"You're right," Charlie added. "With his rep, he should at least give you two."

I laughed despite myself, glancing back over my shoulder just in time to see some girl yell, "Baylor!" before suctioning her lips to the O'Brien who'd been frowning at me from across the room. My blood stilled as I noticed the half-empty vodka bottle in his hand.

Oh goodness.

Pushing the girl away, he said one last thing to

his grinning brother, who just shook his head, then began to make his way up the stairs.

On the third step, he glanced back, his gaze unerringly finding mine. The heat, the pull, it was all still there. But now, he was the first to look away, continuing his trek up the stairs and to what I assumed was his dorm room.

Last door on the left, according to Charlie.

I didn't even want to know how she knew that—though she had assured me, in no uncertain terms, that she'd never done anything with Baylor. *Too easy, not enough challenge*, she'd said. Great news for me because I wasn't looking for a challenge. I was looking for a sure thing—and he was getting away.

Now or never, Honor.

Tugging down my dress a final time, I made my way to the stairs, carefully so I wouldn't trip in the dang heels. It was slow going, but that gave me enough time to work up some courage.

So, this was Baylor. The guy whose scowl had made my blood hot from across the room. That was a good thing, right? I didn't know much, but I knew sex was theoretically better if you were attracted to your partner. This was just one night with a super hot guy. A steamy, meaningless fling that would induct me into what Charlie called The Wonderful World of Sex. I couldn't have a better, more experienced teacher than Baylor O'Brien.

One night with the playboy.

What could possibly go wrong?

2

Archer

Seriously, why me?

This night needed to end, ASAP, before I killed one of my brothers. I'd nearly punched Baylor. Fists-clenched, nostrils-flaring, I'd almost hauled off and punched the idiot. I mean, yeah, it wasn't the first time I'd wanted to smack him. I'd wanted to do that nearly every day since he turned into a little brat at the age of 13, who loved talking back and looking up girls' skirts. But now that Baylor was an "adult," his particular brand of stupid had evolved. The girls were still there; that hadn't changed. But now he'd added alcohol to the mix— lots of it—too much, and that loosened his tongue, obliterating his already non-existent filter, making him say a whole lot of stupid. Despite all that, tonight was the first time I'd ever come close to losing it.

Had to be the girl, I thought.

There was no other explanation.

Walking to the end of the hall, I closed myself in my room, sat heavily on the bed, elbows on knees. *I should be downstairs looking out for my team.* I shook my head. Those guys needed a babysitter 24/7. And being Captain meant the responsibility was all mine.

Yippee.

Not that I wasn't used to it. Being the oldest of six, I'd always been looked to as the responsible one. The sensible one. The one who'd bring my brothers back from the brink whenever they got out of control—which they seemed to be doing a lot more recently.

Instead of relaxing on weekends, I got to break up fights if it was Dex. The fourth oldest in our O'Brien clan was always getting into trouble. People saw his face, the scar, and thought he was a badass. Girls wanted to fix him. Guys wanted to fight him. What's worse? The guy seemed to like it.

Then I had the twins to worry about—well, one twin. Baylor was a hot mess. He loved to party; he loved to drink; he loved girls. All were present here tonight, and for Baylor, it was the trifecta of doom. I didn't even want to think about what was going on downstairs.

Thank God for Chase, I thought.

17

At least I didn't have to worry about him getting piss-your-pants drunk or ending up with a broken nose. Unlike his twin, Chase made me nervous for an entirely different reason. The guy was a junior in college, and where Baylor had added way too many notches to his bedpost, Chase had exactly zero. Nada. No dates, no girlfriends, nothing. Wasn't that girls didn't find him attractive, but the guy turned them away, didn't give one a second look. Chase'd told me he believed in "soulmates," and he'd know her when he found her.

But he was downstairs reading for crying out loud.

At a frat party.

Giving my head another shake, I looked down at the vodka bottle in my hand. The thing was nearly empty thanks to Baylor. I could still hear the words he'd said before I finally managed to confiscate it from him. In my head, the scene played back in perfect HD.

"Whoa, never seen her before."

I grunted, too busy staring at the girl in the red dress.

"Nice choice, brother." I could hear the grin in Baylor's voice, but didn't respond.

Who was she? I wondered. My gaze traveled over her, doing a slow up and down, even though I knew I shouldn't. Long, silky-looking hair, sweet hourglass figure, and eyes that captured mine, made my chest tight.

Made other parts of my anatomy tight, too.

I frowned.

A girl like that didn't belong here around these jerks. Yeah, a lot of the guys were my teammates. None of them bad guys per se. Okay, maybe one or two were Neanderthal material. But all of them liked to party and most used their jock status to hook up. And yeah, I'd seen her eyes linger on two of my brothers—which annoyed the hell out of me—before she'd looked my way. But this was no place for someone so, so...innocent.

"Hey Arch, whenever you're done imagining her naked, feel free to use my room."

The words had me whipping around to Baylor so fast I might've pulled something.

The idiot shrugged despite my glare. "Just trying to be helpful."

"Yeah. Thanks," I said. "You do know it's my room, too, right?"

"Well, I use it more," Baylor said, "so de facto, it's mine."

"Don't use big words when you're drunk, brother."

"Whatever. Just use the room. That's what bros are for, right?" He raised the bottle of vodka to his lips. "I got your back, especially when it comes to getting laid."

"Alright, that's it." I ignored the squeak he made

as I snatched the bottle out of his hand. "I'm cutting you off."

"But...wha...you—"

I gave him the hard stare. "You've had more than enough. Wouldn't want you to piss your pants in front of your fangirls."

"That was one time," Baylor huffed, "and it wasn't even a lot of pee."

The two girls hanging onto him giggled like lunatics but clutched him closer.

He winked. "I'll be with you ladies in a second."

Good God, I had to get out of here.

Baylor grabbed my arm before I could leave, leaned in and said, "Look around, man. Everyone's having a good time except you. And here you stand, looking like someone pissed in your lemonade. Why can't you just relax?"

Because you're too relaxed, I thought. *Because if I let down my guard for just one freaking second, one of my brothers could end up in the emergency room.*

It hadn't happened yet, but with Baylor and Dex's I-don't-give-a-crap attitude, I lived in fear of the day it did.

"We done here?" I said.

"Seriously, how long's it been since you got some?"

Before I could tell him to back off, this girl threw herself at me, thinking I was Baylor, too plastered to tell the difference. My brother did nothing to help. He just stood there, grinning.

Again: why me?

I managed to free myself and was about to head upstairs, when Baylor said, "You need to get laid, Archer. The sooner the better."

Couldn't say I disagreed.

I hadn't answered Baylor's question—and I never would—but it had been a while for me. A looooong while. I'd say, besides my saint of a brother, Chase, I was probably the most sexually *inactive* person on the team. Between games, course work, taking care of my siblings, I hadn't had the time. Girls were great, but I didn't want a different hookup every night. That life just didn't appeal to me. Baylor had a short attention span and valued quantity over quality. I was a one-woman kind of guy. Now, I just needed to find the right one.

Upstairs, alone in my and Baylor's room, I chucked the vodka in the trash, closed my eyes...and saw red.

Damn.

I could still see her in my mind. Could recall every detail about the girl in the red dress with perfect clarity. Even with the loud music, she'd cut through the noise. She was beautiful. She was hot. And she'd been looking at me...right up until I left.

Running my hands through my hair, I sighed heavily.

Now, she'd probably end up going off with one

of my teammates.

Or one of my brothers.

Just the thought made me feel ill.

"Ah, fuck," I said, flopping back on the bed.

A sound near the door drew my attention. Squinting, I turned my head, thought I might've been seeing things, but no. Like something out of a dream, the girl in the red dress stepped into the room and quietly closed the door behind her.

Reaching for the lamp, I sat up, clicked it on...

And yeah, she was still here.

"Hi," I said when she just stood there, something small and square resting in her right hand.

She took a deep breath, seeming to steel herself. And damn my eyes, I had to fight to keep my gaze on her face. She was even more beautiful up close.

"Are you looking for someone?"

After a moment, she nodded and met my gaze. "You."

"Me?" I repeated like some kind of idiot.

"Yes," she said. "I've been looking for you all night actually."

When something amazing like this happens, you're not supposed to question it. I knew that. I did. Hell, it wasn't something that happened every day: girl you've been dreaming about literally appears seconds later. But I had to ask, "Do we know each other?"

"No," she said, a small smile on her lips, "but we

will after tonight."

I swallowed. "That sounds good."

Right as the words left my lips, I felt like a fool, but her laugh was like music to my ears. The swaying of her hips as she crossed the room distracted me completely. There was no room for embarrassment. I was too focused on her slow movements toward the bed.

"Those are nice shoes," I said, noticing the red hot heels.

"Thanks," she said, taking another step, "they're—"

A gasp left her lips as she seemed to trip on air, started to fall, but my reflexes kicked in, honed from years of baseball practice. Something fell to the floor, but it barely registered. I was there in a heartbeat, catching her in my arms, her hands gripping my biceps for dear life.

"Easy there," I mumbled, the feel of her cheek on my chest nothing short of amazing. "You were saying...about the shoes?"

"Borrowed," she finished, frowning as she regained her footing. "They're obviously not mine which is why I almost faceplanted. Stupid heels. I swear they have it out for me."

I felt my lips twitch—which was odd for me. I hardly ever smiled, but it was hard not to laugh.

"Thanks," she mumbled, peeking up from beneath her lashes. "For catching me."

"No problem," I said.

She looked down, a blush rising to her cheeks, and I tilted her chin back up to meet my gaze. I was still at least a head taller than her even with the sky-high heels.

"We should probably sit down though. You know, in case the shoes decide to make another attempt on your life."

Rolling her eyes at herself, she took my hand and led me the rest of the way to the bed. We were nearly there when she tripped—again. This time she was in front of me, so there was nothing else to do. I twisted, hoping to stop us both from going down, and ended up plopping on the bed with mystery girl landing right in my lap.

"Ugh," she said, ducking and shaking her head. "I am so not good at this."

I had to disagree. If "this" meant making me curious as heck about her while turning me on at the same time, she was doing a damn find job. I had to know who she was.

"What's your name?" I asked.

She looked up. "Why do you want to know? You going to tell all your friends downstairs about this, the girl who trips over nothing, the one who tried and failed so miserably to seduce you?"

I had to laugh at that. "First, you tripped over this," I said, leaning down to grab the thing she'd stumbled over. It was a book, and as I held it up, I saw her eyes widen. "This must be yours? It's not mine, and I'm pretty sure my brother's never read Brontë in his life. Second, we've known each other less than five minutes, and you're already in my lap." She blushed again, and I had to stop myself from kissing her right then. She just looked so dang kissable. "I think you're doing pretty well on the seduction front."

"Honor," she said softly.

"What was that?" I asked.

"My name," she said, her eyes meeting mine as she took the book and placed it in her lap. "It's Honor. Nice to meet you."

I felt the corners of my lips turn up. "Honor," I repeated, testing the name on my tongue. "That's beautiful. It's nice to meet you, Honor. I'm—"

She cut me off by placing two fingers against my lips.

"I know who you are," she said, seeming to regain some of her courage. "That's why I'm here."

I raised a brow.

"I've heard a lot about you, how experienced you are, and I was hoping you could help me with something."

Pushing her hand away, I said the first thing that came to mind. "Anything. I'll help you however I can."

She took a deep breath.

"Would you...be willing to sleep with me?"

I blinked, thinking I must've misheard.

"Excuse me?" I said. "I think I just hallucinated. Could you repeat that again?"

Her face was redder than ever, and she looked so embarrassed it made me think I'd understood perfectly. Still... There was no way she'd just said *that*.

"I—" she gulped, voice whisper-thin, "I was hoping to have a one-night stand. With you. Would you sleep with me? Please?"

My jaw dropped, and I could only stare.

"This was a mistake," she mumbled, starting to stand, avoiding my eyes. "I can't believe I just... Geez, what the heck? I'm sorry for putting you in such an awkward position—"

"I'll do it," I said suddenly.

She stopped. "You will?" she said in surprise.

I nodded. Hell yeah, I would.

"But you seemed really not into it a second ago."

"Oh, I'm in," I said. "I'm so in. You just shocked the hell out of me."

"Oh," she said, smiling a shy smile. "Well...thank you."

"You're welcome," I said, feeling like this was all a dream, but again, who was I to question it? Obviously, I must've done something good in my life. Here was a girl, one who I was really freaking attracted to, and she'd just asked me to sleep with her.

Turning to me, eyes full of wonder, she said, "So, how should we do this?"

"Well," I said, sliding one hand up her back, the other to her cheek, loving it when she shivered, "I'm going to kiss you. If that's okay?"

She nodded, her hands coming to grip my waist, and that was the green light I needed.

My mouth was on hers in an instant.

Warmth like I'd never felt before, puzzle pieces fitting together, fireworks and all that romantic crap I'd ever seen in movies but never thought was real, I felt it all at once. My lips glided over hers, and she pressed back with a sweetness I couldn't deny. Not that I wanted to.

I'd never known lips could be so soft.

Honor tilted her head with a sigh as I deepened the kiss, my hands pulling her closer. She was already leaning into me, but I couldn't get enough. Her body was just as soft as her lips, her curves molded to my frame perfectly.

And the sounds she was making.

Those breathy sighs would've brought a lesser man to his knees. Actually, it was probably a good thing I was already seated. Her nails raked my scalp down to my shoulders, and it awakened my inner caveman. That was the only explanation for what happened next. One second, I was kissing her softly, exploring that sweet mouth. The next, I'd flipped her around in one smooth motion, and with a squeak, she was suddenly straddling my lap, a knee on either side of my hips.

And through all of that, I never stopped kissing her.

Never wanted to. I was convinced it would take an act of God to pry my lips from her body—or her saying no, of course. She'd stilled in my lap, and when I looked up, she was staring at me, those big brown eyes of hers wide.

"Do you want to stop?" I asked, fearing the answer. I'd never been this hot for a girl this quickly. But if she'd changed her mind, I'd stop in a heartbeat.

"No, definitely not," she said, and I could breathe again. I'd been so afraid I was moving too fast, but the smile in her voice and on her lips put me at ease. "I'm just impressed. Those were some nice moves."

"You're good for my ego," I said.

"Hmm, those other girls weren't lying."

My brow furrowed. "Other girls?" I asked.

"Yeah," she breathed, dropping a kiss on my cheek, jaw, neck and then up the other side. It was having a drugging effect, my eyelids dropping as I tried to make sense of what she said. "You're definitely living up to your reputation."

Her kisses were making me woozy, but still I had to ask.

"Girls talk about me?" I said.

"Oh yeah," she said, running a hand up my cheekbone. "All good things, all the time."

Huh, I thought while kissing her neck, running the tip of my nose behind her ear. As I watched goosebumps appear there, I fought back a smile. This girl was *definitely* good for my ego.

"I didn't know I had that kind of rep," I said. "It's usually my brother who gets all the girls."

"Your brother?" she asked.

"Yeah," I said, placing a kiss against a spot on her neck that made her gasp. "I have a few of those."

"Oh, I know. But my friend Charlie called you the hot O'Brien."

I wasn't going to argue. "Sounds like a smart girl."

"I don't see why anyone would talk about your brother anyway," she said. "You're so good at this."

This girl was something else.

"Honor," I said, voice rough.

"Yeah?" she said.

"No more talking. You good with that?"

She nodded as I got closer to her lips. "Yes, please."

And things escalated from there.

Her hands were everywhere, my chest, shoulders, stomach, her hips pressed tight against mine. I couldn't stop kissing her neck, her mouth, anywhere I could reach. It was like a game of give and take, but all I wanted to do was give her the best night of her life, so she'd want to have me back for another...and another. I never wanted her to forget my name.

My hand traveled up her thigh until it was just beneath the hem of her dress.

"This okay?" I asked between kisses, my fingers brushing against her upper thigh, waiting for the go ahead.

"Yes," she breathed. "Please."

It was the "please" that did it.

My fingers traveled the rest of the way, under her skirt and up to find her core. She was wet already. Damn.

I kissed her deeply, rubbing my thumb in a circular motion against her, slanting my mouth over hers, learning what she liked. Her eyes were shut, cheeks flushed, mouth parted slightly, and I didn't think I'd ever seen anything more beautiful in my life. As she raised her hips to meet the movements of my hand, I nearly exploded. Leaning in, I placed another long kiss against her neck, my other hand supporting her back.

"Oh," she breathed as her movements became faster.

"That's right, Honor," I said. "I've got you."

"I feel like..."

"It's okay," I said again. "I've got you, baby."

She gripped my shoulders, one moving to my neck as she threw her head back. I'd never felt more like a man. Never felt more powerful than in that moment of giving her pleasure. Never felt more proud of myself as she suddenly tensed and stilled, her mouth dropping open. And then...

"Oh Baylor!" she said as she came.

I couldn't believe it.

My hand still between her legs, I froze. "What did you say?"

"Hmm," she said, eyes opening slowly as she came down from her high.

But I knew what she'd said.

I'd heard it loud and clear. *My brother's name.* My freaking brother's name, falling from her lips after a climax that I brought her to. Was this some kind of cruel joke?

As if in answer, two seconds later, the door burst open and in walked my idiot brother with the two girls he'd been toying with downstairs.

"Oh crap," he said, coming to a halt just inside the doorway. "Sorry man, I forgot the room was in use."

As the girls giggled, Honor was mortified. She shot up off my lap, readjusted her dress and ran/hobbled from the room in her high heels, fleeing as fast as she could. The look she gave me over her shoulder as she left was anything but romantic. She regretted it. I could tell. If her disappearing act didn't say enough, the look of horror mixed with humiliation on her face did. But

I regretted it, too, just not for the same reasons.

The name she'd shouted kept replaying on a loop in my head.

"How many times have I told you?" Baylor said, shaking his finger at me. "The sock on the doorknob is a powerful tool, my friend."

My eyes shot daggers at Baylor as he kept talking.

"Congrats though, my brother. It looks like you finally got some. She was a hot one, too, which makes me wonder why she chose you over me, but whatever. It's cool. I guess you need love, too."

Thank God, he hadn't heard, I thought.

If he did, I'd never hear the end of it.

"Can you give me a second?" I said, straightening up, trying to calm myself down.

"No problem," Baylor nodded. "I'll just go use Chase's room. It's not like he's up there anyway."

As the door shut and I was left alone, I couldn't stop thinking about Honor and everything she'd said *before* shouting my brother's name. It was all starting to make sense now. How she'd heard about me and my experience, my well-known rep with girls. So, she'd thought I was Baylor. She'd come here for my playboy brother, not me. The whole time, she'd thought I was him.

I frowned, remembering that first kiss, how she'd felt like my missing piece, how we'd just fit. I wasn't a romantic, but I knew that was a rare thing.

Did it really matter that she'd thought I was someone else? It wasn't Baylor who'd kissed her like that, I thought. It wasn't Baylor who'd made her shiver. And it certainly wasn't Baylor who'd made her come in such an earth-shattering way.

Lying back on the bed, I pulled something from beneath my back and smiled. I'd never been so happy to see a book in my life. The inside flap read—

This book belongs to: Honor Tierney.

If lost, please give it a good home with lots of readerly love and no bent pages.

Grinning, I placed the book on my chest.

Honor had said she wanted a one-night stand, and if the way she'd ran out of here was anything to go by, she wasn't expecting to see me again.

Too bad I wasn't Baylor.

If I was, she might've been right.

But if she thought I'd just let her go without a word when I knew how amazing she was, after an unforgettable night like that, she had another thing coming.

3

Honor

"I can't believe you didn't call me last night," Charlie said.

"Charlie, can we talk later?" I said, walking as fast as I could. "I'm late for a meeting."

"No, you're not. If I know you, you're running at least ten minutes ahead."

Fifteen, I thought. But that was typically when I liked to be wherever I was going. The fact that I was still on my way meant I was behind schedule. I'd hated being late for things ever since I was a kid.

"Well, you know how Walter gets when one of us isn't on time."

She scoffed. "That old coot? I don't think he'd do anything. He looks like a pushover to me. Plus, aren't you like his favorite?"

"Yeah," I said, passing through the doors of the Communications building. "He loves me because I actually try and write good stories—even though nobody reads them. But trust me, Walter is deceptively calculating. He once saw me eating a bacon, egg and cheese biscuit then had me attend a pig auction just so I could write an article from the pig's POV."

"Sounds like a real ballbuster," Charlie said, and I could tell she was rolling her eyes.

I shrugged. "He's a vegetarian. Put me off bacon for the rest of my life."

"But what happened after you went upstairs with O'Brien?" she said.

Everything, I thought. And nothing I wanted to talk about. Good lord, how was I supposed to explain this to Charlie? She'd never had trouble with men. Guys would just roll over for her if she snapped her fingers. I was pretty sure Charlie had never tripped (twice) while trying to hook up with someone, let alone had that awkward moment at the end where his brother walked in on us. Ugh. The only saving grace was at least I'd never have to see Baylor or any of the O'Briens again. It was senior year. We'd never had any classes together, and I figured they were more into sports anyway. Southern University was a big place. The Omega Beta house was across campus from where I lived. There was a very good chance our paths wouldn't cross again.

I frowned. Why did I feel so down about that?

"Hellooo," Charlie said. "Honor, you still there?"

"I'm here," I said, stopping just outside the journalism room.

"Well? You've got to tell me about your hot night with Baylor O'Brien. Are the legends true? Is he a master of the bedroom?"

I closed my eyes, thinking about last night, how his kisses had set every part of me on fire, the way he'd touched me like he couldn't get enough.

"Yeah," I sighed, "it's all true."

Charlie whooped so loud I had to hold the phone away from my ear.

"I knew it!" she said. "I knew he was the one. How does it feel on your first day as a non-virgin?"

"Well...technically," I said, "I'm still a card-carrying member of the V-club."

"What? But I thought you said it was all true. I thought the two of you hooked up. Did he at least give you the O?"

"He did," I said, then lowered my voice. "But we didn't have sex."

"Huh," she said after a moment.

"What's that supposed to mean?"

"It's just...you sounded so dreamy; I was sure you'd gotten some."

I sighed. It wasn't for a lack of trying, I thought. But instead of Baylor simply taking me like I thought he would, his first priority seemed to be making me feel good—which in turn seemed to make him feel good. What kind of player does that?

"Not to be weird or anything," Charlie said, "but this is the first I'm hearing of anyone *not* sleeping with Baylor O'Brien."

"That is totally weird," I said.

"Sorry, but a guy like him doesn't get that kind of rep for nothing. He supposedly goes through girls like water."

"You know that part didn't really seem to fit." My brow furrowed. "He didn't seem like much of a player to me—besides his skills in the bedroom. He was thoughtful and sweet."

"Huh," she said again, "if he was so good, then why stop? Did something happen?"

"Not really." I blushed, memories of the other night flashing through my mind: the moment when the door opened right after such an intimate act, how I tried my best to run away, hindered by Charlie's dang stilettos, my last look at the first guy I'd actually felt a connection with—and that was before we'd done more than kiss.

"Was it the virgin thing?" Charlie said. "I bet it was, right? Guys can be so weird about that sometimes."

"No, Charlie," I hissed. "It wasn't that, okay? It may have had something to do with his brother walking in on us. But to be honest, I'm not sure—"

"Wait, wait," she said, and I could hear the laughter in her voice. "Did you just say his brother walked in? While you guys were...oh my gosh, Honor! Why didn't you say so before?" She howled. "That is priceless! Seriously, I can't...I just..."

I tapped my shoe, waiting on her.

Charlie was laughing so hard. It sounded like she was gasping for breath.

"Well golly gee," I said, "I can't imagine why I didn't tell you, best friend. Especially when you're having such a super reaction."

"Sorry, sorry," Charlie said between laughs. "But can't you see how hilarious this is?"

"Hilarious," I deadpanned, "scarred-for-life, whatever you want to call it."

Charlie tried to pull it together.

"You finished?" I said.

"Yes," Charlie squeaked, obviously trying to hold back. "But can I ask you just one thing?" She was silent a beat then, "What did the brother say?"

I thought back. "He said something about not knowing we were in there and putting a sock on the doorknob—which I didn't really understand, sounds pretty gross, but whatever."

That set my best friend off again.

I rolled my eyes as peels of laughter came through the phone.

"This has been fun," I said, "but I have to go now. Walter's probably got a great assignment just waiting for me."

"He...you...sock," was all she managed.

"See you at home."

Hanging up, I shook my head.

My attempt at a one-night stand had definitely been a bust. But, I thought, pushing through the door to the newsroom, at least I'd have those memories to look back on. Not all of them were bad. In fact, a lot of them were out-of-this-world spectacular. I'd had my one walk on the wild side. Now I could return back to my normal, boring life, writing for the campus newspaper, hanging at the library and watching Netflix in my pjs.

And I'd never have to face O'Brien again.

Which was a good thing, I told myself, even as a pair of gorgeous gray eyes flashed in my mind.

"Honor," Walter said as he spotted me, "there you are, girl! Ooh, I've got a winner for you this time, a story that's sure to rescue this paper from the depths of oblivion."

I smiled. He said this every other week. "Sounds awesome, Walter."

"It sure is," he said, his white whiskers all aquiver. "It's a sports piece mixed with a human interest bent sure to please the masses. I really think it can save us. So, what do you say? Are you in?"

"Of course," I said. "Why wouldn't I be?"

"Wonderful," Walter said. "I've set up an interview for you at the end of the day. I'll send you all the details then."

"Can't wait," I said. I was excited to get started. This was just what I needed to get my mind off of a certain pair of gray eyes. A new project sounded like the perfect distraction.

* * *

This has to be a joke, I thought as I walked to the field.

When Walter had mentioned something about sports, it hadn't raised any red flags. I mean, how many sports teams were there on campus? There was soccer, football, basketball, volleyball, softball...basically everything under the sun with a ball was played here. Not that I followed any of them. But how was I supposed to know that Walter had arranged a meeting with the baseball team?

Our school's title-winning baseball team as it turns out.

He'd sent me the basic info for the article in a text about ten minutes ago. That was around the time I started scanning the details which included players' names and stats...at which point I started freaking out.

Of all the sports in all the world, why did it have to be this one?

Honestly, I got why it would make a great story. This was the first time in the school's history that they'd had four brothers playing on the same team, and said team was in a good way to make it to the national championship (again) under the coaching of the mother of said boys. It doesn't get much more news-worthy than that. But did it have to be these four brothers? And why did I have to be the one covering the story?

Again, I thought for about the millionth time since getting that text. This had to be a joke.

I almost tripped when I noticed the four O'Brien jerseys out there on the field.

Geez, Honor, get a grip.

That was all I needed. A busted ankle in addition to the utter embarrassment of last night. Luckily, I'd come incognito. The last time Baylor O'Brien had seen me I'd been dressed like a pin-up, my hair straightened, my face covered in makeup perfection (courtesy of Charlie). But today, I was back to my old self: baggy t-shirt, jeans, sneakers and my hair pulled back into a ponytail. With the addition of my ball cap and faux glasses, there was a good chance he wouldn't even remember me.

I mean, O'Brien supposedly had a revolving door of female companions. What were the chances that he'd recall one girl, even if she had been his clumsiest conquest?

Standing on the sidelines, I stopped next to a big, burly man that looked important.

"Excuse me," I said, tapping him on the shoulder.

He turned with a scowl, looked me up and

down, and said (growled really), "You need something?"

I swallowed. The tag on his shirt read, Assistant Coach Green, but I was thinking Grouch fit him better.

"Yes, I'm sorry for interrupting your practice. My boss said he contacted you guys. Spoke to Coach O'Brien? I'm Honor from the campus newspaper, and—"

"There's a campus newspaper?" he said.

"Yes," I said. "*The Howler.*"

He grunted. "Never heard of it."

I gave a mental sigh. Wasn't the first time I'd heard that.

"Well, I'm supposed to be interviewing someone from your team. Anyone would do really. How about we start with the second string or whatever you call it?" I said, hoping to avoid a certain someone. "I'll try and be as quick as I can."

Without looking away from me, he blew a whistle then to my horror yelled, "O'Brien!"

My eyes widened as I watched all action on the field cease. Suddenly, four heads turned to look our way. Rolling his eyes, the man said "Captain! This girl wants to talk to you."

One of the broad shouldered players broke away from the group.

As he got closer, I could make out the gold "C" on his jersey, the way his uniform fit him just right, tight enough across the chest and thighs to make a girl weak in the knees. I knew it was one of the O'Brien brothers from what Coach Grouch just shouted. But I found myself hoping it wouldn't be him. My prayers went unanswered. A second later, he stopped in front of us, as gorgeous as last night as he readjusted his cap.

"What's up, Bear?" he said, eyes moving between me and the older man.

He grunted again. "Got a reporter here. Didn't think any of the other hooligans could string two coherent words together after last night."

O'Brien ran a hand across the back of his neck. "It wasn't as bad as all that. I tried my best to keep them under control."

"And you did a great job—for the most part." The man shook his head, hands on hips as he looked over the field. "Bay's not looking so hot out there."

I felt my face fall. *Bay?* Did he mean Baylor? Why would he say that when...

"Now that we've got reporters coming around, you want to tell your brother to clean up his act? Nobody's gonna recruit him if they think he's trouble."

"I know." Those gray eyes were watching me as he responded. "We've had that discussion more times than I can count."

"I get it. Baylor O'Brien is a tough nut to crack," Grouch said, confusing me further. "Worrying about that boy keeps me up at night—not to mention Dex. He's on a whole other level. But you keep at it, Archer. If anyone can convince them to straighten up, it's you."

Archer? My face paled. As in Archer O'Brien, the oldest brother of the O'Brien family, the guy who, according to Charlie, never breaks any rules, always wears a frown, and wouldn't know how to have fun if it kicked him in the face. That Archer?

"You just be glad Coach had an appointment and isn't here to grill you. If she was, all of your asses would be toast."

"Yeah, I know, Bear. She raised me remember?"

As if just realizing I was still there, Grouch said, "Listen girl, I'm fine with the interview, especially if Coach agreed to it."

I'd lost the ability to speak a while ago, so instead I nodded.

"Just don't keep Captain over here too long. This team would fall apart without him."

And then he left me there.

Not with Baylor, I gulped. But with the guy who'd I'd *thought* was Baylor. The brother who I'd so brazenly made a pass at, the one I'd straddled and kissed was actually...

"Archer O'Brien," he said, holding out a hand for me to shake, his eyes shining in the afternoon sun. "Sorry, you had to hear all that."

"No problem," I said, voice paper thin as I took

his hand. I couldn't believe it. Only I could've made such a terrible mistake. Only I, Honor Tierney, bookworm extraordinaire, writing recluse, and apparent virgin-for-life, could've confused one O'Brien brother for another.

But at least he didn't seem to recognize me. I took a deep breath. That was something, I guess. Part of me was bummed, but the other part was incredibly relieved.

"Do I know you from somewhere?" he said. My relief died a quick death, suddenly replaced with panic. "You look familiar."

Heart in my throat, I said, "I don't think so."

He just kept staring at me, eyes narrowed.

After a moment (that felt like an eternity), he nodded.

"Guess you just have one of those faces," he said, releasing my hand, lifting his chin toward the bleachers. "Why don't we go over there, so you can ask your questions?"

"Oh yeah, thanks." I tried not to think about the fact that he was behind me as we walked, tried not to trip because I knew that might jog his memory.

Once we got there, he took the space next to me, not too close, of course. Not like he'd been the one to give me the most amazing kiss of my life. At least as far as he knew.

"So," I began, taking out my notepad and pen, trying to pretend like this was just another interview, nothing special, no reason to be embarrassed. "How long have you played baseball, Archer?"

I watched as one corner of his mouth twitched.

"Since I could walk," he said, leaning back. "Never really wanted to do anything else."

"Have you always played with your brothers?" I asked.

"Yeah, pretty much. Mom and Dad loved the game and passed that love down to us. Baseball has always been a big part of our family."

"So everyone in your family plays?"

"Well, not my little sister," he said. "She's always been a bit of a rebel, but all five of us boys play."

"Five," I repeated. "You have another brother who's not on the team then?"

"Oh yeah, Finn, my youngest brother. He's seventeen, still in high school." Archer nodded. "He's not as into baseball as the rest of us, more of an academic type, but he throws a mean curveball."

"Speaking of which," I said, "did you know this is the first time the University's had four brothers playing on the same team? That's a lot of O'Briens."

"Yeah," he said, "there are quite a few of us. It can be hard to keep track sometimes."

My brow furrowed, wondering if he meant something by it, but he went on.

"Luckily, we're all so different, and our personalities kind of match our positions."

I leaned in, forgetting to take notes. "Oh, how

do you mean?"

"Take Dex," he said, and I looked to where he was gesturing. "He's up to bat right now. Kind of a hothead, but that works if you need someone who'll go up to bat and isn't afraid to swing, even at a nearly unhittable pitch."

I watched as the pitcher threw, and the batter, Dex, got a piece of it, landing it right in center field.

"That was a line drive." Archer pointed to the pitcher now. "And Chase is almost always perfect. He's was born for this, one of the main reasons we're in contention for a national championship. If you wait for him to mess up, you'll be waiting a long time."

Another batter stepped up to the plate, and I watched as Chase pitched him three strikes, one after the other. It was the same story with the next batter. The last one just stood there dumbfounded.

"Up and down," he said. "My brother is a beast on the pitcher's mound. Which brings me to his other half."

I knew there was only one name left I hadn't heard and waited to see what position he played.

"Baylor isn't like the other two," he continued. "He's a little...unpredictable. Some would even say wild."

When the next batter came up to the plate, he did this odd little dance, where he hit one shoe then the other with the end of his bat, swung it around once and then pointed to the outfield. There were groans from his teammates. He was the one who'd done the keg stand, I thought.

"Let's go, Chase," Baylor said from the batter's box as he finally assumed his stance. "I'm not getting any younger over here."

"Cocky, too," Archer added.

The pitcher, Chase, just shook his head at his brother's antics. Took his time, readying the pitch, and fired it off. The sound as the ball collided with the catcher's mitt was loud.

"Strike!" the Grouch said.

"Oh, come on, Bear," Baylor said. "It was high. Anyone could see that was a ball."

"It was a strike," Archer called out. "Stop being such a baby, Bay, and get ready for the next one."

Baylor, for his part, just shot his brother the bird, muttering under his breath as he got back into position.

"Maybe if you hadn't spent all night partying," Chase called, "you'd be able to get a hit off me."

"Oh, I'll get a hit," Baylor said. "Just need you to throw me a clean pitch."

"Stop playing around and bring me in already," Dex shouted from first.

The pitcher shook his head, and as I looked on, he threw a strike right down the middle. The third pitch was fouled out to right field. Each time, Baylor seemed to settle in a bit deeper, leaning in a little more, looking more determined.

"And this is where things get interesting," Archer said to me.

"Really why?" I said.

"Because Baylor hates to lose. And besides me, he's the only one that's ever been able to—"

Just as he was about to finish, a loud crack rent the air. The ball was soaring out of the park before I could even blink, and there was Baylor, celebrating his win with a whoop before rounding the bases.

"—hit a homerun off of Chase," Archer finished.

I turned to him with a smile on my face, watching them together was just too much fun.

"And what position do you play?" I asked.

"Usually catcher," he said, "and third base, but I'm good at bat, can play any position."

I nodded. "You're the best. That's why you're team captain."

"Ah I don't know about all that," he said, and my eyes widened as I thought I saw a blush sweep up his cheeks. "Chase is the real all-star. He could go pro if he wanted to."

"You look like all-star material to me," I said, feeling my cheeks heat as he looked my way, piercing me with his gray eyes.

"You sure we don't know each other?" he said.

"Yep, I'm sure," I said, ducking my head and packing up as quickly as I could. I had enough here for an article. It was time to cut and run.

49

"Because I could have sworn—"

"Nope," I said, getting to my feet. "Like you said before, I just have one of those faces."

Bear blew his whistle then.

"Captain," he said, "if you're done chatting, we need you back over here."

I released a breath. Saved by the Bear (aka Coach Grouch). I owed him one.

"We're done here if you need to go back," I said, still avoiding his eyes. "Thanks. For the interview, I mean. I think we're good."

"No problem," Archer said, "I'm glad you got what you needed."

I had just turned to go when he leaned down, his lips right next to my ear.

"And I like the glasses," he said.

My breath caught as he ran a hand up my arm.

"I didn't think you could look any hotter than you did last night in that red dress, but it's a good look on you. Kind of like a sexy bookworm."

When I turned to look back over my shoulder, his face was right there, close enough to see the small scar bisecting his upper lip.

"And again, the name's Archer," he said, the corners of his lips turning up. "That might be helpful for next time. I'll see you soon, Honor."

As he released me to run back onto the field, I just stood there like an idiot.

So...he remembered.

Not just remembered, he'd recognized me, had known who I was all along.

And had he just called me a sexy bookworm?

And implied there would be a "next time"?

Good grief. I didn't think I could handle that. Nope, I decided. There was only so much awkward one person could take. If I didn't see another O'Brien for the rest of my life it would be too soon.

4

Honor

It didn't hit me until much later.

The full extent of the awkward.

After the interview, I'd retreated to my haven, my favorite place on campus. The library welcomed me with open arms. It was quiet as usual; there were students scattered here and there, but I easily found myself a quiet table, lost in the stacks, where I placed my bag, computer and notepad, sat back and prepared to do my thing. I was on a mission.

You'd think after that practice and my time on the baseball field I'd be ready to escape, and I was. But my escape came in the form of research. I threw myself into it, learning more about baseball and the O'Brien legacy than I ever wanted to know.

I found out that Coach Daisy O'Brien had been with the school for nearly thirteen years. She and her husband, Tyler O'Brien, according to web articles, were two of the best, most well-respected baseball/softball coaches in all of collegiate history.

Until about eight years ago when Tyler O'Brien died after a battle with cancer.

Coach Daisy had taken the reigns of the baseball team after his death and continued to raise her six children on her own. My heart ached for all of them. Despite the tragedy, the Wolves baseball team, under the direction of Coach Daisy, kept winning, earning several bids to nationals.

But the streak hadn't started until four years ago.

That was exactly when Archer O'Brien had joined the team as a freshman, where he broke nearly every baseball record the University had. The Wolves had climbed the ranks, had an awesome season, and finished it with a national championship. Then came the twins, Baylor and Chase. That season they built upon the success of the previous year, winning another championship, and with Chase breaking all of the records Archer had set the year before. Those guys really were born to do this, I thought, reading through the impressive stats, making notes along the way. When Dexter O'Brien joined the team, they took home yet another championship, though this one was hard won since everyone in college baseball seemed to be gunning for them.

Legacy was an understatement, I thought.

These guys and their mother had built a dynasty on that baseball diamond.

And Archer had led them the whole way.

His stats were out of this world, his work ethic supposedly unmatched, and the love he obviously had for his family when he'd spoken about them would've endeared him to me even if he hadn't given me the hottest night of my life. Or called me a sexy bookworm.

I still couldn't believe he'd said that.

I was so engrossed in my article that by the time I glanced at the clock it was already 10:00 pm. Quickly finishing up before sending it off to Walter, I was packing my things, double-checking all the names, when a memory of last night hit me with the force of a wrecking ball.

"Oh no, no, no," I said, then closed my eyes on a groan.

I'd said the wrong name.

Holy wow, I couldn't believe I hadn't realized it before.

Without the haze of pleasure, I recalled everything from that night with perfect clarity. Me, head thrown back, calling out "Oh Baylor" as I...after Archer made me... Ugh, was it possible to die of post-orgasmic embarrassment? Was that a thing?

Because if it was, I was definitely destined for the grave. Oh gosh, what Archer must think of me.

His last words from today replayed in my mind.

And again, the name's Archer. That might be helpful for next time.

His meaning suddenly became clear—and I wanted to die all over again.

How did one apologize for something like this? Was it even okay to bring it up? Certainly I owed him an apology for calling out not just anyone's name, but *his brother's*. Oh Lord, please just kill me now.

After a moment, I forced myself to breath, my heart to calm.

No worries, I thought. I'd completed the interview, turned in my article, and now, the O'Briens would disappear from my life as quickly as they'd entered it. I'd never have to face him again. And, I told myself, I wouldn't speak of that night to another living soul. Though...I knew Charlie would probably wrinkle it out of me. She was my best friend. I'd never been able to keep anything secret from her for long. But besides her, I was determined to never speak of it again. Even if I did still feel kind of bad and want to apologize to Archer. This was it. Case closed.

Time to go home for some ice cream therapy and a little R and R.

* * *

"You didn't," Charlie said, staring at me wide-eyed, the spoon full of Rocky Road paused half-way to her mouth. "Don't mess with me, Honor. You've got to be making this up."

"I wish," I said, taking a bite of chocolatey goodness.

"So let me get this straight," she said, putting her spoon down. "You went upstairs, following the person you thought was Baylor O'Brien. But it turned out it wasn't Baylor but Archer." She looked to me, and after my nod, she continued. "And then after the most glorious make-out session of your life, he gave you an O with just his hand, and you shouted his brother's name right at the moment of climax."

I nodded.

Charlie sat back, shaking her head. "Honor, this is better than a freaking soap opera. You should seriously consider selling your story to *Cosmo* or something."

"Thanks," I said, frowning down at the tub of ice cream. It hadn't taken very much for Charlie to drag the truth out of me. She was good at it sure, but I blamed the ice cream and my guilt. "But do you think I should say I'm sorry?"

"For what?" she said. "It sounds like Archer nearly got off on you getting off—which is a rare trait in a male. I'm jealous that you found such a rare specimen. But seriously, you don't need to apologize."

"Yeah, but I kind of feel like I owe him."

"Hold up, chickadee." She leaned closer, though it was only the two of us in the living room. "You owe this guy nothing, okay? Sure, he was the first person to ever see your O-face."

"Charlie," I said, smacking her with a pillow, but she just laughed.

"It's a really common thing. People say crazy things in the heat of passion."

I tilted my head. "Have you ever said the wrong name?"

"Sure, sure," she said, and I began to relax. "Though I don't think I've ever said the brother's name. That's just you."

I groaned and flopped back.

"I'm kidding," she said. "I'm sure it happens. For real, Honor, don't sweat it."

We both turned as the door opened. It was a little past 1:00 am, but it was normal for Rose to walk in late. Younger than Charlie and me, she was a total night owl.

"Hey ladies," she said, taking a seat next to me on the couch. "I see the ice cream is out. What happened this time, Charlie? Did you finally find a guy who told you no?"

Charlie smiled. "As if," she said, "and this isn't about me. It's all about our little Honor over here and her naughty night out."

"Oh really?" Rose said. She grabbed my spoon then helped herself to some ice cream. We'd been living together for a while and weren't weird about things like that. "Tell me more. Work sucked, as usual, and I could use a good distraction."

I shot her a frown. "Don't you have to get some sleep?"

Rose shrugged. "Not really. I'll sleep through the afternoon like always and wake up for my night classes, go straight to work at the tattoo parlor from there. These are like my peak hours of wakefulness."

"Ooh, can I tell her?" Charlie said. "Please, please, can I tell her about you and the brothers?"

"Brothers," Rose repeated with a smile. "Well, this just got more interesting."

With a sigh, I nodded. "But only if you try not to laugh at the embarrassing bits."

"Yes!" Charlie fist-pumped. "And I promise no laughter—or very little laughter, like the most miniscule amount I can manage."

"I promise nothing." Rose held her hands out. "I'll try not to laugh, but you know, I'm always a little punchy at this time of night. Plus, I have no idea what I'm in for."

"Oh, it's good," Charlie said with a grin. "Trust me."

"Can't wait. Oh and don't forget girls, our new roommate moves in tomorrow. Someone else has to be up to greet her because I'm probably going to be out like a light."

"No problem," I said. "We'll both be here."

Charlie waved her hands in the air. "Yes, yes, we'll be here. But Rose, just wait until you hear about Honor's night of debauchery. It's so much fun. I can't even."

Shaking my head, I watched as Charlie re-told Rose everything that'd happened. Even I found myself laughing a bit at her enthusiasm. We made it through about half the tub of ice cream before the three of us called it a night. Before going to bed, Rose took me aside and said, "Listen Honor, I know you're embarrassed, but just remember. Tomorrow's a new day with no mistakes in it."

"Yet," we both said at the same time, completing the *Anne of Green Gables* quote.

"And at least if you do decide to go and apologize to this guy, you can get your book back."

With that Rose left, and I went to my bedroom. It was my one huge regret from the night I'd spent with Archer (besides calling him Baylor, of course). My beloved copy of *Jane Eyre* was still in his room somewhere, probably gathering dust. I'd had the book for years and noticed it was missing immediately after leaving the party. Maybe if I had more courage I would've gone back for it, but my humiliation had been too strong. Even Mr. Rochester's brooding loveliness wasn't enough to entice me back.

Oh well, I thought, closing my eyes. Archer was a good person, so at least I knew it was in safe hands. I fell asleep to that thought and dreamed of his eyes gliding effortlessly over the words, holding his full attention, his hands caressing the pages.

Never in my life had I been so jealous of a book.

* * *

The next morning, I stirred awake at the sound of arguing in the living room.

I'd been dreaming about books and baseball of all things, so I wasn't exactly upset to be woken up. But that sounded a lot like Charlie's voice. And boy, she did not sound happy.

I opened the door to my room, closing it quickly and quietly behind me. Rose's room was across from mine, and I always tried my best not to wake her.

"I know *you* didn't mean anything by it," Charlie said to a small brunette, who I noticed had her arms crossed. "But *he* came into my room, uninvited, and we have a strict policy at Magnolia house."

The brunette frowned. "Oh, and what's that?"

"No boys allowed. Ever."

"You realize how absurd that sounds, right? You expect me to believe that with three female roommates, you've never had a member of the opposite sex up here? Yeah, okay," she said sarcastically, and I watched Charlie's eyes widen. Uh oh. So not the right thing to say. "I call bullshit."

"Honestly, I don't care what you think," Charlie said. "Who are you again? You haven't even lived here five seconds, and you're already breaking our only rule."

"The name's Emilia," the mystery girl said, "like I told you a minute ago. And it's my house now, too, so I should get a say in the rules."

"One," Charlie repeated, holding up a finger. "We had one rule, and you already broke it. You're a freshman, right? I'm sure we can find a change of living situation. There's usually plenty of room in the dorms."

"No. No way," the girl said. "I signed a contract, Charlene, so you're stuck with me."

"Like I told you, my name is Charlie," my best friend said. "And nothing's written in stone. But don't worry. Some of the dorms are co-ed. You'd probably like it better there anyway."

"Been there already. The girl I was supposed to room with liked to cut up and burn my clothes for fun, called them 'too promiscuous'. Ironically, I later caught her and her boyfriend having sex—on my bed. I'm never going back there."

Charlie and the newcomer looked like they were both about ready to blow, so I stepped in, hoping to keep the peace. Or create some peace because this was roommate war, right here.

"Hey guys," I said, walking up to them, settling

on a spot between the two so that it didn't look like I was taking sides. "What's all the fuss about?"

"I'm trying to tell the freshie here about our rule," Charlie said, gesturing to the other girl, "but she's not getting the message. Maybe she's deaf in one ear or something. I don't know."

"I can hear you fine," the girl muttered, and I turned to her.

"Hi, I'm Honor," I said, holding out a hand. "You must be our new roommate. You'll have to excuse Charlie, seems like she hasn't had her morning coffee yet. It makes her irritable."

The girl glanced at my hand then took it in a firm grip. "I'm Emilia. My friends call me Emmy. I was told it was okay to move in today, but apparently it's some big inconvenience."

Charlie grunted in agreement, but I shot her a glare.

"It's fine," I said. "Our other roommate told us you were coming. I don't understand what the problem is."

"The problem," Charlie said, "is that she brought guys here. And I came out of the bathroom to find one of them twirling a pair of my underwear around his finger, saying 'Look, what I found on the floor'."

My eyebrows lifted as Emmy blushed. "Is that true?"

"Yeah," she said quickly, "but I didn't even invite him. He just showed up and was checking out my new living arrangements."

Charlie's eyes narrowed. "He was holding up my favorite pair of panties."

"The pink lace ones with the cute little bow?" I asked.

Charlie nodded in the affirmative.

I sucked on my teeth as Emmy buried her head in her hands. "This doesn't look good," I said to her. "That's pretty sacred right there."

"Listen, I'm sorry," she said, "but he's my brother. Can you really hold me responsible for something my immature, deviant brother did?"

"Ouch," said a male voice, and all of us looked to the door...only to see one of the O'Brien brothers standing in the entryway. It could've been Baylor or Chase—they were identical after all—but I thought it was Baylor based on the mischievous twinkle in his eyes. He was holding a cardboard box, feigning a wounded expression. "That really hurts, Emmy. I always thought I was secretly your favorite."

Emmy just rolled her eyes, but my heart began to beat faster as another voice spoke up from behind him.

"Move, Bay. I'm carrying like twice the weight you are." Pushing his brother out of the way, Dex suddenly appeared, carting two boxes of his own. "And stop pouting. Everyone knows Emmy loves me best."

"But she called me a deviant," Baylor said. "And

all over a pair of panties." At Charlie's glare, he was quick to add, "A very nice, hot pair. They were just so colorful and right there out in the open. I was just curious and couldn't seem to help myself. You understand, right?"

Charlie sniffed. "I understand that you have no self-control, are completely ruled by your impulses and probably run after anything in a short skirt."

"Finally," Dex said, the left side of his lip, the one with the scar, pulling up in a grin, "a chick that actually gets it."

"I love you, Bay," Emmy said with a smile, "but you gotta admit. That's pretty accurate."

Baylor nodded. "Oh, I see how it is. So much for family loyalty."

And there it was.

Proof of what I'd been secretly dreading. This was Emmy's family. Emilia, my new roommate, was an *O'Brien*. Which meant...

I was so screwed.

"Where do you want these?"

A new girl appeared then, walking into the living room, followed by what had to be another O'Brien brother. He had all the same attributes as the others: dark brown hair, piercing gray eyes, nice bone structure—though his face was a bit softer, still holding onto a hint of baby fat. And I hadn't seen him out on the baseball field the other day.

"You're my best friend, Emmy, and I love you,"

the new girl added. Her blonde hair was pulled back into a ponytail. She wore a baseball t-shirt and jeans, no makeup and had a smile like sunshine. "But seriously, did you have to bring everything you own? I told you already I don't think it's all going to fit in here."

Emmy shrugged. "You never know what you'll need, June."

June shook her head. "But all those books, your entire wardrobe and your movie collection?"

Emmy shrugged again. "I might get bored. I mean, my best friend decided to stay at home instead of renting a place with me, so..."

"Yeah, that wasn't really by choice," June said. "But it's fine. I'll still see you tons, and we'll hopefully have some classes together. But let's return to your crazy amount of stuff. Finn here's already complaining about his back," she added, patting the guy next to her between the shoulder blades.

"I was not," the guy, Finn, blushed, which was so adorable. He was carrying a large suitcase and a lamp while the blonde girl had a smaller suitcase. "Despite my appearance, June, I can outlift any of these guys."

Dex and Baylor scoffed, started to rib Finn, but Charlie just sighed.

"You see, Honor," she said, holding out a hand to encompass the room. "Testosterone and Magnolia

House just do not mix. This is why we never allow men into our sacred, private lady space."

Baylor smiled at that. "I'd like to get to know your lady space. Privately."

Everyone in the room seemed to let out a collective groan—except the new girl, June. I'd been looking between her and Finn and noticed her tense.

"You want to go out sometime?" Baylor went on, eyeing Charlie.

June seemed to be waiting with bated breath. There was obviously something going on there, I thought. I really hoped Charlie didn't go against character here. Baylor was *so* not her type. Plus, he seemed to have an admirer in June despite his playboy ways.

The girl had hearts in her eyes for goodness sakes—not that Baylor seemed to notice.

"Aw shoot, but you've already seen my best panties." Charlie shook her head in feigned dismay. "The mystery is totally gone. What would we even have to talk about?"

Baylor threw Charlie a wink. "Oh, I'm sure we could find something."

That move might've worked on ladies all over campus but not my bestie.

"I'll pass, but thanks," she said.

"Your loss." Baylor shrugged, and June visibly relaxed. "So Emmy, the boxes, where do want them?"

Before she could answer, a door opened, and Rose poked her head out of her room.

"What's going on in here?" she said, clad in her silk pajama set and open comfy robe. Her words were raspy with sleep. "Everything okay? I heard voices."

"Everything's fine," I said.

"Yeah," Charlie added for the first time looking a bit sheepish. "Sorry for waking you, Rose. I know you've got to get some sleep."

"S'okay," Rose covered her mouth on a yawn. "But if it's all good, I'm going back to bed. See you ladies again when I'm not so dead."

"Sweet dreams," I said as she shut the door.

All was quiet a moment—and then suddenly the sound of something hitting the floor broke the silence.

We all looked to the source of the noise, only to find Finn, standing there, his mouth slightly parted, his eyes glued to the place Rose had just been standing. He'd dropped the suitcase he was holding. If the look on his face was anything to go by, the guy was spellbound. And I could totally understand why. Our roommate didn't know it, but her natural beauty paired with that curvaceous figure was a two-punch shot to the gut. One that Finn was currently trying to recover from as Dex laughed and elbowed him in the arm.

"Close your mouth, Romeo," he said. "She's

gone, and you're drooling."

Shaking himself, Finn blushed again, pushed his brother away—but I thought I caught him sneaking another glance at the door to Rose's room.

"Come on, Junebug," Baylor said, missing the wince June directed his way. "Let's put this stuff down. There's still more to unload."

"Ugh, I hate that name," she mumbled, but he didn't seem to hear. "And of course, you'd choose me to do the grunt work and help you unload more stuff."

"Don't be silly." Taking the suitcase from her, placing both it and the box he'd brought up next to the couch, he pulled June to him in a one-armed hug. "These women desire me to leave their sacred lady space," he said. "Plus you know, I'd rather move boxes with you than anyone."

"Alright fine," she sighed, though she was smiling as she said it.

Baylor seemed oblivious to that as well as they left the room.

"Listen," Emmy said then took a deep breath, "I know you guys have this big rule and everything, but..." She lifted her chin. "They're my brothers. And I didn't even call them; I only told June and Dex, who must've spread the word."

"Hey," Dex scoffed, "I only called Finn because I thought we could use the help. Not to be rude, Emmy, but you do have a lot of stuff for such a little person."

"Yeah," Finn said, "and Bay kept bugging me about where we were going until I finally told him. The way he gossips I'm actually surprised Chase and Archer aren't here, too."

My heart skipped a beat at the last name, and I almost missed what was said next.

"They had extra practice with Bear," Dex said. "I'm guessing they were too tired to come."

A sense of calm washed over me at that, but I also felt a sting of disappointment. Had I actually wanted to see Archer again? And risk the embarrassment that had followed each and every one of our encounters so far? The answer was a bit surprising even to me.

Emmy shook her head at them. "You're lucky I love you all so much." Then turning back to Charlie and me, she added, "I promise, I never intended to break any rules or invade your space. Sorry about that. It won't happen again."

I looked to Charlie, and after an eyeroll, she nodded.

"Okay," she said. "But if I catch another one of them with my underwear, somebody's losing a finger."

Emmy laughed. "Agreed. Though they're not so bad once you get to know them."

Footsteps sounded on the porch, and suddenly, more people filed into the room—but it wasn't who

I expected.

"Aw love you, too, sis," Chase said, Baylor and June following close behind. Archer came in last, bringing up the rear. Even with his head down as he adjusted the box in his arms, he was just as beautiful as I remembered.

"What do you have in here, Emmy? Rocks?" Archer said as he stopped just inside the door. My heart began to beat triple-time as our eyes locked.

Beside me, Charlie threw up her hands. "And they just keep multiplying!"

I wanted to laugh and cry as Archer's lips turned up at the corners. But strangely, I couldn't do either. My fight or flight response should've kicked in, but instead, I just froze. Waiting for...well, I didn't exactly know.

His steps were sure as he walked toward me, and that's when I realized.

Him.

I'd been waiting for him to make the first move, so I could figure out how to proceed, which was all kinds of stupid because he looked completely okay with that role. More than okay. Unlike me, Archer looked confident as heck as he stopped right in front of me, wearing a barely-there smile that could make a girl do crazy things.

The only thing I knew for certain: Guys like him and girls like me didn't mix.

This couldn't end well.

My brain was in full agreement, but by the fluttering of my heart, she hadn't gotten the message. Ugh, my heart was such a hopeless romantic.

5

Archer

I couldn't believe it.

My little sister was rooming with the bookworm who had fully captured my attention since the night she'd decided to seduce my brother and ended up in my bed instead. I knew myself, and I knew I'd find her again. There were no two ways about that. Coach and Bear always said I was the most stubborn person they'd ever met—well, besides my dad. That I never knew when to let things go. I'd been planning to look Honor up in the school registry and ask around about her.

But it seemed like I wouldn't have to.

Here she was standing in front of me, the girl I hadn't been able to get off my mind, like some kind of gift in a Harry Potter t-shirt and yoga pants, her hair tied up in a messy bun. I was staring which I knew was rude, but I just couldn't stop drinking her in.

The only bad part was she didn't look as excited to see me as I was to see her.

I'd have to fix that.

Right after I got my fill of her—which was looking like it might be never.

"Why are you looking at her that way?" Baylor said with his usual tact. "Did she murder your favorite puppy or something?"

"Why do you say that?" I said, never removing my eyes from Honor.

"Because you've been staring at her for at least a full minute without saying anything. There are definitely some weird vibes going on over there."

Honor shrugged. "Plus, you're frowning at me again."

"I am?" My brow furrowed. "Sorry, I didn't realize."

"It's okay," she said, gesturing toward my face. "Though I see now why you're so good at sports. With a frown like that, one look, and it probably scares the crap out of the other team. Totally intimidating."

"Do I scare you?" I asked.

"No," she said, and I exhaled in relief. Then she muttered, "Though you probably should."

"Oh, why's that?"

"Well, look at you," she said. "You're all tall, dark, broad-shouldered and broody. Plus, you pretended not to know me yesterday which means you're either clever or devious." I choked as she went on. "Probably a bit of both. God help us if the good-looking jocks are smart, too. That's like girl kryptonite right there."

There was a beat—and then suddenly her face turned red.

"Oh my God," she said, covering her mouth. "Did I just say all that out loud?"

Out of nowhere, a sound exploded from my lips, my eyes widening a moment later.

"Did he—" Dex tilted his head.

"I think he did," Emilia said.

"It sure sounded like one to me," Chase confirmed.

Finn grinned, nodding his agreement.

"Holy shit," Baylor said, "she made Arch laugh! It's a Christmas miracle."

Chase sighed, sounding put out. "It's the end of January, dumbass."

Baylor waved him off. "Yeah, I know," he said. "Season's about to start. But doesn't it feel like Santa just entered the building or something? Arch, I don't think I've heard you laugh like that since—"

I shot him a glare, and he got quiet real fast.

"What?" he mumbled a second later. "I was just saying you don't laugh much anymore."

"Yeah?" I said. "Well, I think you laugh enough for the both of us, Bay. Somebody has to take life seriously."

My brother ducked his head, and I was surprised there was no quick comeback. Either my glare had finally worked on him—doubtful—or maybe he realized how messed up it would be to bring up dad's death in front of strangers. Whatever the reason, I was glad to turn my attention back to Honor, the girl who'd just managed the impossible and made me laugh for the first time in years.

She was the one frowning now.

"Sorry," she said. "I didn't mean to cause any issues between you and your brother."

I raised a brow, thinking of the name she'd called out the other night. My issues with my brothers were many, but that one stood out like a sore thumb.

Apparently, she was thinking the same thing because she pulled me further away from the others and lowered her voice.

"I also wanted to say I'm so sorry about...well, you know," she whispered.

I shook my head. "No, I don't. You're going to have to spell it out for me."

"I'm sorry for saying what I did. It was a total accident. I wanted to apologize when I figured out my mistake but wasn't sure I could handle the embarrassment."

75

I crossed my arms and waited, knowing there was more.

"My brain was addled by pleasure," she went on. "You were just so good at, well, everything. I mean, what do you expect? I can't be blamed for what I said in the heat of the moment. At least, that's what Charlie said. Right?"

"What did you say exactly?"

She gave me a look, realizing I was playing with her.

"What? I'm just a dumb jock. I can't remember."

"Archer."

I felt the corner of my mouth tip up. "No, that's what you should have said."

"Ugh." Honor raised her hands. "Can't we just pretend like it never happened? I'd be okay with that."

"Well, I wouldn't," I said seriously. "If you think for a second I want to forget what happened between us, you're dead wrong. That was one of the best nights of my life."

"It was?" she said.

"Yeah." I reached up, catching a strand of her hair that'd escaped, and tucked it behind her ear. Her shiver felt like hitting a homerun with all the bases loaded.

"Even after I said Baylor instead of your name?" she said quietly, and I closed my eyes.

That memory would haunt me the rest of my

days—or until I replaced it with a new one.

When I re-opened them, she was watching me closely. "Even then," I said. "But that's gotta be the worst case of mistaken identity ever."

Honor winced. "Seriously Archer, I don't know how I can make it up to you, but I really am sorry."

"Keep saying my name," I said and watched her blush reappear, pink spreading all over her cheeks. "I like the way it sounds coming from your lips."

"Okay..." she said softly.

"And I hope I've made enough of an impression that you'll remember who you're with next time. Speaking of which...you want to go out?"

Her eyes widened. "Did you just ask me for a date?"

"Yeah," I said, pushing my hands into my pockets. "So are you in?"

"This is so easy for you; isn't it?"

"What is?"

"Being charming and laid back and sexy."

I smiled. "You think I'm sexy? Good to know."

"But don't you see? That's exactly why this thing"—she gestured between the two of us—"can't go any further."

I frowned. "Sorry, you lost me."

"I don't think it's a good idea," she said, crossing her arms, bringing my attention to her sweet curves, but I fought to stay focused.

"And why is that?"

"I thought it would be obvious."

I tapped the side of my head. "Dumb jock, remember? I have trouble understanding complex concepts and theories. Just put it out there, so I can prove you wrong."

She sighed then seemed to gather herself.

"Archer," she said, "you're a super talented, athletic, quick-witted-possibly-devious man."

"And sexy. Don't forget the sexy." I nodded. "Continue."

"You're confident, and judging by our night together, you seem experienced." Her cheeks went red again, and I counted that as a win until she added, "You've probably had a ton of women."

"I wouldn't say a ton."

"And I'm...me," she finished. "Just an introverted bookworm, who'd never been to a college party before last weekend, one who was desperate enough to ask you, a complete stranger, to be my one-night stand. I read romance novels. But that's as racy as it gets with me."

She finally took a breath, and I waited until she met my eyes.

"You done?" I said. "Because the only thing I heard are excuses."

"But—"

"Honor, you didn't say you don't like me."

"I—"

I held up a hand. "And you didn't say you didn't

78

want to go. In that case, I'd take your refusal and go lick my wounds in private."

She laughed suddenly. "I don't get it. You should be the one who doesn't want anything to do with me. I thought you were a player, and I approached you to...to *use you* as my one wild hookup. Ugh, I'm awful."

"I'm not complaining," I said, taking a step closer. "And if you still want that one-night stand, I volunteer as tribute."

Honor's face was a mixture of disbelief and delight.

"What? You think jocks don't read," I said. "I devoured the *Hunger Games* the same as everybody else. I'm a Slytherin, too, in case you're interested. Majoring in Sports Sciences with a minor in English. We have an aunt who's a big book collector, got most of us kids into reading when we were young. Which reminds me, I still have your book. You should agree to go out with me to make sure it gets back to you safely."

She shook her head. "You are such a surprise."

"That depends." I shrugged. "Do you like surprises?"

"Not usually," she said. "Only if they're the good kind."

"What am I? Good or bad?"

"Oh, definitely good."

"Okay, then you'll go out with me?" I said,

startled by how much I cared about her answer.
There was no way it should mean so much to me.
I'd just met this girl for crying out loud. I'd never
been like Bay, never needed a girl at my side to feel
fulfilled, hadn't really wanted one either. But man,
this girl...I wanted more than just one night. "Way I
see it, it's the only sure way to get your book back."

Honor put her hands on her hips, her face a
stern mask, trying to look scary. It was so cute I
nearly kissed her.

"Are you seriously threatening to hold my book
hostage until I go out with you?"

I gave her my best, most intimidating frown.
"Hey, a man's gotta do, what a man's gotta do."

She started to smile—but then her phone went
off in her pocket, and she shook herself as if waking
from a dream. As Honor looked away, she took one
step back then another.

"Sorry," she said. "I do like you, Archer. But I
still don't think it's a good idea."

"But—"

Before I could say more, she was staring down
at her phone and walking quickly to what I assumed
was her room. "I need to get this," she said. "Family
emergency. Anyway, it was nice talking to you.
Bye."

The sound of her door clicking shut was as final
as a death knell, her absence taking all of the air and
life out of the room.

80

Actually, it *was* suspiciously quiet. Looking around, I noticed everyone had stopped what they were doing, standing frozen, carefully avoiding my eyes. Great. They'd heard everything. My family had just witnessed my failed attempt at wooing Honor. Oh yes, and her friend from the party, and June had seen it, too. Just great.

Emmy was the first to speak.

"Hey," she said to no one in particular, "are we moving me in or not? I still have a couple more boxes downstairs. They aren't going to lift themselves."

It was as if someone had pushed play on a movie. All the people in the room started moving at once. Emmy gave me a wink, and I mouthed "thank you" to her as she walked into her new room with June. Chase and Finn went outside presumably to get the other boxes while Baylor made his way over to me.

"Tough break," Baylor said, dropping a hand on my shoulder. "We all crash and burn sometimes, Arch. Don't take it personal."

"Yeah," Dex said, coming up beside him. "Plus, that was damn entertaining. Who needs movies when you have real life drama like that?"

"Haha," I said drily.

"No really. I was just waiting for the pig's blood to drop on your head or something."

"You're hilarious."

As Dex walked off, I noticed Baylor's silence which was so out of character I grew concerned.

"What's up, Bay?" I asked. His brow was furrowed, and he seemed to be deep in thought. That was odd as well. "You want to take a crack at me, too, go right ahead. I can take it."

Baylor waved me off. "Too easy," he said.

"That's never stopped you before," I replied.

"Did I hear my name?" he asked a second later. "That girl, Honor, I thought I heard her say something about me. What was that about?"

I made my face blank. "I don't know what you mean."

"You do," he said, pointing accusingly at me. "Your face only gets all smooth like that when you're hiding something. Just tell me."

"No."

"Aw, come on. Just say it."

"Not in a million years," I said back.

Baylor smiled, shook his head. "Oh now, I'm curious. You know, I'll find out what it is. In addition to my devastating good looks, I'm also a great detective. You can't have secrets in this family. The truth always comes out."

I just shook my head, knowing he wasn't going to let it go but unwilling to reveal the truth. Let him dig for it. I had my doubts that he could stay focused that long anyway.

"Alright." Baylor sighed. "If that's how it's going

to be, fine. I'll find out on my own."

"Good luck with that," I said just as Chase and Finn walked back in.

"What's going on?" Chase said.

"Nothing," Baylor said. "Just Archer being closed-off as usual. But I'm going to give him a pass since he just got rejected. You'll find someone else, Arch. No use getting so wound up over one girl. They're not worth it."

Taking the box from Chase, Baylor and Finn carried the last of Emmy's things into her room.

"The sad thing is he really believes that," Chase said, looking after his twin.

"I know," I said back. "I worry about him, probably more than I should."

"You're not the only one." Chase started to turn away but then stopped. "And hey, Arch?"

I met his gaze as he looked over his shoulder. It was crazy how much he looked like Baylor, I thought. It came with the territory of being twins, but we all had our father's gray eyes.

"About the girl?" he said. "Don't feel bad about going after what you want. Like Dad used to say, tenacity is a great trait to have."

Chase nodded then walked away after delivering that bombshell. He'd always been the most introspective of all of us. I think it had something to do with all the reading he did.

"Hey," a new voice said, and I turned to find the

girl Honor had been with at the party staring at me, seemingly sizing me up. "I'm Charlie, Honor's best friend and your sister's new roommate."

I nodded. "I'm Archer."

She bit back a smile. "Oh, I know. Honor's told me a lot about you already."

"She has?" I said. So Honor had talked to her best friend about me? That had to be good, right? "All good things, I hope."

"Uh uh," she said, waving a finger at me. "Don't try that charming act on me, oldest O'Brien. It won't work. I'm not telling you anything unless I think it would benefit my best friend."

"I can respect that."

After giving me a quick look up and down, she nodded. "Lucky for you, I think you may be just what she needs. Honor's special, you see. She's not like other girls."

This was so surreal. I felt like this was some kind of test.

"I agree," I said. "That's why I'm so interested in her."

Charlie nodded again. "Well, it was a good try with the book. She loves those things. Smart move on your part."

"Thank you?" I really didn't know what to say to this girl Charlie. "So, you think I have a shot? With Honor, I mean?"

"Yeah," Charlie said and flipped her hair over

her shoulder, "you may have one—if you're lucky."

"Any advice?" I said.

"Hmm," she said. "Just keep trying."

With that, she turned on her heel and left.

I'd never been one to give up. Like Chase said, quitting didn't really run in the O'Brien DNA. I was stubborn, and I had a feeling that would serve me well where Honor was concerned. If I needed the green light to pursue something with her, I'd just gotten it from Charlie, her best friend.

I just hoped Honor was ready.

Because I was more than ready for her.

6

Honor

As soon as the door closed, I leaned my head against it.

My eyes fell shut as I listened to the conversation on the other side. The sound was muffled, hard to understand the words. The voices were deep, clearly masculine, and I knew for a fact there had never been this much testosterone in Magnolia House since I'd moved in. That was thanks in large part to Charlie's rule (one we'd all agreed to without objection) about not letting men into our space.

But despite the distortion the door created and how similar the brothers' voices sounded, I could've sworn I knew which one belonged to Archer.

"So not a good idea," I mumbled.

As if I needed the reminder.

Opening my eyes, I made my way over to my bed and plopped down. I remembered the first time I'd laid eyes on Archer O'Brien with perfect clarity. Even though I hadn't known his name at the time, one of my first thoughts still rang true.

This guy could ruin me.

Would if I let him.

Luckily, my hang-ups wouldn't allow me to throw my heart out there so carelessly no matter how sweet, clever, and irresistibly attractive he was. I knew what he felt for me was just a passing curiosity. He would get bored the second he realized I wasn't actually as confident and bold as I was in our first meeting. Even with the awkwardness, something must've tripped his guy switch. But I wasn't like Charlie, who could entrance men at a glance. No way would I be able to hold his attention. And when he decided to throw me away, I was sure I'd be crushed. I was just cutting it off before it could get that far.

I sighed, wishing things were different—that I was different—so we could have had a shot.

But like I'd told Archer, I was just me.

And despite my answer to his question, he did scare me. Just not for the reasons he was thinking.

My phone pinged again, and I looked down to see the same text from earlier.

Mom: Honor, call as soon as you get this! It's an

EMERGENCY!!!

I sighed, wondering what it could be this time, debating whether I should even respond. Mom hadn't contacted me in over a month, and she only ever called when she needed something. But what if this was a real emergency?

Hitting the call back button, I waited for her to pick up.

"Oh, I'm so glad you called," she said, sounding out of breath. "I need help."

"Hi Mom," I said. "How are you? Is everything okay?"

"No, Honor. No, it's not. I'm overwhelmed, and I don't know what to do."

I sat up straighter. "What's wrong? Did something happen?"

"I can't find it," she sniffed, sounding like she was close to tears. "I've looked everywhere, but it's just not here."

"What's not there?"

"My favorite sweater," she said as if it should be obvious. "You know, the baby blue wrap one with the deep V? Dave really likes it on me, and we have a big dinner to go to with his colleagues. I need to look my best."

I shook my head, lifting my eyes to the ceiling. "That's the emergency? This is why you called, a sweater?"

"Well, yes! And you don't have to be so rude

about it. That's not how I raised you."

"Sorry," I said. "Have you checked your closet?"

Her voice was all sarcasm. "Of course, I checked the closet."

"What about your drawers? Did you look there?"

"Yes."

"How about—"

"Do you have it?" she said.

I felt my lips pull into a frown. "What? Why would I have your sweater?"

"Oh, I don't know. It's just sometimes you like to borrow my things without asking. Remember the time you took my lipstick."

"I was six, Mom," I said deadpan.

She didn't even pause. "And then there was the time you took my best robe to school."

"That was for a project. I told you. I had to dress like Julius Caesar."

Her patience had obviously run out. "Still, it just proves you've never respected my things. If you took the sweater to college, it's not okay. I need it back now. Dave has been staying late at the office a lot more. He's not engaging with me as much as he used to. It's really important that I show him what he's missing."

Taking a deep breath, I said, "How about underneath your bed?"

"Why would my sweater be there?" she asked.

"You keep some of your winter clothes there

during the summer to give you more space."

I heard her moving things, presumably looking for the missing sweater, until finally, I heard a gasp.

"Oh my God," she said, coming back on the phone. "I found it! Thanks, Honor, you're a lifesaver!"

"You're welcome," I said. "I'm glad—"

"Me, too! But I need to go get ready. The dinner's only a few hours away. Talk to you soon, baby girl!"

The next sound I heard was nothing but dial tone.

"Love you, too," I said, even though she was already gone. Incredible, I thought. Throughout the span of that short conversation, I'd gone from an accused thief to a lifesaver all because of a stupid sweater. Nice to know Mom thought so highly of me.

I was still stewing when another text came through.

Walter: URGENT, contact me ASAP. It's a newsroom emergency!

Seemed there were a lot of "emergencies" today. As I was reading it again, a second text joined the first.

Walter: Honor? Did you get my text? I have news. It concerns you, and it's important. Please call me immediately!

I hit the call button, and Walter picked up on

the first ring.

"Did you see?" he said, his voice full of barely repressed excitement. "Have you been on *The Howler* site yet?"

"No," I said, already reaching for my computer, "I haven't had a chance. Was something wrong with the article? I triple-checked to make sure I had all of my facts correct."

Walter laughed. "Something wrong? Goodness no! Your article is a revelation, a Godsend to this tiny paper. Everyone's raving about it!"

"Walter," I laughed, "be serious. It was just a small 500-word piece. And who's everyone? Our 10 loyal readers don't usually rave—unless it's about the crappy campus parking situation."

He sighed. "It really is a travesty how much you kids pay in tuition only to never find a decent parking space."

"Hey, preaching to choir."

"But Honor, focus please. Have you seen the page yet?"

The Howler site was finally done loading. "I'm on there now, but I really don't know why...you..."

My words trailed off because I'd just seen the visitor count and had to do a double take. The counter on the main page was now at 91,502.

"Wow," I breathed. "Weren't we sitting at something like 800 a few days ago?"

Walter sounded smug. "It was at 804 two days

ago. Since you posted your article on the O'Briens, the count has risen by astronomical proportions. This is all thanks to you and that wonderful family, my girl."

"This can't be because of my article," I said, clicking on the picture I'd paired with the story. It was a great shot I'd managed to get before leaving the practice field. Archer, Baylor, Chase and Dex had their backs to the camera, and I'd captured the moment when one of them (Baylor, I think) had made a joke, and they'd turned, all smiling to each other. Well, Archer had just been frowning less than usual, but still. "It has to be something else."

"Have you looked at the comments?" he said.

"Doing that now." I began scrolling, getting all the way to the bottom and finding...a crap ton of comments. They were mostly from students, but there were some left by alumni, professors and just people in the community as well. Walter was right. They loved the story. If I needed something to erase the crappy convo with my mom, this was the perfect pick-me-up. "That's...that's...incredible! Walter, your idea about covering the team and family was a definite winner. Congratulations!"

"Thank you, my dear, but you're the one who wrote it," he said. "And you did a brilliant job at giving people a taste of what *The Howler* has to offer. Bravo!"

"Aw thank you, I—"

92

"Now, for your follow-up," he cut in, "I was thinking of delving even deeper. People can't get enough of the O'Briens. They are salivating for more."

"More?" I said faintly.

"Well, of course," he said. "I was thinking to start we'd do a series of profiles, one for each brother."

I swallowed. "You really think people would like those?"

"Honor, did you even read the comments? These guys are like a boy band, only instead of music, they play baseball. Each one has their own fangirls and fanboys. The O'Brien brothers are talented ball players, and it certainly doesn't hurt that they're easy on the eyes."

"I hadn't noticed," I lied.

"Hmm, well, that's probably because you are such a professional and would never let a pretty face turn your head." Walter was a fantastic investigative journalist, and I was sure he could smell my lie from a mile away, but he didn't call me on it. Bless his heart. "This would obviously require more time spent with the team, more in-depth interviews. For all intents and purposes, you'd be living and breathing all things O'Brien. I know it will be a lot, but I think you're up to the task."

He sounded so confident, but my pulse rate was rising at the thought of spending more time with the O'Briens. One O'Brien in particular if I was being honest.

"I don't know," I said. "The idea is wonderful, Walter. And I'd hate to let you down, but—"

"Honor, I know this is your senior year, and you've got a lot going on. But there's a big story here. I want my best reporter on it."

I took a deep breath.

"In case you didn't know, that's you," he said with complete sincerity. "So, will you do it?"

As if I could say no to him?

"Of course," I sighed. "Just let me know what you need."

"I knew I could count on you."

Walter sounded like he was smiling, but I didn't know what he was so dang happy about.

His faith in me was totally misplaced. I'd been this close to chickening out, still wasn't sure I'd made the right decision.

But the deed was done. Right or wrong, I was in this for the long haul. I just hoped it wasn't the dumbest decision I'd ever made.

* * *

When the call ended 20 minutes later, I had my first follow-up interview scheduled for Tuesday at 2:00 PM.

With the Head Coach of the Wolves, Daisy O'Brien.

AKA Archer's mom.

Not that that would be strange or anything. It

wasn't like I'd propositioned her son at a party then turned him down when he'd asked me out for a proper date. I mean, what kind of person does that?

I sighed as I stood, walked to my door and opened it.

The scene that greeted me was completely different than the one I'd left earlier. First, there were no O'Brien men around—for which I was grateful. Second, Charlie and Emmy were on the couch together watching the Hallmark Channel, not looking like they were seconds away from an impromptu catfight. Definitely a good thing. Rose was there as well, making herself a coffee, looking like she'd just woken up at two in the afternoon—which was actually early for her.

"Shouldn't you still be in bed?" I asked.

Rose shrugged. "Couldn't get back to sleep. Too much excitement going on out here."

"You can say that again."

"So Archer." She smiled. "Charlie said he stopped by."

"Him and every other O'Brien on the planet," Charlie piped up from the couch—to which Emmy rolled her eyes.

"Hey," she said, "it wasn't that bad."

Charlie scoffed. "They were everywhere, Rose. Men in our sacred lady space. Can you imagine? I know you were half-asleep, but you must've noticed the difference."

Rose shot me a smile. "I thought I sensed a disturbance in the Force."

"A manly disturbance," I said. "There were tan muscles and chiseled jaws as far as the eye could see."

"And tight butts," Charlie added.

Emmy scrunched her nose. "Ew, those are my brothers you're talking about."

"Exactly," Charlie said. "Our new roomie has a plethora of brothers, and apparently, none of them have girlfriends."

"Not for a lack of trying, I hear," Rose put in as she and Charlie cut their eyes at me, but I ignored them and walked over to the couch.

"Where did June go?" I asked and took a seat. "She seemed really nice."

"She is nice, probably too nice sometimes," Emmy said, still staring at the TV. "June had to go home and help her dad at the garage. They own one about 15 minutes from here. It's a good place if you need any work done on your car."

"Hmm, I'll keep that in mind," I said.

"So, what's going on with you and my brother?"

The question caught me off guard. "Nothing," I said quickly.

Emmy looked away from the TV and straight into my eyes.

"It didn't seem that way to me," she said.

"Me either," Charlie agreed, and she smiled as I

shot her a glare. "It seemed like a whole lot of something in my humble opinion."

"Humble?" Rose laughed. "Yeah, right. But really Honor, what's up with you and this Archer guy? Did he ask you out? And did you seriously turn him down?"

"Yes to both," Charlie said.

I didn't know where to look, so I ducked my head with a shrug. "It wasn't a big deal. He's a baseball superstar whose final season in college is about to start. He's probably forgotten all about me."

"Hmm, doubtful," Emmy said. "Just so you know, Archer never acts like that."

"Like what?"

"He doesn't usually go after girls," she said. "They pursue him."

I nodded, feeling a slight pang in my chest. "Got it. I'm just another girl he met at a party, nothing special. I suspected as much."

Emmy's brows furrowed. "That's not what I meant."

Rose shook her head at me sadly, and Charlie said, "Honor, I love you, but why are you being so dense? He's totally into you. The guy looked like he'd got punched in the stomach after you turned him down and left."

"Hey, it's cool," I said. "Besides, it's not like it could've gone anywhere anyway. This will actually make spending more time with him easier."

"Ooh, and the plot thickens," Charlie said, her eyes bright as she and the other two girls leaned forward. "What do you mean more time?"

"I got an assignment from Walter," I said. "He wants me to do interviews with the team, follow them around, write an entire series."

"On my family?" Emmy asked.

"Yeah," I said, "which means—"

"More time with Archer," Rose said, fighting back a smile.

"More time with the hot baseball player who's into you and rocked your world at that party," Charlie said. "It's a sign."

I tilted my head. "Of what?"

She shrugged. "Fun, sexy times ahead?"

"Charlie, be serious."

"I don't know, okay? But it has to mean something."

Yeah, I thought, it meant I needed to get all these feelings locked down, stop thinking like a girl with a crush. Getting to my feet, I shook my head and walked into the kitchen for some water, not realizing Emmy had followed me until she spoke.

"Listen Honor," she said, "I don't know you, and you don't know me. I have no idea what kind of person you are, why you said no or what your game is."

She held up a hand as I started to speak.

"But Archer's my brother. He may be older than me; he may be bigger and a guy, but I've never subscribed to any of that females-are-weaker B.S. My brothers can be annoying and way too over-protective, but they're the best." Emmy narrowed her eyes. "If you hurt Archer, you'll have me to answer to. Understand?"

"Yes," I said after she was done. It was so refreshing to see a sister standing up for her big brother that I had to smile. "But you've got nothing to worry about. At least not from me. I like Archer." *Probably more than I should*, I added mentally. "I don't want to hurt him, Emmy. I don't want anything from him."

She nodded as she searched my face. "I believe you...but I don't think you know what you want."

Truer words had never been spoken, I thought.

"Just know, you'd be lucky to have him," she added before walking away.

Actually, on second thought, those were the truest words ever spoken.

Too bad I wasn't brave—or stupid—enough to try my luck where Archer was concerned.

7

Archer

Honor's hands in my hair, her lips sliding against mine, the feel of her as she moved in my lap. I remembered it all like it was yesterday. And yeah, I couldn't stop thinking about that either. How surprised she was to see me at her house, her smile from the other day—and the look of distress that crossed her face before she turned me down cold.

"O'Brien, get your head in the game!"

Bear's shout pulled me right back to the practice field.

Which was where my focus should've been in the first place.

Heat raced up my neck as I looked around at my team. All eyes were on me, but I had no idea what had already been said. Had we been discussing defensive strategy? Offensive? The lineup? How important it was to not make stupid mistakes like the one Declan made on the other play by bobbling the ball on what should've been a perfectly easy grounder? I tried to keep my comment as vague as possible.

"Guys, we can't afford to make any errors," I said, pulling my cap lower. "Like Coach says, perfection is impossible, but that's what we're shooting for. Our first game is next week. Let's practice like champions."

Bear nodded to me, and my brothers all looked amused.

"You heard your Captain," he said. "Get back to work."

"Nice save," Chase mumbled next to me as we all dispersed.

"Thanks," I said, handing him the ball and then walking behind the plate.

Parker Graves was doing practice swings just outside the batter's box. "Okay, so who is she?" he said.

"Who's who?" I asked.

"The girl in your head."

As Honor's face flashed across my mind, I cleared my throat. "Man, you have no idea what you're talking about."

"Think I do," he said, digging his cleats into the

dirt, turning once in a circle like he did before every at bat. "Only one thing distracts a guy like that, and it's a female. So, what's her name?"

I just shook my head and pulled down my mask before dropping into a squat.

"Fine," Graves said, assuming his stance. "Don't tell me. Just know this: once you let a girl in, it's hard to get 'em out of your thoughts."

"Maybe you should concentrate more on your swing," I said. "Probably get more hits that way."

"Just trying to be friendly, Captain," he laughed. "The others aren't going to take it so easy on you."

And he was right.

Graves hit a pop fly to left field that was caught, no problem. Automatic out. Next up to bat was T.J. Perez, a sophomore who seemed to a have a love of women that rivaled even Baylor's. Actually, the two liked to hang out a lot.

"So, I hear you've got your eye on someone," T.J. said as he stepped up to the plate.

I frowned behind my mask. "And who'd you hear that from?"

"From your loudmouth brother. Who do you think?"

I cursed underneath my breath.

"She pretty?" he said, throwing me a grin. "Baylor said she was. Rejection always hurts worse when they're pretty."

"And you would know, wouldn't you Perez?" I

said and got down into position.

"Hey, I'm on your side, Captain. Bros before hoes, am I right?"

God bless Chase for striking out that fool.

Hunter Bly came up next and just said, "T.J. told me. Sorry man, her loss."

He got on base with a single down the middle, but I couldn't even be mad about it. Did everyone know Honor had turned me down?

Chase struck out the next batter, and I went to the dugout, stripping out of my catcher's gear as we changed up positions. It wasn't like I hadn't expected something to leak. I swear, these guys gossiped worse than any girls I'd ever met. But I hadn't thought my whole team would be jawing at me the entire practice. I was fifth in the batting lineup, so I closed my eyes and leaned back against the bench. My mind usually blanked when I tried to relax.

But this time was different.

She was right there, unbidden, floating just in front of me. I could picture Honor's face, down to the little dimple on her left cheek. Her smile was like the sun, and it immediately warmed and set me at ease. Somehow, I had to figure out a way to spend more time with her. I could definitely start hanging around her house. Emmy was her roommate, my excuse if I ever needed one for why I was there so much. But I didn't want to come off as desperate. Plus, her other roommate/best friend, Charlie, might have something to say about it.

Still, it was the best plan I had.

Maybe I could invite her to a game? I thought.

"Hey," Dex said, and my eyes flipped open. "Let's go, Archer. You're up."

"Thanks," I said, taking the bat he held out to me, and slipped on my helmet. Quickly taking stock, I noticed we had a man on first and second with two outs. Time to get my head in the game.

I was loosening up my shoulders when Mitch Snider had a go at me.

"Word is you got rejected," he laughed. "Can't say I'm surprised. The ladies don't seem to like you much, O'Brien."

As Captain, I got along with most of the guys on the team. But Mitch had always had a chip on his shoulder. He was a senior like me, and he thought my brothers and I got special treatment since we were the coach's kids. He couldn't see the truth, that he just wasn't as great as his big head lead him to believe, and that was a problem for two reasons. 1) It made him an arrogant player without the talent to back it up, and 2) It made him say and do stupid things.

"She probably wanted a real baller," he added. "Not one that's all hype."

"You'll have to do better than that," I said.

"What?"

"You heard me, Snider," I said, warming up my arms, practicing my swing a couple times as I looked down at him. "The insults only hurt if they're true, and I've got the stats to back up my game."

That shut him up—for about a second.

I had just assumed my stance when he said, "I bet I could've bagged her."

I froze. "Excuse me?"

"You heard me," he said, throwing my words back at me. I looked down, and he was smirking. "Girl in the red dress, right?"

The first pitch blazed past me without my even seeing it.

"Strike one!" called Bear, but I was hardly listening.

Mitch threw the ball back then said, "I saw her at the party. Girls like that are so easy."

"What?" I said softly.

The ball whizzed past again. I didn't swing, heard the muffled "strike two" being called, but I was too blinded by his next words to care.

"I bet I could've had her on her back in 10 seconds flat."

One moment, I was standing there frozen. The next I was up in his face.

"Asshole," I said, pushing him back, hard. "What did you just say?" Another push. "You stay away from her."

Bear blew his whistle and tried to get between

105

the two of us.

"Break it up," he said, pushing Mitch back as Dex pulled me from behind. "What the hell was that all about?"

Mitch shook his head. "I was just joking, and he came at me out of the blue."

"Out of the blue, huh?" Bear turned his scowl on me next, his voice a mix of anger and frustration. "You're supposed to be the captain of this team, Archer. You know you can't go around pushing your teammates. What's gotten into you?"

Glaring at Mitch, I said, "I don't know, but you're right. It won't happen again."

Bear grunted then walked away, shaking his head, and I noticed Coach/my mom standing there on the sidelines watching the whole thing. She hadn't come over. She hardly ever intervened in scuffles like this, tried not to get in the middle of fights when it was one of us and another player to avoid talk of favoritism. I could see her disappointment from across the field. But I couldn't regret it.

What Mitch said had been out of line, and captain or not, I just couldn't let it stand.

"You okay?" Dex said. "Don't let Snider get to you. You know he's an ass."

"Yeah, easier said than done," I muttered.

"This girl, Honor," he said. "You really like her, don't you?"

I just gave him frown in answer, but apparently it was enough.

Dex nodded. "That's what I thought."

Before I could respond, Snider came up next to me.

"Sorry man," he said, placing a hand on my shoulder. "It was just a joke."

I shrugged his hand off. "It's cool. Let's just play ball."

"And you know I lied." He smiled again. "Girl like that? She would've been begging for it in five seconds, not ten. Virgins never stand a chance with me."

My vision went red, but before I could do anything—possibly kill the SOB—Dex had already delivered a solid left hook to the guy's jaw, knocking him out cold.

I looked to him, and he just shrugged.

"Hey, it's not like I'm Captain," Dex said, the scar on his face pulling up as he grinned. "And come on, the douche was just asking for a punch to the face."

"That he was," I said, giving him a pat on the back.

Bear's whistle shrilled through the air, his bellow following soon after. "Laps!" he shouted. "Ten of them around the field. If you can't play like a team, you'll run like one. And if I need to add more to get you hotheads to cool down, I will!"

The running was great conditioning, and we

were all in good shape. That's a lie. We were all in the best shape of our lives. But the heat made it a challenge. By the time we were done, everyone was panting—this included Mitch who had recovered in time to run, his eye now swollen, the color purple like the inside of a grapefruit—and my mother was waiting for us on the pitcher's mound. We gathered around her, taking a knee like we always did when she gave one of her speeches, which she usually waited to do until the end of practice. There'd been a lot going on today, though, so I didn't think much of it.

"Guys," she said, looking around at each of us, her blonde hair pulled back in a ponytail, catching in the breeze, "I'm not going to lie. You're looking pretty good out there."

Some of the newbies puffed up at that. But I'd heard one too many of Coach's talks, so I knew where this was headed.

"But pretty good unfortunately isn't good enough."

They deflated just as quickly.

"Now, I'm not saying this to discourage you," she said, walking around in a small circle, making sure everyone was listening. "You are Southern. You represent one of the winningest teams in collegiate baseball history. There's been blood, sweat and tears spilled on this field, and the results are indisputable. Three consecutive championships. All of them belonging to the Wolves. You should be dang proud of that."

Finally, her eyes landed on me.

"And you've done all that as a team. But I am not seeing a team playing out here today, and that's a crying shame."

Her words hit me right in the solar plexus. Man, that hurt.

"These past seasons you've won together. You've lost together. And now, I need you to buck up and start acting like a team together. Am I understood?"

Everyone nodded.

"I know about last practice," she went on, and out of the corner of my eye I saw Baylor wince. "A lot of you like to party, stay out late and have fun with your friends. It's college after all, right? That's what you're supposed to be doing. Having fun."

Her hands went to her hips.

"But you're not just here for that. Are you gentlemen?" She didn't wait for an answer. "No sir, you signed up to come here and play ball for the Wolves. This is where you get to use your God-given talent to show everyone what you're capable of. This is where you get to be Sandy Koufax on the mound, Willie Mays in the outfield, Babe Ruth at bat, and Johnny Bench behind the plate. This baseball diamond is my church, guys, so you better treat it with respect. You treat yourself and your bodies with respect, too, you hear? And we will win."

All was silent as Mom nodded, the sureness in her voice filling everyone in that circle with confidence. This was why she was such a good coach, I thought. Break us down, only to build us back up, better and stronger than before. We all had talent as individuals. *She* was why we were such a great team.

"This is our season, gentlemen. Everyone is gunning for us. Everyone wants to take the Wolves out of contention. But we work hard now. We focus. We practice harder than everybody else, so that no one can defeat us on the field. And if they do, they're going to have to work like hell for it. We go out there knowing this is ours." She nodded to herself. "That's how we're going to bring another championship home to Southern."

Coach looked around at the group again, and though no one else probably saw it, I noticed how her eyes lingered on her sons. There was so much pride there. It made me ashamed of how I'd acted earlier in practice. Made me want to do better.

"Now," she said, clapping her hands, "I've got a meeting to get to, but I know you'll do me proud. Get some water, guys, and then get back out there. Let's practice like champions."

Cheers went up, and when we went to our bags, Chase and Dex came over to me.

"What's up with that?" Dex said.

"Don't know," Chase said, "but I'm definitely curious."

"What do you mean?" I asked, squirting some water into my mouth and over my head. Shoot, it was hot out here.

"Arch," Chase said, "when's the last time you remember mom missing two practices in a row?"

I thought back but couldn't think of one.

"Never," Dex cut in. "She's always here, especially this close to the season. Something's got to be up."

"Last week, she had a dentist appointment," I said.

Chase nodded. "Nothing suspicious about that."

"But this meeting? Who do you think it's with?"

Nobody had an answer for that.

"I know who Mom's meeting with," Baylor said, tossing his water bottle from one hand to the other, looking like the freaking cat that caught the canary. "Got it out of Bear. Took some prodding, but in the end, he told me everything."

Dex gestured to him to go on. "Well?" he said. "You going to tell us who it is or what?"

"Hmm," Baylor said, pretending to think about it, "I'm not sure if I should. Arch is already distracted enough as it is."

"Me?" I started. "What's this got to do with me?"

"Nothing," Baylor said. "Just a piece of info you might be interested in. Snider had it coming by the way. He's got a big mouth, talks way too much trash, which I think says a lot coming from me."

Chase rolled his eyes. "Just tell us, Bay."

"Yeah," Dex said, "cut the crap, and get on with it already."

"Okay, okay," he said, "but only since you asked so nicely."

We waited.

"Mom is meeting...with a reporter at 2:00 pm," Baylor said. I didn't understand the grin on his face—Mom met with a lot of reporters—until he added, "She's actually been to the field once before, works for the school paper."

My heart pounded in my chest.

"Bear wasn't a big fan of how much of our captain's time she took up," he added.

"No way," Chase said. "You mean—"

"Mom's got an interview with Honor"—Baylor checked the time on his phone—"in about 10 minutes. Too bad practice lasts another forty. It's kind of cool if you think about it, Arch," he said. "Your almost-girlfriend is about to meet our mother for the first time."

I shook my head. "She's not my girlfriend."

"But you'd like her to be," Dex said.

Couldn't argue with that.

"Like Bay said, your concentration was shot before this. Think you can snap out of it?"

Chase crossed his arms. "Bear isn't going to take

any more crap. He's already breathing down your throat."

"Hey, no worries," Baylor said. "She's just a distraction. Right, Arch?"

"I'll be fine," I said, my focus more concentrated than it had been all day.

First, I'd get through practice. Then after rushing through a shower, I'd be on my way to Mom's office, hopefully, to catch the end of that interview. I was quick, one of the fastest on the team. I could make it.

Knowing Honor was about to meet my mom probably should've made me nervous, but it didn't. Getting to see her again. That's what drove me through the rest of practice.

Baylor was right. Honor was a distraction.

But she was also my motivation.

I couldn't wait to be with her again. And as it turned out, my mind loved being distracted by her.

8

Honor

I was out of breath.

And nearly late for my meeting.

Ugh, and I'd wanted to make such a good impression.

Taking a moment—but only one—to breathe, I knocked twice on a closed door with the words **Head Coach Daisy O'Brien** sprawled across it. The answer was immediate. A strong female voice from the other side said, "Come in."

With one last breath, I opened the door and stepped inside.

The woman's head had been down as she worked on a few papers, but her eyes met mine as I entered.

"Hi," she said, smiling, "you must be Honor."

"Yes." I noticed her lips and high cheekbones looked just like Archer's. Unfortunately, this did nothing to calm my racing heart. "Nice to meet you, Mrs. O'Brien. I'm sorry I was almost late. My British Lit class usually ends at 1:45, but it ran over today."

She gestured to the seat in front of her, which I gladly took. "So you came all the way from the Browning Building? That's clear across campus."

I nodded.

"Nice cardio," she said. "Do you run a lot?"

"Not unless you count running to the bookstore when a new release from one of my favorite authors comes out," I said.

She laughed, thank goodness. "I'm the same way, and so is my older sister, Genevieve. When a new Patterson book releases, I'm one of the first in line."

Okay, this I was more comfortable with. I could talk books all day, every day. "I'm more of a romance person myself."

"Nothing like a good romance," she said.

"I like happy endings."

"Who doesn't? There's so much sadness in the world."

"Exactly. Real life has too many tragedies. Happily-ever-after is something to strive for not scoff at. Being happy is one of the bravest things you can be."

"Amen to that," she said.

I flushed, knowing I'd gotten carried away—book talk tended to do that to me—but I liked her already. I just hoped the feeling was mutual.

"I hear you have some questions for me."

"Yes, of course," I said, giving myself a mental slap. Come on, Honor. Be professional. Just because you've got a woman crush on the guy-you-like's mom is no reason to drop the ball. "It's just a few interview questions. My boss asked me to profile you and your sons."

"Well, that should be interesting," she murmured, more to herself than me. "Bear said you came to one of the practices. What did you think?"

"I was very impressed," I said, looking around at her walls. She had tons of pictures, most featuring either her family, baseball or both. "You have a talented team, Mrs. O'Brien."

"Hmm. And have you met my boys?"

Archer's eyes, the intense focus in them as he leaned forward just before pressing his lips to mine, the feeling of his hands as they brushed the sides of my hips.

I cleared my throat as heat rose to my cheeks. "Yeah, I mean, yes. I met them. Just briefly though, we don't know each other well or anything."

Her brows rose at my reaction. "No?"

I shook my head, tried to change the subject. Grabbing my notebook, with my pen in hand, I asked, "So, have you always known you wanted to be a coach?"

"Pretty much," she said. "There's magic in this game, a romance about it that no other sport can touch. Before I met my husband, baseball was my first love. Luckily, the kids love it, too."

"Was that because of you or your husband?"

"Both, I'd imagine. Tyler and I met at a baseball game."

I smiled. "Oh really? Was it love at first sight?"

"More like hate." She laughed. "We were rooting for opposite teams. I love my Mets, but he was a Yankees fan. Can you believe that? There are actual people who like the Yankees."

I smiled, taking notes, as she faked a shiver of disgust.

"Anyway, we met through friends, and he and I had it out, arguing most of the night about which team was better, who would win the game. The loser had to buy the other drinks at the end."

"And who ended up buying?" I asked.

"He did, of course. My Mets took that game in awesome fashion. It was a beautiful sight. Tyler, though, didn't seem half as sad as he should've been to see his team lose. He was downright happy about it." She sighed. "He told me later that his Yanks did him a solid that night. That he wanted to take me out to dinner instead of drinks, and by the end of that dinner... Oh Honor, I was a lost cause. A year later, he asked me to be his wife—at a Mets-Yankees game—and then we got married, had a wonderful family. It was such a good life with him."

I was taking notes furiously at this point, trying to get it all down. Theirs was such a beautiful story. It sounded like a real-life fairytale, and I couldn't believe I was getting to hear it all like this.

"Did you guys ever switch teams?" I asked.

"No way," she said. "Tyler, well, he always told people the damn Yankees were the ones who brought us together. He laughed long and loud at the face I made whenever he said it, too. Correcting him was futile, but I didn't think it was the Yanks or my Mets. Like I said, it was baseball, that indefinable magic of the game, that first made us dislike each other and then fall in love."

"Well, I'm honored that you told me your story," I said. "It sounds like one for the record books."

"Have you ever been in love, Honor?"

The question was so unexpected it took me a second to respond. Looking up, I met her steady gaze.

"I don't think so," I said.

"Why not?" she asked. "You seem like a smart, sweet girl, and you said yourself you love romance."

"In books," I said. "In real life, not so much."

She tilted her head, so I went on.

"To be honest, it's always seemed like such a huge risk, putting all of your trust and heart into the care of one person? Trusting them not to leave, to love you back? Being constantly afraid of losing them? Love is scary."

Mrs. O'Brien smiled sadly. "Love is the most terrifying thing in the world, but trust me, it's worth it."

I blinked, taking that in. I couldn't explain all my doubts to someone I'd just met, could barely explain them to myself. But here I was talking to a woman who had lost her husband to cancer about love and loss, and here she was telling me it was worth it. If that wasn't a ringing endorsement of love, I didn't know what was.

"I know it's your interview," she said, "but could I ask you a few questions?"

"Sure," I said, thinking/hoping/praying, *please let them be easier than the first one.*

"Are you a baseball fan?"

So much for easy.

"Will you throw me out if I say no?" I asked.

Mrs. O'Brien laughed while shaking her head. "I guess I'll let you stay. Though maybe you're a bit more of a fan then you're letting on. You are doing these profiles."

"Until recently, I didn't even know what a line drive was," I confessed.

"Hm, and I wonder who taught you that term..."

Archer had, I thought, fighting down another flush at her shrewd look.

"One of your sons actually," I said. "They're all amazing from what I can tell. Do you think any of them will go pro one day?"

She sat back in her chair, drumming her fingernails against the desk. "I think any of them could play professionally—if they really wanted to. But I'd never force that on them. They'd have to want it for themselves."

That sounded fair.

"Would you ever date a pro baseball player?" she asked.

Wow, I thought, trying not to read into that question but failing miserably.

"Not sure," I said slowly. "Why would you ask me that?"

Mrs. O'Brien shrugged, but her eyes seemed tighter than they were a second ago. "Just curious. A lot of girls would love to date a pro baller or even a college starter with a lot of prospects. They have a lot going for them: fame, good looks, potentially a great salary."

"Well," I said, tapping my chin, "in that case, I might date one. But it would depend."

"On what?" she asked.

"Are they a Yankees fan?" I said. "Because I've heard those can be trouble."

There was a moment of silence, and then suddenly she smiled.

"Good answer," she said.

"I thought so," I said back. "But seriously, what was that all about? I'm not secretly some baseball bunny who's searching for her ticket to fame and fortune. I'm just a reporter looking for a good story."

"I get that," she said. "I just wanted to be sure. You'd be surprised how many young ladies with less than honorable intentions come around here looking to get to my team."

"Okay...but why did you doubt me in the first place?"

Mrs. O'Brien sighed. "Honestly, I heard about you before this meeting."

I blinked at that. "Oh?"

"Yes," she said. "Apparently, you caught the eye of my son, Archer. He asked you for a date, and you turned him down. Is that right?"

"I did." I swallowed, only now realizing she'd asked me more questions than I'd asked her during the time we'd spent together. And no wonder. I was being interviewed as well. I just hadn't known it. "And Archer...he told you all this?"

She scoffed. "As if. He never tells me anything about his love life. Good Lord, girl, no. I got the info from my daughter Emmy. My son Baylor may have mentioned something, too."

I closed my eyes.

"It was just a surprise. Archer's usually so guarded, doesn't wear his heart on his sleeve," she added. "He's nearly as bad as Dex in that way. I'm sorry I didn't mention it before, but I wanted to get to know you for myself."

Opening my eyes, I met her steady gaze. "I understand. You're just being a good mom."

"Exactly."

"So, what do you think? Are my intentions honorable?"

She tilted her head as I waited.

"I think so," she said. "Though we'll have to do something about the whole not-a-baseball-fan thing. You still need to interview my sons, correct?"

"Yes, I was hoping to come to practice again, and—"

"Why not come to a game?"

Startled, I looked up. "What?"

She shrugged. "For that matter, why not travel with us a bit this season? You're obviously not a... What did you call it again? Oh yeah, a baseball bunny. That's a good one. I'll have to use it sometime."

She threw me a smile, and I smiled back.

"If you come on the road with us, you'd get to see what baseball is all about, get to spend more time with the team, get to know my boys better and question them at your leisure."

"Sounds good," I said carefully. "But are you sure you're okay with that? Me, traveling with the team?"

"Why wouldn't I be?" she said. "Students from the physical therapy track travel with us sometimes. I want the stories you write about us to be the best that they can be."

"Well, thanks," I said. "I'll definitely think about it."

"Great." She stood and came around her desk to meet me on the other side. "In the meantime, I'll send you the game schedule. Look it over and let me know."

"Awesome, thanks again for the interview, Mrs. O'Brien. It was so nice meeting you."

As we stopped at the door, she turned to me and said, "It was nice meeting you, too, Honor. I look forward to seeing more of you."

"Can I ask you one more thing?"

"Shoot," she said.

I took a deep breath, steeling myself to ask the question that had been on my mind. "You never asked why I said no to Archer, but you invited me to travel with you guys. No offense, Mrs. O'Brien, but you're not trying to play matchmaker. Are you?"

"Honor, I'm a coach and a mom," she said. "Not a matchmaker."

"Oh my gosh, I know." Embarrassment washed over me like a wave. I felt like a fool for even asking. "I'm so sorry. Please just forget it."

She nodded graciously. "That's okay," she said. "My reason for inviting you is simple. I just want you to be able to experience the romance of baseball."

As she shut her door, I walked away in a daze. Her last words played on repeat in my head, the implications anything but simple—and was I dreaming or had there been a twinkle in her eye when she'd said *romance*? The whole interview was interesting to say the least. It hadn't taken long, lasted only about 45 minutes, but all together, her answers would make one heck of an article.

Looking through my notes, my mind was so caught up that I wasn't even looking where I was going.

That's probably why, just as I turned the corner, I ran headfirst into a solid wall of muscle.

Or to be accurate, it ran into me.

Surprised, I stumbled backward, losing my balance, and the wall grunted. Strong arms banded around my waist a second later, pulling me in before I could fall. My trajectory suddenly changed, and the next thing I knew I was pressed up against a warm body.

A very big, fit body.

Looking up slowly, my eyes traveled over a broad chest...a very nice neck...an angular chin...paused briefly on a familiar frown...and finally met a pair of gorgeous gray eyes.

"Archer," I said, my voice far more breathy than I'd intended.

"Honor." He nodded then groaned.

"What's wrong?" I asked in concern. "You okay?"

"Yeah," he said, still wearing a frown. "Just hit my head on the wall when I saved you."

"Saved me? Guess that's one way to put it." Smiling, I reached up to run my hand along the back of his head. I was very gentle, watching for even the slightest sign of discomfort, but he seemed to relax at my touch. "You're the one who came tearing around the corner at a hundred miles per hour. Why were you running anyway?"

"Hmm," he said, closing his eyes. "Had somewhere I needed to be."

"Ah," I said, "and you literally sprinted to get there. Must be pretty important."

"It was," he said. "Plus, I gotta keep in shape somehow."

I had to laugh at that. "I don't think you have anything to worry about there."

Eyes opening slowly, he captured my gaze with a look so intense I nearly lost my breath. My fingers stilled in his hair.

"Was that a compliment?" he said.

"It...I—"

"Because it sure sounded like one."

I shrugged, trying to get past my lack of flirtation skills and just talk like a normal human being. "You can take it any way you'd like."

The corner of his lip turned up. "Really? Take

it...any way I'd like?"

"Seriously, do you have to make it sound so dirty?"

"Hey, I'm just repeating what you said."

His eyes were smiling even if his lips were not, which let me know that *he* knew exactly what he was doing. "In a sexy low voice with tons of innuendo," I accused. "That makes the meaning of the words completely different."

"Oh," he said, "I see."

"I know you do," I said, narrowing my eyes. "You're just teasing. Which is strange because I thought you were supposed to be the responsible one, Archer."

"I am responsible," he said and then leaned closer, speaking directly into my ear. "But that doesn't mean I'm immune to hearing you say certain things"—His hands tightened around my waist, making me gasp—"or feeling you pressed up against me like this."

It was at that moment I realized several things. Since we collided, we had been standing like this: Me, draped across his chest, while his back was leaned up against the wall. Archer's arms were wrapped around me, his hands splayed on my lower back. Our legs were tangled together and my hand, that treacherous hand, was still buried in his hair while the other rested near his heart. The position couldn't have been more intimate. If anyone saw us, they'd definitely assume there was some hanky-panky going on.

My body warmed, aware now of everywhere we touched.

"And just so we're clear," he said, still speaking low, "I wasn't teasing."

His cheek brushed against mine as he leaned back, so he could meet my eyes.

"I would love to take you—any way, anywhere, anytime."

I tried to speak but couldn't; my throat was too dry. It was probably a good thing, since I had no idea what to say back. *Yes, please. I'd love to be taken. Is right now good for you?* That was just asking for trouble—again, not that I could say it anyway. Archer O'Brien literally left me speechless.

As I stood there unable to respond, Archer's frown came back full force.

"Honor?" he said after a beat. "You all right?"

Before I could respond, another voice spoke over me.

"Archer," Mrs. O'Brien called out. "Is that you?"

Eyes wide, I scrambled away as fast as I could, putting a safe distance between me and her son, worried she'd catch us in such a compromising pose. That would definitely put me smack dab in the "baseball bunny" category in her mind. But she never came around the corner. With a sigh, Archer pushed off the wall and stepped out into the main hall.

"Yeah, Mom, it's me," he said.

"Well, what are you doing over there, talking to yourself? Come into the office. I was hoping to speak to you about something."

"Sure, be there in a second."

"Okay," she said, and I heard her footsteps disappear.

Archer looked at me again, pushed his hands into his pockets.

"Guess I'll see you around," he said.

"Yeah, sure," was my brilliant reply. And if that wasn't bad enough, I gave him a thumbs-up, and added, "You bet."

I saw his lips twitch again, thought he might've wanted to laugh, but instead he walked away, moving toward his mother's office while shaking his head.

For my part, I left the building in a daze. How did he do that? How was it that Archer could talk to me and just make the whole world disappear? More importantly: How was I supposed to profile Archer and not fall for him? This was going to be an absolute disaster.

9

Archer

My day had gone from bad to worse.

After next to no sleep, I'd woken up to the sound of my phone alarm, followed by a text alert. My neck and back ached. The couch in the Omega Beta house wasn't exactly comfortable, but when Baylor had company, it was understood that I would bow out and let him have the room. I'd spent way too many nights on that lumpy couch.

I'd also spent way too many mornings getting him out of this exact predicament.

Checking my phone, I saw an S.O.S text from Bay. Apparently, the girl from last night was refusing to leave. Baylor had gotten himself another clinger.

What a surprise.

Sighing, I made my way up the stairs and opened the door to our room. There was a girl draped over Bay, who sat at his desk, looking very uncomfortable as she ran her fingers through his hair. They were both dressed, thankfully, though her hair was a mess, and his shirt looked like it was missing the top two buttons. When Baylor saw me, his eyes lit up.

"Archer," he said, sounding relieved. "Great to see you, brother. Did you need something?"

I was used to this, too. It was an act we'd perfected over the years.

"Yeah," I said, "I need to get dressed."

"Oh shoot," Baylor said, disentangling himself from the girl. "Sorry, sweetheart. Now that my brother's back, I guess you'll have to leave."

She looked over her shoulder, eyes roving over my body as if she hadn't just had her hands all over Bay. "I don't mind. If you want to get dressed, you're more than welcome." Her eyes met mine as she smiled. "I'm not shy or anything."

I cocked a brow. "But I am. Sorry, you'll have to go."

She harrumphed and pouted. "You're no fun, Archer O'Brien."

Wasn't the first time I'd heard that, so I took it in stride.

"You're right. He isn't," Baylor said, ushering her to the door. "But last night was fun. Thanks for that, sweetheart."

"No, thank you." She turned at the door, planted a kiss on his lips then pulled away slowly. "You're a good time, Baylor. Don't lose my number, okay?"

"Hmm," he said, watching as she sashayed out the door.

I couldn't contain my eyeroll. "Her number? Do you even remember her name?"

Baylor grinned. "Course, I do. It's sweetheart. That's all their names."

"Don't be a jerk," I said.

"Oh come on, Archer." Baylor closed the door and plopped down onto his bed. "She knew the score. And did you or did you not notice how she checked you out right in front of me? That was classy."

He had a point, but...

"Just be careful," I said, pulling off my old shirt and grabbing a towel. "You need to tone it down with all the girls and the drinking. Bear's worried, and so am I."

"Yeah, yeah, I've heard it," he said dismissively.

"Well, maybe you need to hear it again. Some of these girls might want to get you into trouble. Did you ever think of that? You're smarter than this. Hell, you're better than this, Bay."

"Actually, I'm not," he said, putting his hands behind his head, "but I'm glad you think so."

Shaking my head, I went to the door.

"Rest easy, Arch. I've got it under control."

"Do you?" I asked. "Because it sure doesn't look like it."

Baylor lifted his shoulders. "A little fun never hurt anyone. It's all good."

"Whatever you say. But you are better than this. I hope you know that."

Baylor just scoffed.

I went to my classes. The exam in Principles of Physiology was no cakewalk, but I'd studied hard last night, probably pulled at least a B, maybe an A minus. Either way, my GPA was solid. Management of Sports Organizations was usually my favorite class because everything about it interested me. But during today's lecture, my mind was still on Bay, thinking about what I could do to help him. If Dad was here, he would've known exactly what to say. He always did. My siblings and I had an unspoken agreement not to involve Mom in any of our crap. She'd already gone through so much. Dad's death devastated her. Though she smiled and was still the kindest soul ever, she'd never fully recovered from his loss. As the oldest, I'd tried to fill his shoes as best I could, be there for her and my younger brothers and sister ...but it was never enough.

Speaking of which...

I got a call later that night around 9:00 pm from Garret, the bartender at *Shake & Pour*, asking me to come get Dex. He'd been fighting again. Wonderful.

I drove to the bar as fast as I could without getting pulled over. I'd only taken a few steps inside when I spotted them. Garret was sitting on a stool next to my brother, who had an ice pack pressed against his face. Dex had his elbow propped up on the bar, lips set in a sneer, but from where I stood, he didn't look the worse for wear. It was only as I got closer and saw his eye that I blanched.

"What the hell happened?" I asked and gave a thank-you nod to Garret as he left to go serve his customers.

Dex shook his head. "This guy challenged me Archer, said a few choice words about our mother, too. What was I supposed to do? Let that slide?"

"Yes," I said, pulling the ice pack away. Seeing all that black and blue near his left eye made me nauseous. "That's exactly what you do. Walk the heck away. Why can't you ever just walk away?"

Dex didn't answer, just cocked his head.

"You look like hell," I said after a moment.

He grinned at that, the idiot. "You should see the other guy. He was such a poser. Couldn't take a punch for nothing. Didn't last five minutes."

I sighed, helping him up, looking sharply as he winced.

"You okay?" I asked.

"Yeah," he said, "lucky shot to the ribs. That's

all."

"Dex. You've got to stop doing this."

Dex frowned as we made our way to the door. "Stop what? Sticking up for my family? Never gonna happen."

I understood where he was coming from. Really, I did. If someone had been badmouthing Mom in front of me, I didn't know how I would've reacted. But this fighting shit had to end.

"Mom would never want you to get hurt over her," I said.

Dex grunted.

"Maybe instead of accepting the challenge, just try to talk it out next time."

"Yeah, sounds good," he said, and I looked to him in surprise. "Then maybe, we could braid each other's hair and go out for ice cream after."

The grin he threw me was pure defiance, and I knew he hadn't heard a word I'd just said.

I dropped him off at home, but I needed something to lift my mood after this crappy day, something just for me. And as I spied the copy of *Jane Eyre* on my nightstand, I knew exactly what I wanted.

* * *

"Arch, I don't know what you're thinking. But this isn't going to go well."

Chase was probably right, but heck, what did I have to lose? She'd already turned me down once.

It wasn't like I expected anything different—though I hoped for it. Seeing Honor would be a boon after everything that'd gone down this morning. After our little meeting in the hall and what Mom had told me, it looked like we'd be seeing more of each other. Plus...

"I told you, Chase," I said and held up Honor's book. "I'm just here to return this to her. Might need it for a class or something."

He shook his head then knocked to let Emmy know we were waiting outside.

But it was Charlie who answered the door.

"Well, well, well," she said, looking the two of us over. "If it isn't Archer and the panty thief."

I kept my frown, but inside, seeing the initial look of shock on Chase's face, I died laughing.

For his part, Chase just shrugged. "I think you're confusing me with my twin, Baylor."

She squinted at him. "Hmm, seriously?"

"It happens a lot," he said. "But yeah, I've never had any contact with your panties."

"Your loss," she said, pretending to study her nails, then looked up from beneath her lashes right at my brother—who wasn't paying her any attention. It was kind of funny actually. Chase was checking his phone, completely oblivious to her flirting, while Charlie wore a look of surprise. "There are so many of you O'Briens coming in and out of here it's hard to keep track. What did you say your name was again?"

Chase kept his head down. "I didn't. Can we come in? Archer has something for Honor."

Charlie crossed her arms. "I think I mentioned our rule before about not allowing men into our space. But maybe if you ask nicely..."

It was like watching a cat try to attract a mouse. In this case, Charlie was the cat and Chase was the mouse, but instead of trying to catch the mouse outright, Charlie was pretending like she didn't want him to notice her. I could've told her that approach would never work, not with Chase, but I was enjoying this way too much.

Raising my hand, I said, "Hey Charlie."

She stared for another second before turning her eyes to me.

"Sorry about him." I laid a hand on my brother's shoulder, and he looked up. "Chase isn't always the best conversationalist."

"Obviously," she said which cut off Chase's protest. His mouth snapped shut as he looked at her, seeming to really take her in for the first time. "I guess it's a good thing he's so cute."

Chase blinked, and his cheeks got red. Oh man, was he blushing? We seriously had to get him out of the house more often. Women would eat him alive if he couldn't take a little harmless flirtation.

Charlie smiled slowly. "I'll go get Honor. Emmy went for a drive. You two can wait in the living room if you want. But don't get too comfortable. The no guys rule exists for a reason."

I nodded, pulling Chase inside along with me. "And we fully support that rule. One hundred percent. Don't we Chase?"

"Yeah," he said then cleared his throat, "yeah, we do."

"Wouldn't want a whole bunch of guys hanging around Emmy," I said. "Especially not in her apartment."

Chase nodded as we sat side-by-side on the couch. "That's like my worst nightmare."

"You and me both," I said, frowning.

About a minute later, Honor and Charlie came back into the room.

"But I never have visitors," Honor was saying. "This had better be good, Charlie. I was just watching the end of *Pride and Prejudice* and—"

I stood, my eyes meeting hers.

"Oh," she said in surprise.

"Yeah, oh," Charlie said. "Now, will you stop complaining, and just see what he wants so we can get them out of here?"

"Sure," she said but didn't move toward me.

I felt kind of bad about leaving Chase to fend for himself, peripherally noticing him tense as Charlie came closer to the couch, probably to take a second chance at talking to him. *Sorry brother, you're on your own*, I thought, knowing he'd understand. Honor was here now, and my attention was all for her.

I walked around the couch and stopped in front of Honor, my eyes moving over her outfit. Her hair was up and kind of messy, little tendrils falling around her face, and she was wearing an oversize t-shirt that had the silhouette of a male holding something over his head. It said "Mrs. Lloyd Dobler" across the top. My lips turned down, the frown getting deeper. I didn't know who this Lloyd Dobler guy was, but I was instantly jealous. She had his name written over her chest for crying out loud. Her pajama pants looked big and had little dogs on them while her feet—I nearly smiled when I saw the fuzzy socks covering her toes.

"What are you so happy about?" she said, and my head popped up immediately.

"What do you mean?" I asked.

She pointed at my face. "You're smiling."

"I was not," I said, knowing my frown was still firmly in place.

"Not your mouth." Honor shook her head. "There, your eyes are smiling."

This was news to me. "They are?"

"Yeah," she said, pulling her hand back and crossing her arms. "I've noticed they do that sometimes."

Only when I'm with you, I thought.

"Did you need something, Archer? I wasn't expecting anyone—which is why I'm dressed like this, obviously. Sorry you had to see me in my crappy pajamas."

You look good to me.

The words went through my head, but I didn't say them. She looked self-conscious enough as it was. And beautiful, even if she didn't think so. It wasn't so much about what she wore as who was wearing the clothes. Honor could probably wear a potato sack, and she'd still make my eyes smile.

Wanting to cheer her up, I held out her copy of *Jane Eyre*. "Just came to return this to its proper owner," I said.

"Ah." She took the book from my hand and pulled it to her chest. "That's...great. Thank you."

My brow furrowed. "I thought you might need it for class. Thought you'd be happy to get it back."

"Oh no, I definitely am, and it's not required reading," she said then laughed at herself. "It's just one of my favorites. My shelves have been missing Jane. Thank you so much again for returning it."

Maybe I'd imagined the note of sadness I detected in her voice?

"So I guess this means you don't want to date me anymore," she added.

"What? Nah, I still definitely want that. I just felt bad."

"About what?" She sounded surprised.

"Keeping your book," I said and ran a hand over my neck. "Plus, now I don't need an excuse to see you. I hear you'll be coming to some of our games, hanging out with the team. That's cool."

Honor blinked.

"Did you really think I'd give up that easily?"

"Most guys would," she said with a shrug.

Yeah well, I wasn't most guys.

"Honestly, it might make things easier."

"In what way?" I asked.

Honor tucked a strand of hair behind her ear and looked up at me. "Well, I have a proposition for you. If you're up for it."

I knew I'd agree to anything she asked at that point. "Okay, what did you have in mind?"

"Maybe we can start over and try being just friends."

Friends. I actually was okay with that. It was the "just" I didn't like. My mind balked at the word, but for the first time tonight, Honor looked sure. She was smiling up at me hopefully, and though I wanted more from her than friendship—so much more—I didn't have the heart to tell her right then.

"Hm, sounds interesting," I said.

Not exactly a lie, right? But not an agreement that we should be "just friends" either. I knew she wanted more from me, too. We couldn't just start over, forget about what happened at the party where we met and everything since. I had to figure out what was holding her back and how to convince her to give us a go.

"Awesome," Honor said. "I've thought about it a lot. I'm actually going to need to profile you at some point, Archer, and this will make it so much less complicated."

I nodded. "I heard about that. Speaking of, I brought you the game schedule. My mom asked me to drop it off."

"She did?" Honor took the paper with a frown. "I thought she was just going to send it through email."

"Well, technically, I volunteered," I said and saw her eyes flare. Ah, that was not the look of someone who wanted to be just friends. I could work with that.

"You seem to do a lot of volunteering," she said suspiciously. I couldn't be sure, but I hoped she remembered the way I'd volunteered to be her one-night stand before.

I took a step forward. "What can I say? I'm a giver."

"Oh great." She cleared her throat. "Well, I'm glad you stopped by so we could have this chat."

"Me, too," I said, stepping into her space.

Honor's eyes widened.

"What?" I asked innocently. "Friends hug each other, right?"

I thought I heard a chuckle from the other side of the living room but ignored it.

Honor shook her head with a smile. "I guess so."

Yes, I thought, as she stepped into my arms. It was brief, but I milked that hug for all it was worth. Feeling her breath speed up as I turned my head into her neck, I grinned before pulling back.

"I guess I'll see you at the game next week," I said. "It's at home, should be a lot of fun."

"Yeah, my first game ever," Honor said. "I'm excited."

"Your first baseball game?" I couldn't keep the surprise out of my voice. "You're serious?"

"Yeah."

"Well, that's special. We should do something."

"I don't think that's necessary."

"Oh, it definitely is," I said. "As your new friend, I insist. If we win, you come out to celebrate with us."

Honor raised a brow. "But that's only if you win, right?"

"Yeah," I said, "but we'll definitely get that W. So, you better be ready to go out after."

"So sure of yourself," she said.

I shook my head. "I'm sure of my team. They'd never let me down—especially when I tell them it's your first game. So, you'll come?"

"Just as friends, right?"

I shrugged. "Whatever you say."

She shook her head, but I knew I had her even before she said, "You're on."

In my mind, I was still trying to figure out why

Honor insisted on the whole just friends thing. Maybe she wanted to see how we'd get along first? Maybe she really wasn't attracted to me like I was to her? But no, I'd seen the look in her eyes, felt her reaction whenever we were close. Regardless, I was excited about next week. She'd agreed to come out to the game, and she'd be rooting for our team.

One thing I knew for sure: My boys better be ready to play their hearts out because I was not letting this one get away.

Not the win or the girl.

10

Honor

Every surface in my room was covered in clothes, the closet empty.

And still, I couldn't figure out what to wear.

"I just can't believe it," Charlie was saying. "I mean, he basically ignored me the whole time. I know you were over there talking it up with your boy toy. But Chase didn't even try to ask me out. Can you believe that?"

I sighed and looked over at her. "You are a hard person to ignore."

Charlie nodded. "Damn right, I am."

"And he's not my boy toy," I mumbled. "Like I told you, we're just—"

"Friends?" Charlie rolled her eyes with a scoff. Reclining back on my bed, laying on all of the clothes there, she grinned. "Oh please, I saw the way the two of you were looking at each other."

"How were we looking at each other?" I asked, putting another shirt up to my chest for a second before throwing it aside.

"Like you wanted to go at it right there in the living room."

I gasped, nearly swallowing my tongue at her words. "We were not."

"Were, too," she said, sitting up. "Archer definitely was. And I could tell you how this is going to end, but I think I'll just sit back and watch it all play out. You guys are too cute together."

Shaking my head, a blush was permanently etched on my cheeks as I held up another shirt, raised my eyebrow at Charlie. She bit her lip a second before shaking her head. With a groan, I joined her on the bed. It wasn't like I was getting anywhere clothes-wise. My whole wardrobe seemed to be against me today. At this rate, I'd be showing up at the game in my PJ's.

"Just to be clear," I said again, "he wasn't looking at me like that."

"Okay...but yes, he was," Charlie said then groaned a second later. "Which is exactly how his brother should've been looking at me. Seriously, I gave him all my best cues. The hair flip"—she pushed her hair over her shoulder—"the flirtatious glance"—she looked at me then away—"the pout"—

she pursed her lips, making them seem even more lush—"and the words which you know I'm awesome at. What is this Chase guy's deal?"

I was having a hard time not laughing. She sounded so put out. "Maybe he was just having an off day and couldn't read the signs."

"You think?" she asked, then looked down at her body. "My boobs still look good, right?"

I did laugh at that. "Yes! Oh my gosh, Charlie, please. They're just as perky as ever. If Chase didn't notice you, that's his problem. Not yours."

She smiled as her gaze came back to mine. "I know, right? Now, remind me. Why are you going through all of your stuff again?"

Looking around the room, I frowned. "It looks like a tornado hit. Doesn't it?"

"Yeah, kind of."

"Ugh, I don't know what to wear."

"Why does it matter so much?" Charlie asked. "It's just a baseball game."

In my head, I knew Charlie was right, and maybe if I felt more rational, it wouldn't be such a big deal. It shouldn't be. But...

"Well, it's my first one, and I'm not sure what to expect."

Charlie nodded. "And?"

"And important people are going to be there."

"Oh, important, you don't say. And?" she prompted again.

"And...well..."

"Yes..."

I shot her a glare. "You know I hate you, right?"

Charlie just smiled. "No, you don't. You love me like I love you. Now, what were you going to say?"

Taking a deep breath, I said, "I know I shouldn't care, but so far, Archer's only seen me in a red sexy dress looking like a pinup or dressed like a bum how I was that first time I went to the field so he wouldn't recognize me. Or," I closed my eyes, "in my comfy pajamas. There was also the time outside his mom's office, but that was really brief. I want to look like me, but I...want to look nice."

"There," she said. "Was that so hard?"

Yes, I thought. "So, will you help me or what?"

"Of course, young grasshopper," she said and patted me on the shoulder. Standing up, she eyed my clothes for a couple of minutes, then picked up my favorite pair of light wash jeans, a plain white t-shirt that I loved because of how laid back yet feminine it made me feel, and my nicest pair of sneakers. "What about these? Or we could even get a jersey at the student store before the game if you want."

My jaw dropped as I stared. "I've been at this for an hour. How did you manage to pick out the perfect outfit so fast?"

Charlie shrugged then handed me the clothes.

"I have an eye for fashion. It's no big deal. Plus, I know you and what you're most comfortable in."

"Thanks," I said.

"Welcome," she said then stopped at my door. Turning back to me, she added, "Oh and Honor, wear your hair down. I bet Archer would love that."

My cheeks flushed hot as I looked away. "Like I said, we're friends."

I couldn't see it, but I knew she was grinning.

"I hate to point it out, but I'm your friend," she said. "And you've never cared this much about what you wear in front of me."

Embarrassment rolled through my body, but it was only because she was so right. I had never cared what I wore in front of any of my other friends.

"Hair down," she said again.

"It'll probably be hot," I said stubbornly. "I think I'll just wear it up."

Charlie chuckled as she left, leaving me there with my mess of a room and lots to think about.

* * *

I wore my hair down.

Well, half-up, half-down, which was the perfect representation for how I was feeling. Confused, like I didn't know quite where Archer and I stood. Friends didn't get excited about hugging their friends, right? I'd definitely felt breathless when Archer had pulled me into his arms the other day. And they also didn't go all googly-eyed when they saw said friend run out of the dugout onto the field to warm-up. And when that friend looked for them in the stands and waved, their bones didn't get all weak and melty, right?

Gah.

Okay, I was going to have to work on the friend thing.

But geez, he looked good in that uniform.

A female voice spoke, breaking me out of my Archer daze. "Hey, Honor. Would you mind if I sit here?"

I looked up and smiled when I saw June. "No, go ahead. Hey June, I didn't know you'd be here."

"Oh yeah," she said, taking a seat beside me. "I never miss a game."

"Big Wolves fan?" I asked.

June shrugged. "I guess you could say that."

As her eyes roamed the players and got stuck on one in particular, I knew it wasn't just the team she was here for. I could totally relate to that feeling. Though her eyes were only on Baylor.

"This is my first game," I said.

"Really? Emmy's going to freak when she hears that. Wait until you see them play. They're really incredible."

"I saw the team practice once," I said. "Do you have a favorite player?"

June laughed, but it looked like she was blushing. "Oh, not really. Chase is a great pitcher, and Archer does amazing things behind the plate. Not to even mention Dex, who's always ready for anything."

"And Baylor?" I asked gently.

"He's good, too," she said all nonchalant. "Baylor's really smart, and he doesn't ever get scared. Statistically speaking, he's probably got the best batting average and RBIs—but it's not like I follow all of his stats or anything."

Jeez, was this what I sounded like when I tried to deny my feelings? No wonder Charlie hadn't believed me. As the players came in from warm-up and walked past us in the stands, Baylor looked up and threw June a wink. She smiled and bit her lip.

"June seriously, don't encourage him," Emmy said, sitting down beside her. She was carrying a bottle of water and a towel. I noticed then that, for the most part, we were all dressed the same—jeans and t-shirt—and gave a sigh of relief. Thank you, Charlie. "You know he's a player," Emmy went on. "Plus, you're my best friend. He knows better than to try something with you."

June rolled her eyes. "As if I'd be interested."

"Do you know how many friends I've lost because they went behind my back and screwed him? Not to mention how many have tried to befriend me to hook up with my brothers? Too many to count."

"Nothing to worry about, Em," June said. "It's

not like he'd ever notice me anyway."

Emmy shot her a look that said yeah-right before switching her gaze to me. "And how are things with you and Archer?"

"We decided to just be friends," I said.

"Who decided? You or him?"

"Well, I came up with the idea, but—"

"Ah," she said. "I see."

June sat forward. "So, you're going to try and be friends? With Archer?"

"Yeah," I said slowly as the two of the exchanged a significant look. "Is there something wrong with that?"

"Oh no," June said at the same time Emmy said, "Not really."

I waited, knowing there was more to it.

Emmy sighed after a moment then added, "Arch isn't really a just-friends type of guy. I don't remember him ever having a friend who was a girl. Do you, June?"

"Nope," June said. "Can't say I do. The others yes, but not Archer."

I laughed but stopped just as quickly, noting the looks on their faces.

"You're serious?" I said.

They nodded.

"But I'm sure he's had girlfriends, right?"

Emmy nodded. "Yeah, about three."

My eyes widened. "Three? But he's so

wonderful and attractive and—"

Emmy held up a hand, feigning sickness even as she smiled. "Please stop. I can't take anymore."

I laughed. "Okay but come on. Only three girlfriends? All his life? Archer O'Brien? I don't believe it."

"Hmm," June said, "she's right. I'm not sure if we should count Annabelle. That was like what? A few days during his freshman year? That wasn't really a romantic relationship."

"That's true," Emmy said. "Annabelle shouldn't count—plus, she was rude and only wanted him as arm candy." She nodded at June then looked to me. "So yeah, two girlfriends."

I felt like all the wind had just gotten knocked out of me, my whole view of Archer trying to reconfigure itself. But it just didn't make sense.

"But how?" I asked unable to let it drop. "He had to have had girls who wanted him."

"Oh yeah," Emmy said, "he's dated. Don't get me wrong. Girls definitely want him. Archer's just really particular about who he wants back."

Well okay, then.

As Emmy eyed me again, she added, "And he's a natural protector, likes to take care of all of us. My brothers and I call him the momma bear—behind his back, of course. That might be another reason."

It still didn't add up, but what did I know? The fact that girls had thrown themselves at Archer, but he hadn't just basked in their attention like some guys...it made me like him even better. As if I needed that.

June patted my hand. "I think it's a good thing that you two are trying to be friends."

Emmy just grinned. "Yeah, good luck with that."

The game started shortly after, and I was grateful. Curiosity had always been one of my greatest downfalls. But I hadn't meant to ask about Archer's past girlfriends or girls who were his friends—or the lack thereof. I'd probably think about it way too much later, but right now, I welcomed the distraction the game provided.

And boy was it a great game.

Of course, I had nothing to compare it to, but from the first pitch, our guys were on fire.

Chase threw strike after strike, not allowing any hits. He'd nod after Archer signaled him, and it was like clockwork. I was in awe as I watched the ball zoom past the plate, almost faster than my eyes could track. The guys from Young Harris swung, but they didn't stand a chance. Up and down, I thought with a smile, remembering what Archer had told me at practice. Before I knew it, our team was up to bat.

Dex was first in the lineup. He hit a foul ball to left field on the first pitch. The second was called a strike, which Emmy didn't seem to agree with at all, saying any idiot could see it was high. Before the third pitch, Dex stepped out of the box to loosen his neck then crowded the plate like he owned it.

"Why's he standing so close?" I said. "Isn't he afraid of getting hit with the ball?"

Emmy made a face. "Dex? Heck no, he's not afraid of anything. Dex only gets hit if he wants to get hit—and I'm talking more in fights than baseball. But no matter what, he's going to get on base."

"That's why he's the lead-off batter," June put in, like I should know what that meant.

Seeing my confusion, Emmy said, "It means Dex bats first because he's reliable and amazing. Now, watch my brother get a hit off of this guy."

It was like she'd known what would happen.

The next pitch was clean down the middle, and Dex hit a pretty line drive that got him all the way to second base.

"Yeah, double," Emmy shouted. "Let's go, D!"

I quickly scribbled a few of the terms I'd heard so far into my notebook. My "Baseball Notes" sheet was already half-full. I knew I'd need more space before this was over, but at least I had a quick reference guide.

Our second batter struck out, but the third guy got a hit. It was a single, which meant there were players on first and third base when it was Baylor's turn to bat. He walked by right as Archer stepped out to do a few practice swings, so honestly, I wasn't paying much attention.

Unlike everyone else in the stands.

They clapped louder than ever when Baylor was announced. He ate it up, show-boated a bit, blowing the entire audience a kiss, and I noticed he had his own little cheering section, who just happened to be sitting right behind us. It was mostly female.

One girl said, "Baseball has been so good to that family."

"I know. Just look at that ass," said another, and they both giggled.

As Baylor got into his stance, I felt June tense beside me, but she didn't say anything.

He let the first pitch go by, a good thing since it was a ball.

"And those arms." A third voice sighed as he got ready again. "Do you think they'd let me be a water girl for the team or something? I'd do just about anything for a shot with him."

"I hear he's not picky. My friend Marla was with him last year, and she's not half as pretty as you. You've got a shot."

"You think?"

At that point, Emmy turned around. "Excuse me, could you please shut up? I'm trying to watch the game here."

The three girls stared back at her with thinly veiled disdain. Looking at them for the first time, I noticed they all had that sun-kissed look, hair down and flowing, a lot of makeup, but you wouldn't know it unless you were really close to them like we were now. They had on t-shirts, too, but they all matched: royal blue with two white stripes on the sleeves and black letters on the front that said Baseball Babe.

"We weren't even talking to you," one of them said.

The sound of a bat connecting was heard, and we all looked to the field. It was called foul at the last second, and Emmy turned to them once again.

"I know you weren't talking to me, but I can still hear you," Emmy said sweetly.

"Why don't you just mind your own business?" said the one who I thought had wanted to be the water girl. It sounded like her voice.

"That's my brother," she said, tipping her chin in Baylor's direction. "So he is my business. Stop talking about him like he's a piece of meat, and we won't have a problem."

Wow, way to go, Emmy.

That certainly shut them up.

I'd be lying if I said their conversation didn't make me feel bad about how I'd wanted to use Baylor to lose my V-card. But it hadn't happened, thank goodness. Because I'd ended up in bed with Archer instead. A little shiver went through me as he took another practice swing.

A second later, Baylor got a hit to deep left field, bringing both Dex and the other runner in and landing himself on third. Just like that, it was 2-0. The crowd cheered; Emmy and June fist-bumped, and then it was Archer's turn.

The other team's pitcher looked like he was trying to shake off that last play as Archer approached the plate. I knew I was biased. But there was something in the way Archer moved that set him apart. He was all loose grace and confidence as he assumed his batter's stance. There was nothing questioning, no hesitancy.

The first pitch he watched go by.

Strike one.

The second pitch, same thing.

Strike two.

"What's he waiting for?" I asked, getting nervous.

"His pitch," June said.

"Yeah," Emmy agreed as Archer stepped out of the box. "The ump isn't calling them, but those pitches were high. Archer's patient. He's really good about waiting."

That gave me pause, made me realize I knew that about him already—even in the short time we'd shared together, he'd been nothing but patient with me. But then why had he given up so quickly on dating me if he was so good at waiting?—but as Archer got back into position, I found myself holding my breath.

It happened on the third pitch.

The pitcher released the ball, and Archer finally

swung. His bat connected, and a crack rent the air as the ball sailed into left field, back and back, until finally it left the field altogether. The Wolves fans jumped to their feet, and I was right there with them. Homerun! At his first at bat. That had been freaking spectacular.

"Holy crap," I said as Archer rounded the bases, and Baylor whooped as he ran home to score another run. "That was amazing!"

Emmy smiled. "First game of the season," she said as if it explained everything.

A sneaking suspicion hit me.

"What do you mean by that?" I asked.

"Oh nothing, it was just something our parents ingrained in us." She shrugged. "Start strong. Finish stronger. I meant they haven't lost the first game of the season in a long time."

I hadn't forgotten about the wager I'd made with Archer. I'd promised to go out and celebrate later with the team if they won, and so far, he was definitely winning. I watched as he got congratulations from his team, saw him glance up at the stands as he walked to the dugout. Archer caught my gaze, and though his signature frown was still in place, his eyes were smiling like they did sometimes. That look paired with Emmy's words only made me more certain my theory was correct.

"Define a long time," I said.

"Well...I don't think my brothers have ever lost

the first game of the season," she said. "Not even when they were in t-ball, and there were no official 'winners.'"

"Ugh."

"What's up?"

As I relayed all the details of our bet, Emmy and June's smiles got wider. It wasn't like I wanted the Wolves to lose but come on. Never? Since they were playing t-ball? At the end of my short rant, Emmy reached across to pat me on the hand.

"Sorry girl," she said on a laugh. "You've been had."

"It'll be great, though," June said. "We always go back to the Omega Beta house after the games to hang out. It's pretty fun."

I nodded, but my throat was a bit tight, as I watched the Wolves dominate the rest of the game. The team played like they were out for blood. And if the goal was to start out strong and get even stronger, I pitied the other teams down the line. Everything I'd read or heard about the team and the O'Brien brothers was confirmed. That baseball game was brilliant—but honestly? From that point on, my mind was focused on only one thing.

The fact that my "friend" Archer had made a bet that would result in me having to go back to the Omega Beta house. The place where we'd met. The place where we'd had our perfect first kiss—which had   then   turned   into   a   very passionate/sizzling/memorable make-out session.

The place where I'd mistakenly ended up in his bed.

At least now, I knew which brother was which, I reassured myself. There definitely wouldn't be any mix-ups tonight on that front. Plus, there wouldn't be any beds or kissing involved period. Archer and I were friends. Just like me and Charlie, or me and Rose. And it's not like I wanted to kiss him again anyway.

Maybe if I kept telling myself that, I'd actually believe it.

11

Archer

I was still pumped after the game. My team had come through in a big way. It was my senior year, and we'd just won the first game of the season. I couldn't have been prouder. Now it was time to celebrate.

And I knew exactly who I wanted to do that with.

Fresh out of the shower, I walked over to my clothes, dressing in record time. Emmy had just texted to let me know they were out there, and I didn't want to keep Honor waiting.

"Hey, Declan," I said, lacing up my shoes. "That was a great catch in the third."

"Really?" he said like he didn't totally believe it.

"Yeah." I nodded, gave his shoulder a pat. "You

keep playing like that, we'll definitely make it to the championship. Well done."

The kid smiled. "Thanks, Captain."

"No problem," I said, pulling my cap on. "You did a great job."

As I was leaving, Baylor caught up to me.

"Great job?" Baylor scoffed, softly so no one else would hear, not that anyone was standing near us anyway. "I've been making catches like that since middle school. It was easy. The ball came right to him."

I shrugged. "He's a freshman who needs some encouragement. And he did make the play," I pointed out. "Improvement from practice."

"Ah," he said, "you're building him up."

"Just acknowledging that he did something good." I nudged his side with my elbow. "Nice hit in the sixth by the way. I think they heard that grand slam in the next county over."

Baylor threw me a grin. "No use pulling your inspirational mumbo jumbo on me, brother. It's unnecessary."

"Didn't say it because it's necessary. I said it because it's true."

"Keep saying things like that, and my head will get even bigger."

"Wasn't aware that was possible."

"Oh ha ha," he said, and we walked outside together. "What's got you in such a good mood? It can't be the win. You knew we'd take this first game."

"Nothing."

Looking over all the students and fans still milling outside, I spotted Honor and felt my shoulders relax. She was standing with Emmy, June—and was that Mom she was talking to? Anyway, it was a relief to see her. Part of me had thought maybe she wouldn't stay or would go back on our bet.

"Nothing, huh," Baylor repeated. "Does nothing happen to be five-foot-five with brown hair, brown eyes and have a name that rhymes with 'goner'?"

"Shut it," I muttered as we got closer.

"Because that's what you're going to be if you're not careful."

I scowled at him, but Baylor laughed.

"Just don't say I didn't warn you." He ran the last few steps to the girls and Mom. "You see that grand slam, Junior? Was it masterful or what?"

June smiled. "You know it was."

"Yeah, but I like to hear you say it."

"Why don't you go ask your fangirls over there," Emmy said, tipping her chin at three girls who were standing a ways away. I thought I recognized them from our games. "They went crazy when it happened."

"They did, huh?" Baylor eyed the girls speculatively, lifting his chin at them, which set

163

them off giggling. "Good to know."

Emmy groaned after a second, and Baylor looked at her.

"What? I can't help it if they like what they see," he said.

"You were a little slow off the bag," June said, startling everyone. The expression on her face was dead serious while Baylor looked shocked. "And let's be honest, you could've probably made that play on the first strike he threw."

"Maybe I was trying to tire him out," Baylor argued. "Make him throw more pitches."

She shrugged. "Maybe," she said. "But you were still slow off the bag. Scouts could be watching at any time. Wouldn't hurt you to show a little hustle."

Baylor glanced at me then Emmy, Honor and finally Mom, but when none of us contradicted her, he looked back to June.

"Hustle," he repeated, stepping closer to June as she took a step back. "I'll show you hustle. Better start running, Junebug."

June tried to run. I'll give her that. But Baylor caught her seconds later, scooping her up and spinning her around in his arms as she gasped. If I was a goner, well, at least I knew it. Baylor was in deep (or at least he was going to be if he ever confronted his feelings), and he didn't seem to be aware of a thing. Looking back at Honor, I caught her staring and felt my chest fill.

164

"Nice game," she said while pushing a hand into her pocket.

I nodded. "Thanks," I said, thinking damn, she looked good in that white tee and jeans. "Glad you could make it out."

"Me, too."

June screeched again, and Emmy rolled her eyes. "As fun as this is to watch, I need to go check on my best friend. I'll see you guys later. Great playing, Archer—as always."

She gave my arm a squeeze as she walked away, which left me there with Honor and Mom.

"She's right," Mom said to me. "You did great today, Captain. Way to lead your team to victory."

"Couldn't have done it without our great coach," I said back.

Mom smiled, then to Honor, she said, "Glad you came on a day when the Wolves played so well. I assume you and the guys are going to celebrate?"

"We are," Honor said, glancing at me, "though I have no idea what we're doing."

"You'll have fun, I think." Coach/Mom threw me a scowl then. "Though not too much fun. Right, Archer?"

"Don't worry, Mom. I'll keep an eye on them, make sure nothing gets out of hand," I said.

"Oh, I know you will," she said then leaned in to give me a hug. Whispering, she said, "I like her."

"You're not the only one," I mumbled before she

drew back.

"Well, alright." Mom waved at someone who called her name, telling them she'd be right there, before turning back to us. "Again, good game, son. Honor, you'll think over what I said?"

Honor nodded, and as Mom walked away, it was finally just the two of us.

"Do I want to know what that was about?" I asked.

She shrugged. "You'll see."

"Ah, so you and my Mom are keeping secrets now," I said. "Never a good sign."

Honor bit her lip. "So, you won the bet—though as I hear, it wasn't so much of a bet as a sure thing. That was a little sneaky of you."

My chin dipped as I looked her in the eye. "Slytherin, remember?"

She shook her head. "So, what are we going to do?"

"You'll see," I said, throwing her words back.

"I hope there are no dungeons involved," she joked.

Not going to lie. That sent my brain right into the gutter, and an image of Honor dressed in leather went through my mind, but I quickly recovered.

"Nope," I said, "no dungeons."

"Okay then, Captain, lead the way."

Unlike with everyone else, my heart skipped when Honor called me that. I remembered what

Baylor had told me, what I'd already admitted to myself if I was honest. *Goner* was a completely accurate description. Now, I just had to get Honor on the same page.

* * *

"*This* is what you do after a win?"

"What'd you expect?" I asked. "Loud music and beer pong?"

"Something like that," she said.

"We're in training."

"I know, but..." Honor laughed in delight. "This is just *so* not what I imagined. So different than the last time I was here."

I stared at her lips. They were red and smiling, so how could I not?

"Hey, watch out," she said, nodding toward the pan in my hand. "Those are looking a little done."

With a curse, I hurriedly got back to my task, flipping the bacon, removing four pancakes from the opposite pan and adding more batter. In the other pan, the eggs were still looking good—at least I'd remembered to turn those off—but cooking all that food at once required focus. Unfortunately, with Honor standing there, my attention was shot. Breakfast was the closest we could get to eating "unhealthy," and honestly, some of the guys were drinking beer. We knew we'd have to work it all off at the next practice. But man, this was a celebration. It was good food with good people, and it was worth it.

"Thanks," I said, "I haven't burned anything since I first learned how to cook."

"Really?" She sounded dubious as I flipped the pancakes over.

"Really. My dad taught me to be vigilant." I shot her a look. "You're just distracting."

"Hey, that's not fair," she protested. "I'm not even doing anything."

I didn't get a chance to tell her that she didn't have to do anything. It was just her. Honor. She distracted me like nothing else by just being in the same room. It had been that way since day one.

My teammate Shawn Reyes came up asking for more pancakes, so Honor put two on his plate while I cooked and asked about his little brother.

"How's Miles been getting along?" I said. "School any easier?"

"Yeah, your baby bro really helped him," Shawn said, adding syrup then taking a bite of his pancakes, eyes closing on a groan. A second later, he added, "He's passing algebra now, says it's his favorite class. Crazy, right?"

"Finn's good like that," I said, thinking of my youngest brother. "He's basically a genius, always been the smartest of all of us. You think your parents will let Miles come to a game now?"

"Mom and Dad have been holding that over his head," Shawn said. "But I think he's all clear."

"Better keep playing like you did today then."

"Aye, aye, Captain."

As Shawn left, T.J. slid into his place.

"Hey, I'm T.J. Can I get some bacon, eggs, and ketchup, please?" he said and threw Honor a grin.

"You sure can," she said, placing the bacon on his plate while I ladled eggs on next. "And the ketchup's right there, T.J."

"Thanks a lot."

"What's with the polite act?" I asked. T.J. was going to town with the ketchup—I could hardly see any yellow left on those eggs—but what bothered me was the way he kept eyeing Honor. "You're never nice to a girl unless you're trying to get her into bed."

T.J.'s face showed no shame as he shrugged. "First of all, I dispute that. I'm always nice. And second, I heard she was free. So I thought, maybe we could—"

"You thought wrong." My words came out more as a growl, but I couldn't help it. "Honor's my...she's my...friend."

Even I knew it sounded weak.

T.J. blinked. After a moment, he said, "And?"

I crossed my arms, regaining some of my cool. "And if you want me to keep helping you with your swing, you'll back off."

"Okay, okay," T.J. said, holding a palm out. "Let's not get crazy. I just saw a hot chick and

169

thought I'd take a shot. No offense, Honor."

"None taken," she said, though it sounded like she was trying not to laugh.

"But I didn't know she was yours," T.J. added, looking to me. "No harm, no foul. Right, Captain? I'll just be on my way."

"Hey," I said, catching his arm before he could leave. Looking him in the eye, I said, "I meant to ask, how's your grandma doing?"

T.J.'s voice lost its fun edge real quick. "She's okay, got released from the hospital last week. They say her red counts are back up, so that's good."

I nodded. "It is. The team signed a card for her. It's in my bag by the door. Don't forget to take it."

"I won't."

"We're all here for you, you know," I said quietly. "We got your back."

"I do know," he said with a nod. "Thanks, Captain."

I shook my head. "No thanks necessary."

T.J. shot a look over my shoulder, and suddenly his smile was back.

"Well, I'll just get going. Leave you to spend some quality time with your...*friend*."

I didn't miss the emphasis he put on the word or the wink he threw Honor before he walked away, but the guy was gone before I could say anything. T.J. had always been a smartass. As I turned to scoop up the remaining pancakes, I could feel Honor looking at me.

"Do you do that with all of them?" she asked.

"What?" I said.

"Check in, make sure they're okay, ask about their families."

Shrugging, I switched off the burner and picked up a towel to wipe my hands.

Honor continued to stare up into my eyes. "It's sweet," she said. "How you look out for them."

"I don't look out for—" From the corner of my eye, I saw Baylor stealthily trying to grab another beer from the fridge and called him out. "Hey! You know the rules. One and done."

He stopped with his hand on the bottle, turned to me with wide eyes, figuratively caught with his hand in the cookie jar. "But Arch, I was just..."

"Correct me if I'm wrong, but you already had your one beer for tonight. Right, Bay?"

"Yeah, but..."

Hands on hips, I stared him down, waiting for his explanation.

"Fine, geez," he said and shut the fridge door. "But lighten up. It's not like one more Corona would've killed me."

"It wouldn't have made you any quicker either," I said. "June was right. You need to get faster if you want to go pro."

Baylor gave a sober nod but then ruined it with a salute. "Okay, Cap. Whatever you say, Cap."

As he went back to rejoin some of the girls from the game, the ones who'd all been dressed alike, and took a sip of one of their beers, I just shook my head. Baylor threw me a grin in response.

"He seems like a lot to handle," Honor commented.

"He is," I said. "They all are."

"But it's obvious you love them."

I looked around and tried to imagine what it was like to come into this place filled with baseball players, friends and superfans, how it all looked to her. Some of the guys had pulled up a game in the living room. Others were lounging around, digging into their second and third plates of breakfast. A few were playing video games in the room next door. Several were getting their flirt on like Baylor. Everything seemed chill, relaxed. I didn't know if this was Honor's scene, but it was definitely mine.

I shrugged. "They're my family."

"Gotta say"—she smiled as my eyes met hers—"this is a far cry from what I'd imagined 'celebrating a win' would be like. I was worried it would be like the last party."

"You mean, when you came here looking to score with my brother?"

She winced. "Ugh, please don't remind me."

After serving the last of the food, I leaned back against the counter.

"What was that all about anyway?" I said.

Honor's eyes widened. "Are we seriously talking about this?"

"Figured it's what friends do."

"But why?" she said. "You were there. It was a disaster. You know I tried to seduce you thinking you were—"

Honor suddenly cut herself off, and we both looked to Baylor as he let out a loud laugh. Two of my other teammates had gotten up from the couch and were headed this way, looking to grab more food, no doubt, though it was already gone.

"Hey, follow me."

The instant I took her hand a sensation of warmth ran through me. Honor drew in a breath.

"Where are we going?" she asked.

"This is an important talk," I said, walking toward the stairs, leading her up them and down the hall. I kept hold of her hand the whole way. "I thought we could use some privacy."

"Yeah...but your room? What if someone needs you downstairs?"

Opening the door, I walked inside first, and Honor followed. "They can do without me for a few minutes."

"Okay, if you're sure..."

Honor's head was down, looking at our hands, studying them.

"Your hands are really rough," she murmured.

It took me a second to respond. Her thumb had

173

just brushed against mine, trailing down to the inside of my palm. My whole body was focused on that one area. What had she just said? Something about my hands?

"Must be all the baseball," she added a second later.

"Yeah," I said gruffly.

Her thumb was now doing these intoxicating little circles on my skin. They were driving me slowly insane, but I never wanted her to stop. Seeming to realize what she was doing, her hand slipped from mine a moment later. Honor walked over to the desk and sat in the chair there—even though I noticed her eyes kept going to the bed. Each time this happened, her face flushed a bit more.

Interesting.

I closed the door and leaned my back against it.

"So friend," I prompted, "picking up where we left off. The party? Why exactly were you there?"

"I told you. I was there to..." she trailed off, her cheeks flaming.

I decided to help her out. "Get laid, hookup, have sex?"

Rolling her eyes at herself, she said, "Yes. I was trying to be wild and sexy for once which I'm terrible at if you didn't notice."

"I don't know about that," I said, remembering the way the movements of her thumb had made me feel a second ago.

"Oh come on, Archer," she said. "All I wanted was a fling, and it ended horribly."

My eyebrows went up at that. "If I remember correctly, it wasn't all bad."

Honor's lips twitched. "I guess not," she said, and I knew by the way her eyes dropped to my lips before jerking back up to meet mine that she meant it.

"So, why Baylor?" I asked.

"Do we really have to go there?"

"Please, humor me. I've been thinking about this a lot"—only like every day since it happened—"and it's the thing that really bothers me. I have to know. Why did you choose him?"

She wouldn't meet my eyes. "I don't know. I'd heard some rumors, knew he was a player, and I guess I just wanted to experience what it was like."

Tension roiled in the pit of my stomach, but I had to ask. "Being with Baylor?"

"Not him," she said, and I felt my shoulders relax, "it could've been anybody really. And please know, I feel like a total douchenozzle for ever having thought about using your brother like that."

"He would've gladly let you do it." The mere thought of them together made my teeth clench. "Baylor isn't real selective. And even if he was, I can't see him turning you down."

"I just wanted to know what it feels like," Honor

said. "To be wanted, to be desired like that. My romantic knowledge and experience is sorely lacking. I wanted something light with no strings attached before I left college."

"Do you still want that?" I asked.

She looked to me, must've read something in my expression that wasn't there, because she covered her face a moment later. "Oh my God, that sounds awful, doesn't it? You probably think I'm a terrible person. Heck, even I think that."

Actually, I thought she was pretty great, but we'd come back to that later.

Walking to the desk, I bent down and pulled her hands away, so I could see her eyes.

"Do you still want that?" I repeated and then waited for her answer.

Because it mattered, because she mattered, and because this could change everything.

12

Honor

My heart was pounding.

And all Archer was doing was holding my hand.

Gah. It wasn't even a sexy place on the body to be touched. In my head, I knew this, but the reality was more complex. The feeling of his thumb as it swept against my pulse point sent a shiver straight through me. It felt like there was some kind of magic tether between his hand and mine, one that ran to the center of my being, making it feel like he had a direct line to my heart.

Who knew such an innocent touch could light me up like this?

It was a sign, I thought.

A sign that I should be running for the hills,

away from the room and away from him as fast I could. Self-preservation was a real thing. I should get out now while I had the chance.

The problem was I didn't actually want to do any of that.

Especially not with Archer looking at me this way. His gray eyes were intense yet warm as he waited for my answer.

Do you still want that? he'd asked.

"Yes," I said then swallowed. "I still want it."

Archer's eyes were on me. "With Baylor?"

I shook my head. "No, not with him."

Archer let out a breath and dropped his head. After nodding to himself, his gaze captured mine once more. "Then I think you should let me kiss you again."

"What?" I said.

"Well, as your friend, I feel like I should be the one you experiment with. And if you want to increase your romantic experience, I figure now's as good a time as any to start."

I caught my breath as his hand moved to my cheek. "But I...I've been kissed before. You kissed me, remember?"

"Yeah," he said, "but at the time, you thought I was someone else. Now, you know who you're kissing. It might make a difference."

Oh, it definitely would, I thought. Having been around Archer, knowing him better, seeing how he treated his family and his team downstairs, I'd fallen a little more. Knowing I was kissing Archer O'Brien would make it that much more powerful.

"Wait," I said as he leaned in, hoping to talk some sense into one of us. He stopped a breath away from my lips. "This is crazy. No strings attached? No offense, Archer, but you don't seem like that kind of guy."

"None taken," he said.

"And despite what I said, I'm definitely not that kind of girl," I added, looking deep into his eyes. "I seriously have zero experience. Romance is *not* my thing. I'm sure I'll be bad at it. The confidence and sexiness, the red dress and heels, that was all Charlie."

"You looked great in those heels," he cut in, "even if they did try to kill you."

"But don't you see? That's not really me. Charlie gave me the clothes, even coached me on how to get a guy. I came here looking to hook up that night, but...I don't know if I'm ready." I took a deep breath. "So, if that's what you're after, if that's why you're offering, I just want to be honest. I'm not sure it'll ever get to that point."

After a moment, Archer's lips twitched, and I noticed his eyes were smiling—which made me frown. I'd just poured my heart out, revealed my innermost thoughts, and he seemed...amused?

"What's that look for?" I asked. "Are you

laughing at me?"

"No," he said—but a second later a real life smile broke through, and I pointed to his face.

"Yes, you are! I can't believe you!"

I was trying my best not to be affected. But if Archer's frown was sexy-as-hell, his smile was something else entirely. It made my heart ache to see it, even as I struggled to hold onto my indignation.

"I thought you never smiled, and you choose a time like this," I said. "Friends shouldn't laugh at friends—especially when they're admitting heartfelt truths."

"Sorry," he said, "but it's funny."

"What is?"

"The fact that you're so misinformed."

I went to protest, but before I could, Archer had his fingers in my hair, pulling me so close, I could feel each word on my lips as he said them.

"Honor, can I be honest?" he said.

I nodded, unable to speak.

"I went along with the friends thing because that's what you wanted. I'm absolutely willing to try no strings attached, if that's what will make you happy."

He paused, shook his head.

"But I want so much more from you than sex."

I forgot how to breathe.

"I don't want to scare you. I'm down for

however fast or slow you want to take this. But that's my truth. Are you good with that?"

"Mm-hm," I said.

"Okay," he said, dipping his head closer, "I'm going to kiss you now."

God yes, please.

Archer's lips had just touched mine, the barest brush of skin on skin—when the door to the room flew open.

"Arch, we found more bacon. Is there any more syrup? We need—oh sorry. Didn't know you were busy."

Pulling away from me an inch, his eyes closed, Archer said, "Yeah, Dex. There's another bottle in the cabinet above the stove."

"Great," the voice said. "Well, I'll just put the meat on then...?"

"Great," Archer said back, but as the door closed, I saw his shoulders slump. "If I'm not down there in the next ten seconds, someone's bound to start a fire. No one else cooks in the house."

"Better get going then," I laughed, though the sound was a little breathless. Okay, more than a little.

Archer looked at me a moment then stood. He had taken a step toward the door but turned back a second later, pressing his lips to my cheek.

"Like I said, we'll do this however you want. No strings attached."

181

"Sounds good," I said.

"We'll continue this later."

I nodded and watched as Archer smiled for the second time that night. It was just as stunning as the first, but after everything that'd happened it packed an extra punch. So did knowing we'd be continuing this later—whatever this was.

I shivered at the thought.

* * *

A couple minutes later, I heard shouting and ended up shivering for a totally different reason.

The party seemed to be at a standstill as I jogged down the stairs. Archer's smile had disappeared as if it had never been. He was standing with his arms out, kind of like a crossing guard, except instead of directing traffic, Archer was trying to deescalate an obviously volatile situation.

"Get out of my way," some guy said, his expression and eyes angry as he looked past Archer. Following his gaze, I noticed Dex and Baylor, and uh-oh. They didn't look any happier than he did.

"Tell me exactly what happened first," Archer said.

"I don't have to tell you nothing."

"Yeah, Tony, you do." His voice hardened. "This is my house, my team, my rules. Unless you want to be escorted out, you better explain."

The guy, Tony, seemed to get even angrier if that was possible. I didn't remember seeing him on the field, so he must've been a friend or fan. "I caught your brother all over my girl. That's what happened."

"Is that true?" Archer asked, looking to his brothers.

Baylor scoffed. "Hey, she kissed me."

"And you stood there doing nothing, huh? Yeah, right." Tony pressed forward but ran into Archer's still outstretched hand. He also seemed to have a girl who was holding him back; I assumed she was the girlfriend. Her face was bright red but if it was from embarrassment or guilt I couldn't tell. Probably both. "I'm watching the game with my boys. I turn around for one second to get a beer, and when I go to the kitchen, he's got his tongue down her throat."

"Again," Baylor said, "technically, it was her tongue down my throat."

"Oh, you're asking it for it, O'Brien."

Tony tried to get at him, but this time Dex stepped forward.

"Put your hands on my brother again, and see what happens," he said softly, the danger in his words unmistakable.

Tony backed off a bit at that, but he wasn't appeased. That much was clear by his next words.

"So what, Archer? I got pissed and reacted. Your brother was making out with my girl. What was I supposed to do?"

Archer shook his head. "You know there's no fighting here."

"Me and the guys pulled them apart before any real damage was done," Dex said.

"Bay, you have anything to add?" Archer asked.

"Listen, it wasn't like she had a ring on her finger," Baylor said. "How was I supposed to know she had a boyfriend on the premises? Then Tony here, comes in shouting, throwing his fists around. Of course, I'm going to defend myself."

Archer nodded, looking at first one then the other. "Sounds like a misunderstanding to me, one that got out of control. An apology could go a long way."

Tony didn't look like he agreed, but Baylor nodded.

"Hey man, I'm sorry," he said, sounding sincere. "I honestly didn't know she was with anyone. It won't happen again."

Tony glanced back at his girlfriend, who averted her gaze, then to Archer and finally Baylor. His eyes still held that hard gleam. "You know what, Baylor," he said, "you can take that apology, and shove it right up your ass."

Dex looked ready for a fight, but Tony held up his hands.

"I'll let myself out," he said, shrugging off his girlfriend and walking out of the house. She followed a few steps behind. Once they were gone, the crowd kind of dispersed on its own, everyone going back to their own little corners as if nothing had happened. But I noticed the tension still lining Archer's body.

"Well," Baylor said with a grin, "that was fun."

Archer stepped up to his brothers, looking them both over. "That," he said, "was a crisis averted. Nothing fun about it. Are you guys okay?"

Dex rolled his eyes, but Baylor just laughed. "Yeah, mama bear," he said. "We're good. Tony's the one you should be concerned about with a girl like that."

"You're welcome for pulling him off you by the way," Dex muttered.

Baylor shook his head. "Please. I could've handled that guy in my sleep."

"Whatever you say."

"Where's Chase?" Archer said suddenly. "I didn't see him anywhere."

"He's in the kitchen, trying to make the bacon."

"I better go see how it's going."

Baylor patted him on his shoulder before walking off. "Everything's good, Arch. You saved the day again. Now stop worrying."

I watched Archer nod then make his way to the kitchen, to check on Chase, no doubt. His frown was in place once more. I wished he could've taken Baylor's advice, but I didn't think it was a choice. The worrying. His love for his family was one of the things I liked best about him—though that number seemed to be growing daily.

The thought scared me enough that I didn't seek him out again.

* * *

The next couple of days I was like a zombie. Even in British Lit, my favorite class, I wasn't able to pay attention, the words the professor wrote swimming before me. In accounting, the numbers flitted in and out of my mind as if they had wings. Thoughts of Archer, his hands, his eyes, that smile, they'd pop up out of the blue when I was supposed to be concentrating on my studies, and just like that, my ability to apply myself went to mush.

My mother had warned me about this. One of the only things she really had any authority on was men, and she'd told me this would happen.

"Just wait, Honor," she'd said. It was a day she'd forgotten (yet again) to pick me up from elementary school, and I'd had to walk the three miles it took to get home. "When you find the man of your dreams, you'll know what I'm talking about. Everything and everyone else will become a blur, and all you'll see is him. When you're in love, he becomes your whole world."

But I didn't want that.

It was one of the main reasons I was so afraid to let myself fall in the first place. Mom's obsession with love—particularly love of men—had always flashed bright like a warning sign. The way she forgot to care for her family when she was with one, the way she didn't care for herself when they left, I wanted no part of it. And what if that all-or-nothing mindset was hereditary? I'd never been with a guy, so I wouldn't know.

Charlie's parents had basically raised me. It was one of the reasons we were so close, best friends who were more like sisters. Whenever I didn't have lunch money, Charlie would share her food with me. When Mom locked me out and told me to go stay with a friend because she and her beau were expecting company, Charlie's parents let us have an impromptu sleepover. There were a lot of those. When Mom forgot to get groceries or hadn't left me money on the table so I could get them, Charlie was there with sandwiches and apple slices.

Mom's men never lasted more than a year or two, but after getting depressed for a couple weeks, she'd rally and find another who she claimed to be madly in love with. It happened like clockwork. I'd heard Charlie's parents say once that she hadn't always been like this. My father's leaving, that was the thing that changed everything. Mom had been chasing true love ever since—and she hadn't slowed down once to see if her kid was keeping up or falling behind.

Anyway, I knew other people had it worse. My mother's neglect didn't stem from malice or hate,

187

just indifference. And her obsession with love and being loved shouldn't scare me. I wasn't anything like her. Had never fallen in and out of love as easily. But I was her daughter. I'd seen first-hand all the damage love could do and had learned to always keep my guard up.

But Archer seemed to be weakening that resolve every time we met.

I wasn't in love with him—not yet. Still, I could feel myself slipping. Every time my mind turned to him, I reminded myself that this wasn't anything serious. We were friends, and he'd agreed (as a friend) to help me with my romantic experience.

It was that simple.

I groaned.

But...if it was so simple, would I still be obsessing over the sweet kiss he'd delivered to my cheek after we were disturbed or the words he'd said before that?

I want so much more from you than sex.

What did that even mean?

I want so much more from you than sex.

Archer's words played through my head over and over. For some reason, my knees got weak each time. But I had no idea what "more than sex" entailed. Hopefully, he'd explain it to me soon, and then I could stop thinking about it so much.

Maybe it was my inexperience, I thought. Maybe after Archer and I spent some time together

I'd get used to him. I'd become immune to his touches, the feel of his lips, all of these...feelings. A girl could only hope.

It was Friday, and I was on my way to the baseball field, a bag thrown over my shoulder with clothes, a couple books, toothbrush, the necessities. The article I'd written on Daisy O'Brien had been an even bigger hit than the first.

"They love her!" Walter had said to me earlier this morning in the newsroom. "I ran the article on the coach right after their big win. The Wolves fans devoured every word. You really got to the heart of Daisy O'Brien's story, Honor. Well done!"

I'd shrugged. "She's a hard person not to like. Plus, she was really easy to talk to."

"Mothers are like that."

Not all of them, I thought.

"So, when can we expect the next one?" Walter's eyes were twinkling, his excitement clear. "*The Howler* has become a must-read. I can't wait to see what you bring me about the brothers."

"Well..." I was stalling, but in truth, I'd already made my decision. "Coach O'Brien said I could travel with the team. If I wanted to."

"A generous offer. And?" Walter prompted.

"Um, they have a couple of games this weekend. They're away games, so I thought I'd go and try to get some of the interviews done then."

"Brilliant!"

"I was actually hoping to get them done sooner rather than later. That way we can have all the articles ready to go."

Walter had nodded. "You've always been very diligent. Oh, I can't wait to see what you write next."

I didn't tell him that diligence had nothing to do with it. I wanted to get the interviews done quickly for the sake of my sanity. Another reason I might've been so hung up on Archer was this assignment. The articles loomed large in my mind. To keep the pace, we'd have to release one story a week or at least bi-weekly, so I needed to get on the ball.

My plan was to start interviewing the O'Briens while on the bus. I didn't get any sleep last night, spent a long time thinking and coming up with my plan of attack aka my interviewing strategy. But now I was prepared. It would be a long drive. I could at least get one or two done, I thought with a yawn. Then maybe I could take a much-needed nap.

It was early, so the sun was still low in the sky as I approached the Wolves' bus. There was the face of a wolf painted on one side with the words "Southern Baseball" etched underneath it. The bus itself was large, looming over a couple of smaller yellow buses parked beside it in a row. I could see some of the players just arriving. They dropped off their bags to be loaded underneath the vehicle and then boarded.

My phone went off in my pocket, and I took a

detour, walked between the yellow buses and answered.

It was a text from Charlie.

She said: Honor, remember to HAVE FUN! I want to hear everything as soon as you get home ;)

I shook my head, typing back immediately.

Me: What's with the winky-face? It's just an assignment.

Charlie: Yeah okay...it's not like you'll be spending time w/Archer or anything...

Me: Only if I'm asking him interview questions...

Charlie: Aw, you're no fun :(

A beat passed, then another text came through.

Charlie: If any hanky-panky goes on on that bus, I demand to know!!! You must tell me!

I laughed.

Me: I promise—but nothing's going to happen.

Charlie: I'd love to hear what Archer has to say about that.

And she followed it up with another winky-face.

Shaking my head, I opened my bag and dropped my phone in. I was just about to walk back out when a familiar voice said, "Need any help?"

I jumped about a foot then looked to Archer, who was walking toward me between the buses.

"No, I'm good," I said breathlessly. "Where did you come from?"

He shrugged. "I saw you walk back here when I drove up."

As he stopped about a foot away, I couldn't help taking him in. There was a lot of shadow between the buses, but the light that did get in framed him perfectly. His hair was effortlessly styled, his eyes bright as they stared right back at me. For some reason his broad shoulders looked even more pronounced, his legs somehow more fit, and my eyes widened as I realized why.

"Are you...wearing a suit?"

Archer tipped his chin. "Mom likes us to dress up when we travel, says it shows respect for the other team."

My first thought was: God bless his mother.

My second: Bless whoever made that suit because holy hotness. How were women supposed to function in the face of such unmistakable male beauty? The sleek black suit jacket, the crisp white button down, those fitted slacks, and the man who was wearing it all like a second skin. It was so unfair.

I had to clear my throat. "Isn't it uncomfortable? When you're traveling, I mean?"

"Not really," he said, unbuttoning the blazer, pushing a hand into his pocket. "We can change on the bus if we want."

"Oh." As much as I fought it, I couldn't keep the disappointment out of my voice. "Are you going to change then?"

"Probably just take off my jacket."

"Oh, that's great."

"Why do you say that?"

His eyes watched me the entire time as I struggled to find a coherent response. "You—you just look really nice. The suit...it looks good on you. That's all."

"Good," he repeated and took a step toward me. I took one back, matching him step for step, until I felt my shoulders rest against cool metal. "You think I look good?"

I nodded. "You know you do."

If I was being honest, Archer looked more than good in that suit. He was every woman's dream personified. Or maybe that was just me.

"Now, I feel underdressed," I said.

His hand came up to my cheek. "No, you look perfect."

I raised my brows, trying to keep it light even though all I could think of were his fingers running along my skin. "You probably didn't even notice what I'm wearing."

Without looking away, Archer said, "Dark blue sweater, red t-shirt that says, 'All I do is read, read, read, no matter what,' jeans that fit you like a glove, red sneakers."

My jaw dropped.

"I notice you, Honor."

"You do?"

He nodded, his eyes dropping to my lips. "How could I not?"

193

If I wasn't already melting, that turned me into a puddle, my heart stuttering behind my ribs. He could've asked me anything right then, and I think I would've said yes. Without any forethought, I leaned up onto my tiptoes and pressed my lips to his.

Like Archer had said: How could I not?

His lips were warm and soft, and if he was surprised, he didn't show it.

Archer's hand cupped my face while his other hand went to my waist, his body pressing into mine. But I couldn't seem to get close enough. My hands automatically went to his shoulders, feeling his muscles as they tightened, then moved up to his neck, playing with the hair at his nape. This seemed to set something off within him. In the next second, Archer's hands had traveled down to my hips, gripped behind my thighs and lifted. On instinct, my legs wrapped around his waist. At this, he let out a purely masculine sound of approval.

And all that time he never stopped kissing me.

My whole body felt completely attuned to his. It wasn't like any kiss I'd ever experienced. I sighed into his mouth as he deepened the kiss, his hands tightening on my legs. Surely this couldn't have been as earthshattering for him as it was for me, I thought, my self-doubt kicking in. I had no idea what I was doing. My fingers traveled through his hair, and once again, he made that noise of approval in the back of his throat, so I knew I'd done something right.

"Archer," I gasped as his lips moved to my neck.

"Again," he murmured.

"What?"

Lifting his head, he pierced me with eyes so intense, I couldn't look away even if I'd wanted to—which I didn't.

"My name," he said. "Say it again, just like that."

I must've taken too long because dropping his head, he placed another lingering kiss against my mouth.

"My name," he repeated, and then added almost as an afterthought, "please."

Not knowing where the courage came from, I leaned so my lips were right next to his ear.

"Archer," I whispered, smiling when I felt him shiver. "We should get on the bus. Anyone could walk by and see us."

His voice was dark as he said, "If one of my brothers tries to interrupt again, I swear I'm going to kill someone."

I laughed, couldn't help it.

Archer leaned back, searching my face, then he kissed me once more before setting me on my feet. His frown was back, but I could tell he wanted to smile. His eyes were bright as he looked me over, and I wondered what he saw. He didn't seem nearly as dazed as I felt. Archer looked just as good as he had before the kiss, totally unaffected. Well, except for his hair. It was a lot messier—which had to be from my fingers running through it, I realized belatedly.

"Is something wrong?" I asked as he continued to stare. "Do I look okay?"

"Your lips are swollen," he said voice low. "I did that."

Cheeks flushed, I said, "Yeah well...I should probably take a second to get myself back together. You can go on ahead."

Archer nodded. I think he knew I needed some time alone. "I'll see you on the bus."

With one last look, he left, and I grabbed my bag from the ground with shaky hands. I must've dropped it sometime during the kiss. My fingers went to my lips which were indeed swollen.

Archer had done that.

And I was in so much trouble.

13

Archer

Honor.
Her mouth.
That kiss.
The way her fingers felt in my hair.
The sound of my name falling from her lips...
I had to force myself to turn and walk away, and even then, all I wanted to do was go back and kiss her some more. Not going to lie, I hadn't known that was going to happen. When I'd seen her go between the buses, I'd followed, just wanting to make sure she was alright. Never, not in my wildest dreams, had I thought it would lead to the hottest, most sensational kiss of my life.

My lips were still tingling for God's sake. I could still feel her legs wrapped around me—and I needed to calm down. I was about to have to sit through a six-hour drive with my team, and I didn't need everyone knowing how hung up I was.

Plus, Honor had said no strings.

Everything in me revolted at the thought. Honor had been right. I was definitely not that type of guy. But I'd try to be. For her.

My head was in a fog as I made the short trek to the bus. The scene replayed on a loop in my mind. As I made my way up the bus steps and into the aisle, I was still preoccupied with thoughts of Honor, distracted as I greeted my teammates, hoping no one would notice.

But of course, I wasn't that lucky.

"Damn, Arch," Baylor said and stopped me with a hand on my arm. His eyes were sparkling as his gaze went to my hair. "Looks like you've been having fun."

I shrugged. "Don't know what you mean."

"Oh yeah, I'm sure you don't."

"Give it a rest," Chase said from a couple rows back, but of course, his twin didn't listen.

With his lips tilted up in a grin, Baylor said, "Like hell I will. When was the last time I got to tease Archer about anything? Especially for looking like he just finished hooking up with someone?"

Instead of blushing at his too-accurate description, I frowned harder.

"Ah, I can tell by your constipated expression

that I'm right."

Parker Graves spoke up then. "Ten bucks says the captain punches him before this little convo is over. Any takers?"

"You're on," Dex said. "No way Archer would do that. Even if Bay is asking for it."

I wasn't so sure. On the typical, I would've never considered punching him—okay, I might have *considered* it, but the better angels in my mind would've stayed my hand. This time Baylor's smug expression was making me more and more pissed—especially when he mentioned Honor by name.

"I bet it was Emmy's new roommate. Honor, right?"

My hands curled into fists.

"Bay, I would shut up now," Chase cautioned.

"Or maybe you took my advice and moved on," Baylor said, sitting in a seat and pulling me down next to him. "So, who was it? And where can I get her number? She'd have to be something to make you look this out of it. Sharing is caring, Arch."

I distantly heard T.J. say, "I've got ten on Captain decking him."

Dex groaned as my frown only grew. "Baylor, geez man. Why do you got to be such an indiscriminate manwhore?"

Baylor pointed at him. "I take issue with that statement. I am very discriminant. There is no one more discriminating than me."

"Do you even know what that word means?" Chase asked.

"I do," Baylor said emphatically. "And even if I didn't, I'd know it was insult by the way Dex said it."

Dex groaned again, but I was done with this.

"You need to stop," I said, voice pitched low so only Baylor could hear. He looked back to me in confusion. "Even if I was out there 'hooking up' as you crudely put it, that's between me and that person."

"But—"

I shook my head. "It's none of your business."

Baylor couldn't take a hint. "But I'm dying of curiosity over here. Plus, I tell you and the guys everything."

"You are the king of TMI," I agreed.

"At least tell me this," he said. "Who was she?"

Before I could put him off again, Honor stepped onto the bus. The effect she had was instant. Everyone stopped moving, and everything got quiet. I didn't know if it was the novelty of having a female on the bus (other than Mom) or what, but everyone stared for a moment, which obviously made Honor uncomfortable.

"Hi," she said, breaking the silence.

Her eyes searched the faces in front of her before finally stopping on mine.

"Hi," I said back.

"Well, mystery solved," Baylor mumbled,

causing Honor's brow to furrow. "Hey, T.J.? I believe you and Parker owe my brother some funds."

The two groaned as they handed Dex their cash, and they all started moving again.

"Easy money," Dex said. "I knew he wouldn't do it."

I couldn't be sure, but I thought I heard Chase mutter, "I didn't" under his breath. My eyes stayed glued to Honor who still hadn't moved. Behind her, Mom came up the steps followed by Bear. A few of the other assistant coaches were already seated.

"Good to see you, Honor," Mom said with a smile.

"You, too," Honor said. "Thanks for letting me tag along, Coach O'Brien."

"It was no problem at all. Ready to get some more of those interviews done?"

"I hope so."

Bear grunted. "Not to be rude, but can we move this along? It's the crack of dawn, we got a long ride ahead of us, and my ass is freezing."

Honor jumped then moved farther onto the bus. "Oh sorry! I didn't realize I was blocking the way."

"Ignore him," Mom said. "He's just mad because his beauty sleep was cut short. Bear's always a little cranky in the morning."

Bear grunted again while the rest of us who

were close enough to hear scoffed. Beauty sleep? Yeah, right. Cranky was Bear's number one emotion right next to grumpy, disagreeable and irritated. He was a heck of an assistant coach, but look up "curmudgeon" in the dictionary, and you'd find a big old picture of Bear Green.

Situating himself in the first row as always, Bear hunkered down, and Mom sat next to him.

"Take any seat you want, Honor," she said. "We should get going here in a second."

Honor nodded and made her way down the aisle. My gaze followed her the whole way. She looked nervous, eyes flitting from one side to the other. I didn't understand what that was about. After the kiss we'd shared, I fully expected her to sit next to me. My team was awesome, but Honor sitting next to any of the guys for a prolonged amount of time when there was a perfectly good seat next to me? Not happening. But it wasn't until she was closer that I realized, for that to happen, the space would have to be open. And it was currently occupied.

"Move," I said to Baylor. "You're in her seat."

He grinned. "Didn't realize it was reserved."

"Well, it is," I mumbled. Honor was almost even with us now. "So move."

"Okay, okay." Baylor stood. "No need to get all hostile. I'm going."

Honor looked at me then, but to my horror, it

was at the same moment Baylor said, "Hey Honor, sit here! I'm moving, and Archer says he saved you a seat."

My eyes closed on reflex. I was going to kill him.

"That's nice," Honor laughed nervously, "but I don't want you to have to move."

"Ah come on," Baylor said, running a hand through his hair like a little punk. I knew that move. He used it to attract girls, and nine times out of ten, it worked like a charm. "I know it's a little grade school, saving you a seat on the bus and all, but it's kind of cute. Don't you think?"

Strike that. I was still going to kill him, but slowly.

"I'd planned to start my interviews anyway."

"Interviews?" Baylor asked.

"Yeah," she said, her eyes moving to me then away, "I really need to concentrate and get them done. You O'Briens are a hot item in the campus paper."

Baylor's eyes were showing far too much interest. "You don't say? So, you'll be interviewing each of us?"

"That's right."

I cleared my throat. "If you want, you can start with me. I read the article you did on Mom. It was really good."

She blinked. "You read it?"

"Yeah, and I'd love to keep"—my gaze went to her lips—"talking with you. About what we were discussing before..."

"Actually," she said, "I think I see an open seat. Maybe later?"

As she hustled down the aisle, leaving both Baylor and me staring after her, I watched her say something to Chase. The next thing I know, he'd stood up to let her in, giving her the seat next to the window. At my frown, his eyes widened, and he held up his hands as if to say, "Hey, don't look at me. It's not my fault."

And, as I lowered back into my seat, I knew he was right. I came on too strong. And Honor ran as fast as she could in the opposite direction. But why did she run? And why hadn't she wanted to sit with me? I wondered.

The bus started, and we'd gone about five minutes before I heard her laugh. Looking back over my shoulder, I saw her talking animatedly with Chase about something and frowned. It didn't look like they were getting much interviewing done.

Baylor, who'd ended up seated next to me, shook his head. "Archer, whatever you do, do not keep looking back there."

I shifted my scowl to him.

"What? Don't give me that look," he said. "Trust me on this. I aced Psychology last semester. You don't want your mind to start playing tricks, coming up with all these scenarios of what they might be talking about. You'll only be torturing yourself. And over what? It's not like Chase is going to make a move to steal your girl."

As Honor's laugh floated up again, I gave into the impulse and looked back, despite Baylor's warning. Chase and Honor really did look cozy back there. I wondered what they were saying, wondered if she could feel my gaze on her like I always felt hers on me. I wondered if she regretted not sitting next to me in the first place or if she was happy with her choice.

Baylor was right about one thing.

It was torture, the not knowing.

But no worries, I reassured myself. This was Chase and Honor, my younger brother and the girl I was falling for. At least they didn't have much in common—besides a love of books, solid work ethic, quirky personalities that would compliment each other a thousand times better than ours ever would...

Damn.

On second thought, maybe I should be *more* worried.

14

Honor

"I still can't believe you're reading that," I said.

"Re-reading," Chase corrected. "I told you it's really good. I only ever re-read the great ones."

"It's just too strange," I said, digging into my bag.

"What's strange? Anyone who doesn't like Jamie and Claire's story was born without a heart. *Outlander* has to be one of the best books written this century."

I smiled. "Hey, no arguments here, *Sassenach*." I held up one of the paperbacks I'd brought along to read on the long bus ride. The deep blue cover was an exact match to the one Chase held in his hands. "What's weird is we had the exact same idea."

Chase's lips tilted up in a grin. "You know what they say about great minds."

"They like to devour great books," I said.

This was so surreal. I'd come back here to avoid Archer and the pull I'd felt since meeting him, the one that only got stronger every time we spoke—or kissed. My brain was still mushy around the edges, addled by our encounter, my feelings all over the place. Archer O'Brien's kisses really should've been illegal.

Baylor's teasing hadn't helped, but the way Archer had stood next to him, looking so completely unruffled, so unlike me...I knew I needed a little more time before we talked again. After weighing my options, I'd decided to sit next to Chase. He'd always struck me as the least intimidating of all the O'Briens, and today was no different. Unlike Dex, who'd been sitting at the back of the bus, staring at me hard as I walked up the aisle, as if daring me to sit next to him, Chase was head down, reading a book.

There was no choice really.

Of course, I'd asked Chase if I could sit next to him. I just hadn't expected us to be reading the exact same thing. The realization had drawn a laugh from my lips and made me immediately comfortable all at once.

"So, I'm doing a few interviews for *The Howler*," I began, flipping open the notebook I'd pulled out along with my paperback. "And I was hoping to interview you."

"Me?" Chase said, inserting a bookmark and closing his book. His brow furrowed. "Why would you want to do that?"

I shrugged. "You are the star pitcher of the Wolves."

"Yeah..."

"And you're also the golden boy with the golden arm who's lead your team to three consecutive championships. Not to mention, you're the third oldest O'Brien brother—and obviously the one with the best taste in books."

Chase tried to hide it, but I saw the grin he bit back. "I get it from my Aunt Genevieve. She's a total bibliophile. Emmy has pretty good taste, too."

"I'll have to check out her shelves sometime when I'm back home," I said, making a note in my mind to do just that.

He tilted his head. "And you sitting here, starting with me...it has nothing to do with whatever's going on between you and Archer?"

My throat tightened. Was I really that obvious?

I must've been because Chase nodded a second later. "That's what I thought," he said. "You know, he can't stop looking back here."

"Really?" I said, eyes wide, not daring to look.

"Yeah, he's bound to have a crick in his neck at this rate. Well Honor, if we lose the game, you'll know it was all your fault."

That startled another laugh out of me. "And a sense of humor, too?"

Chase grinned outright.

"Oh now, I can't wait to interview you," I said.

"I don't want to disappoint," he said, "but I should probably tell you. I'm not all that interesting."

I shook my head at how wrong (and humble) he was. "We'll let the readers be the judge of that, hm?"

Chase nodded. "Alright."

"I just have a few questions. Fair warning, some are pretty personal because I got them directly from the readers' comments on the site. Your fans are kinda nosey. I hope that's okay?"

"Like I said, I'm boring," he laughed, gesturing with his hand for me to continue. "Ask me anything. I'll try to be as open as possible."

Lifting my pen, I asked the first question, "What do you love about baseball?"

"How much time do you have?" His eyes took on a faraway look. "I love being on the mound, the power that runs through my arm as I release the ball, the satisfaction I get from every good pitch. There's nothing else like it. I love being a part of a team, knowing that I've got their back and they've got mine. Having my family there with me is a huge bonus."

I smiled while taking notes. "Think you'll go pro

someday?"

Chase shrugged. "That's the dream. Not sure if it'll happen, but I've never been afraid of hard work."

"Great answer."

"Thanks."

"Okay, here's where it gets personal," I said. "Do you have a girlfriend?"

"No," he said.

"No one special in your life?"

His eyes lit up at that. "Just baseball and books."

"Okay, I think they'll actually love hearing that," I said. "A lot of them were hoping you were single. Next question: Boxers or briefs?"

Chase blinked. "People actually want to know that?"

I bit my lip to hold back a laugh. "It's actually one of the top things they want to know about each of you. Sorry."

"It's fine," he said as a blush stole up his cheeks. "I was just surprised."

After a muttered "briefs," we moved on to the next question.

"Do you prefer blondes, brunettes or redheads? And as a follow-up, the next question is: Can you please describe your ideal woman?"

"Hmm, I 've never really thought about it before..."

After a beat, Chase shook his head.

"I don't know who my ideal woman is—but I'll

know her when I find her."

I wrote that down as quickly as possible then asked if he could explain what he meant. To say his answer shocked me would be an understatement.

"I'm looking for my soulmate," he said simply without even a hint of sarcasm.

"Seriously?" I asked.

Chase nodded. "If my parents taught me anything, it's that love is real. There's someone out there for each of us. We just have to be patient and keep our eyes and hearts open."

"You really believe that?"

"Hell yeah, I do. And what's the point of dating a whole bunch of women who aren't the one? How do you look at your soulmate once you do find them and explain why you kissed or made love to other women? No way. I'm more than ready to fall in love with my soulmate. But until then, I'm content to wait."

"Chase..." I set down my pen and looked him in the eyes. I tried to hide the incredulity in my voice but wasn't sure I succeeded. "Are you"—I lowered my voice to a whisper—"are you telling me you're a...virgin?"

When he merely lifted a brow, my jaw dropped.

"And you're celibate?"

He shrugged. "I prefer to think of it as waiting for the one—but yeah. I guess you could say that."

My mind was blown. Call me judgmental, but

I'd just assumed with a twin like Baylor and considering he was a gorgeous college guy in his twenties that he'd be sowing his wild oats like the other ninety percent of the male population. Silly me.

I sat back in my chair, needing a moment, then looked to him.

"I don't have to put this in the article," I said.

"Why not?" he said. "I'm not ashamed of it, Honor, and you told me the questions would be personal."

Yeah, I thought, but not that personal.

"And I'm guessing from your reaction it would make a good story."

Was he kidding? Walter would go crazy over this and so would pretty much every girl on campus. "It would make a great story. But really, you don't—"

"Alright then," Chase said, cutting me off. "You have any other questions for me?"

"Only a few more," I said.

"Okay, shoot," he said.

The rest of the questions went by in a snap. And why wouldn't they? Chase had already given me way more insight into him then I could've ever hoped for. My profile of him for *The Howler* was going to be epic.

Afterward, both of us kind of nodded and went straight to our books. Chase was so right. *Outlander* really was one of the best books of the century—heck probably of all time. The characters were just so well-drawn, and you couldn't help but care for them. We were about two hours into the drive, and I'd gotten to the part where Jamie had fallen off his horse, and Claire mended his arm, when the first yawn hit. After reading ten more pages, my eyelids were starting to feel heavy. My sleepless night finally caught up with me. Placing the book into my lap, I leaned my head against the window, letting the coolness seep into my skin. The conversations of the guys on the bus, the crisp sound of Chase turning the pages, it all became dull background noise. My eyes closed as the rhythm of the bus lulled me to sleep.

Archer was in my dream.

And I knew I had to be dreaming—because he was wearing a kilt.

I hadn't thought anything could compare to seeing him in that suit. But I'd been mistaken. His whole form filled out the kilt quite nicely, the green, blue and white plaid hugging his waist, his strong, muscular thighs on display. On top, he wore a loose white shirt that showcased his broad shoulders. It was slit down the middle allowing a hint of skin to peek through. And was it me, or was his hair just a touch longer? It was definitely messier, tousled and windswept like he'd been out riding over the hills.

Yeah, he was gorgeous (just like Jamie Fraser).

And he rocked a kilt better than anyone I'd ever seen (maybe even better than Jamie).

Dream me sighed as he opened his mouth, ready to hear his Scottish burr, but it never came.

"Mind if I cut in?" he said in a completely normal voice.

I should've been disappointed, but the deep, smooth sound did things to me, with or without the accent.

Dream me shook her head, and he took a step closer.

"I was wondering how long it was going to take you to come back here."

That didn't sound like me—sounded a lot like Chase actually—but it was close to what I'd been thinking, so I didn't dwell on it too much.

"I was encouraged to keep my distance, but it looks like that's not happening," Archer said. "You mind if I sit?"

Frowning, I looked down at the grassy meadow, shivering as I felt a gust of air hit my arms.

"Of course not." Again, the voice sounded distinctly different than my own or Archer's. "I need to use the bathroom anyway. Just didn't want to leave her here by herself." After a pause, it added, "She's really great, you know."

Archer grunted. "That your way of telling me you want her, too?"

A choked sound then, "Are you seriously asking

me this?"

"That's not an answer," he said.

A laugh then, "No man, that's not what I'm saying. What I'm saying is: Don't screw it up."

"I'll try my best."

Another gust of wind blew by, and I felt the goosebumps rise on my skin. Dream me sat next to Archer on the grass, shifted to be closer to his warmth. I rested my head against his shoulder.

"What am I going to do with you?" he muttered.

No idea, I thought. *But I can't wait to find out.*

He started humming softly, and though I couldn't make out the tune, it flowed through me, relaxing my body until I was totally content. A sigh escaped, though I wasn't sure if it was his or mine. This was the best dream I'd had in a while. Usually, they weren't so vivid. I could've sworn I felt the brush of his hand against the skin of my cheek as he pushed the hair away from my face.

I wasn't sure how long I slept.

My tiredness hadn't helped, but I'd always been able to sleep in the car, falling right out on road trips. It was both a blessing and a curse. Waking up had always been the tough part. And part of me this time fought to stay exactly where I was, in the warm contentment with kilted Archer as we had adventures together in the Highlands. But the rhythm of the bus had stopped some time ago, a clear signal we weren't moving anymore.

The pillow under my head was just so comfortable. It felt like it was heated or something, and the smell...gah. I didn't know what it was, but it reminded me of clover mixed with clean fresh fields. Burrowing my face deeper, I fought opening my eyes—until the pillow under my head let out a soft chuckle.

I froze.

Slowly, my eyelids lifted, and I sat up, raised my head. Blinking at the sight in front of me, I took note of all the empty bus seats and the black jacket that had just fallen from my shoulders into my lap. A second ago, it had been draped over me like a blanket. I frowned down at it, having no clue how it had gotten there.

"I was wondering if you were going to wake up on your own. Must've been a good dream."

That wasn't Chase's voice.

I looked to my left, knowing who I'd find, but a jolt still went through me when my gaze met Archer's.

"Hey there, sleepyhead," he said, one side of his lips tilted up.

"What happened to Chase?" I said.

"We switched seats a while back." Archer shrugged. "Did you get some rest?"

His voice, just like in my dream, was so smooth. "Yeah, I did. Thanks."

He nodded. "Seemed like you needed it."

Glancing around again before coming back to him, I said, "Where is everyone?"

"Out there getting their stuff off the bus."

And I hadn't even heard them leave, a rowdy bunch of baseball players? Man, either they were the quietest guys alive, or I must've been dead to the world.

The mystery was solved when Archer added, "I told them if they woke you I'd make them do extra sprints."

"Ah," I said, shifting slightly. "Sorry about"—I gestured to him—"you know, falling asleep on you. But in my defense, your shoulder was so comfortable, like a heated pillow."

Archer sounded amused. "Are you saying I'm soft?"

Eyes wide, I turned to him. "No! Not at all. I just slept well."

"Yeah, I know," he said. "You were out. May have even snored a bit, definitely drooled a little."

"Please tell me you're joking," I said, mortified.

Archer shrugged before saying, "So you got to interview Chase?"

I was still stuck on the snoring/drooling comment, trying to discreetly check his shirt for evidence, but I answered in as cool a voice as possible, "Yeah, he was great, gave me a lot to work with."

"That's good," he said. "Want to try me? We

have some time before the game."

"Sure," I said then swallowed. "If you're up for it."

"I told you already," he said. "I'm up for anything when it comes to you."

Swallowing again, I took my time opening my notebook and taking out my pen. It hadn't been awkward interviewing Chase—but Archer was a whole other matter.

"Okay, so first question," I said, deviating from my list a bit to satisfy my own curiosity. "Have you ever worn a kilt?"

Archer's signature frown appeared. "No..." he said, drawing out the word. "I haven't. But I would love to know why you asked. Did Chase say something?"

I shook my head, only slightly disappointed. "Nope, just curious."

"Right," Archer said. "Kilts are a Scottish thing, you know. O'Brien is an Irish surname."

"Of course, I knew that." I rearranged myself again so I could face him, and so he couldn't try to peek at my notebook like I thought I'd caught him doing a second ago. "A lot of these questions came from the fans. Like I told Chase, they can get kind of personal."

"Okay," he said.

"Does that mean I can move on?" I asked.

"Move on from the kilts? Go right ahead."

"Okay, next question"—I was back on script now, even though I felt really uncomfortable asking him this—"do you have a girlfriend?"

Archer tilted his head. "You already know the answer to that."

Sighing, I looked up and met his gaze. Gah, those gray eyes could swallow me whole if I let them. "It never hurts to be sure."

"No," he said. "I'm one-hundred percent single at the moment. Though that's not necessarily by choice."

Feeling my cheeks heat, I took my notes then quickly moved on. "Is there anyone you're interested in?"

"Yeah, I am. But I'm not sure she's into me."

I scoffed. "She'd have to be crazy not to be."

"Honor," he said quietly.

Pretending that I didn't hear the pleading tone, I asked him the next one. "Blondes, brunettes or reheads?"

"Brunette," he said, taking a strand of my hair, before I slapped his hand away. "With natural light brown highlights."

"Boxers or briefs?"

His voice deepened. "Whatever you like best."

With a gulp, I asked another, "Can you describe your ideal woman?"

"I can do better than that," he said. "Get out a mirror, and I'll show you exactly what she looks like."

Looking up, I caught his gaze just as he ran his knuckles along my cheek. The feel of them caused a shiver of pleasure to travel down my spine.

"Better yet, get out your phone, take a picture of yourself. Then send it to me, so I can keep it for whenever some other reporter asks me that question."

"Archer," I sighed.

"Yeah?" he said.

"You're wasting your time on me."

He just shook his head. "I don't think so."

With a sound of exasperation, I pulled away from him, while he continued to sit there calmly, staring at my face. "You don't even know me! I'm not the girl you met at the party. Heck," I threw my hands into the air, "I don't even want to be a reporter. This is just for fun. I'm majoring in accounting to become a CPA. Totally boring, right? And I have so many issues. You have no idea."

"Tell me then," he said.

"I'm not just inexperienced. I-I'm afraid of relationships," I said, deciding to lay it all out there. Archer deserved the truth, and for some reason, I couldn't seem to stop the words from coming. "I have major abandonment issues. I don't expect you to understand. You have a great family. But my dad left when I was young. And my mom, the way she attaches herself to men, the way she's obsessed with their love, she basically gave up on me. It was abandonment, too, just in a different way."

His mouth opened to interrupt, but I wasn't done. Not by a long shot.

"Guys never wanted me in high school either," I went on. "I think it's because I'm not normal and would rather hang out with book characters than real people—plus they knew I wouldn't put out on the third date. So you see? Everyone gets tired of me eventually. And you will, too." I shook my head. "I'm a lost cause, Archer. We can't be together. No matter how much I want you."

Taking a much-needed breath, I watched the emotions flit across Archer's face: concern, sympathy...and then there was the one I hadn't expected. Slowly, almost imperceptibly, Archer began to smile. It started in his eyes, then his mouth bloomed into a full-on grin.

"What are you so happy about?" I asked.

"You want me," he said.

I shook my head, not to deny it but because I was confused. He nodded anyway.

"Yeah, you do." Archer's eyes were alight. "You said so yourself. 'No matter how much I want you.'"

Thinking back, I realized yes, I had in fact said that. But was it the only thing he heard?

"Don't worry, I caught everything else you said, too. But I just want to live in those last words for a bit if you don't mind."

Before I could respond, I heard a ding from inside my bag.

"You should get that," Archer said, tipping his chin toward the floor. "It's been going off for the last half-hour."

With a frown, I reached down, opened the bag and grabbed my phone. The screen lit up, and sure enough, there were five texts from Charlie. They started out simple.

Charlie: Hey girlie, just checking in on you (and all those hot bball players, of course!)

Then about 10 minutes later...

Charlie: Honor!!!!! Come on, text me back, I'm SO bored!

Then...

Charlie: I can't believe you're there w/all those guys. Find the hottest, and text me a pic. So bored here without you :(

Charlie: Hello? Honor, you there? Emmy says you should be there soon. Let me know how it's going, please (and also send pics of hot bball players :))

And then, there was the last one.

Charlie: Has anything happened with Archer yet? ;) Remember you promised to tell me if it does! You and he would make such pretty babies *sigh* Write back soon!

"Pretty babies, huh?" Archer said, and I gasped, pulling the phone to my chest. I couldn't believe

222

he'd read that.

Clearing my throat, I turned away, trying to hide my pink cheeks. "Charlie has an overly active imagination."

It sounded like he bit back a laugh, but I wasn't sure.

"What are you going to text back?" he asked.

"I'm not sure yet," I mumbled.

Leaning in, quicker than I could react, Archer swiped the phone from my hand and held it away from us. When I turned to him, he laid a kiss to my forehead, and I heard the click in the background signaling a picture had been taken.

"Send her that," he said, tossing my phone back, standing and stretching his arms above his head— which made his shirt rise up. He must've untucked it sometime during the ride because I saw a little slice of skin. My eyes latched onto that small reveal, the tan of his abs contrasted with the white of his shirt, like it was the eighth wonder of the world. "I think she'll like it."

"But—" I said.

"In fact, give me your phone back for a sec, and I'll send it to myself, too."

Shaking out of it with difficulty—the trance his naked stomach put me under was no joke—I frowned. "No way. You already stole my phone once. There's no telling what you'd do this time or if you'd even give it back."

With a shrug, Archer started walking away. "Okay...I guess this means I'll have to keep the picture I took of you while you were sleeping. It's going to be your contact pic."

My eyes were wide as they met his.

"Don't worry," he said, turning back just as he was about to step off the bus. His eyes were smiling again. "You look cute in your sleep—even when you drool."

I swear I died right there.

15

Archer

Maybe I shouldn't have teased her

Maybe it would've been better if Chase and I had never changed seats.

As I had that thought, an image of Honor with her head resting against my brother's shoulder went through my mind, and I scowled. Hard. No, I'd made the right choice.

And she really did look cute in the drool pic.

I was in the locker room with my boys, getting ready for the game against Covington when the sound of a text came through. Turning my phone over, I saw it was from an unknown number, but the selfie I'd taken of me and Honor was right there.

Score, I thought.

I quickly saved the pic and added Honor to my

saved contacts. I'd been bluffing before, hoping she either wouldn't remember that she'd never given me her number or assume that I'd gotten it from Emmy. Either way, I had it now, a direct line to Honor—and she could contact me if she wanted or needed anything. That was a win in my book.

I shot her a quick thank you, and she answered right away.

Honor: No thanks needed. Now, please delete and destroy the drool pic!

I typed in my response.

Me: But you look so darn cute...

Honor: You're incorrigible.

Me: I've been called worse.

Honor: Gah, so annoying. Just so you know, I don't usually drool in my sleep. Also...sorry about your shirt :(.

Was she kidding? I was never getting rid of that shirt. In fact, it was my new favorite—possibly/probably because she'd had her lips pressed against it not thirty minutes ago. And though I'd made her contact picture the one with the two of us—it was too good not to. She must've blinked at the exact moment I took it because her eyes were closed, my lips pressed against her skin, a definite keeper—but I'd saved the drool pic as well.

Me: Don't worry about it. Also, incorrigible? Nice vocab for a non-reporter/accountant ;)

Her reply was short and sweet.

Honor: Accounting = Stability. And don't try to change the subject: DELETE the pic!!! Please.

The 'please' cracked me up. Holding back a laugh, I sent her my response.

Me: Okay done. It's gone.

Honor: Hmm, thank you—you really deleted it, right?

She was too perceptive for her own good.

Me: I did.

Though I may or may not have plans to go back and recover it from my recently deleted photos. Hey, it was the only picture I had of just her...and what was the big deal anyway? So my dress shirt had a little wet patch on it. Her lips had been parted slightly in the sweetest way, and how she'd cuddled up next to me? Yeah, I didn't want to forget or delete that memory.

Honor: Well, that's a relief lol. I'd hate to think that was how you'd always see me. Drool pics really aren't all that attractive ;)

Me: Trust me. It was sexy.

It took her a second to respond after that, but I waited to see what she'd say. After several starts and stops, this is what came through.

Honor: Okay well...I'll let you go back to getting ready. Good luck, today, Archer! I hope you guys kill it out there!!!

Me: Oh, we will—and Honor?

Honor: Yeah?

I decided to ask the question that'd been bothering me since the bus.

Me: Who's Jamie?

Honor: ???

Me: Jamie...you said his name a couple of times in your sleep. Was just curious.

I waited with bated breath. Her answer that came a minute later wasn't long, but it told me a lot.

Honor: Oh him! I met him in a bookstore. He was so beautiful, just sitting there, waiting for me to notice him. It was all very romantic.

I was slower this time with my reply, unsure of what to say.

Me: Ah...well that's...nice? I guess...

Honor was laughing at me. I knew it by the tone of her response as well as all the crying-laughing little emojis she included.

Honor: OMG!!! Archer, I'm just kidding! Jamie Fraser is a character from Diana Gabaldon's *Outlander* books. He's one of my many book boyfriends!

The breath that flew from my lips was pure relief.

Me: Oh, good one lol.

Honor: Really? You thought it was funny? There were a lot of ellipses in one text ;)

Me: Hilarious.

Honor: Ask Chase about Jamie if you don't believe me.

Me: That's okay.

Though I planned on doing just that after we got done with this conversation.

Me: So, book boyfriend, huh?

Honor: Yep.

Me: That mean he's imaginary?

Honor: Yes, he's fictional. But that doesn't make my love for him any less real! <3

This girl was seriously something else, I thought, shaking my head.

Honor: Now, go catch some balls and good luck in the game!

Go catch some balls? Who said things like that? I put the phone aside—then looked up to see Baylor staring at me.

"Did you need something?" I asked.

"Nope," he said. "Just haven't seen you smile like that in a while."

Was I smiling? Reaching up for a quick check, I found that yeah. I was. It was entirely thanks to Honor.

With a shrug, I said, "Didn't realize. You ready for the game? Scouts will be at this one."

Baylor stared for another second. "Yeah, I'm always ready."

His tone was off, though, so I stood and placed a hand on his shoulder. "Don't worry," I said quietly. "You've got nothing to be nervous about. Just show out like you usually do, and you'll be great."

"I know this," Baylor scoffed. "Besides Chase is the one who gets nervous at these things, not me. You should go give him some of this pep talk."

But I could sense he wanted to say more. "Something else bothering you?"

"I'm worried about you," he said. "Not the scouts."

That took me by surprise. "Me? Why?" I asked.

"I know you like Honor," he said, "and it seems like she likes you. But just...be careful. Okay?" When I didn't say anything, he added, "If she's playing you, I don't want to see you get hurt."

"She wouldn't do that," I said.

"You never know."

I tilted my head. "Listen, I know you've been burned in the past. That doesn't mean it's going to happen to me—or you again, for that matter."

"Doesn't mean it won't either," he said.

"You sound concerned? That's not really like you."

"No worries. I'll be back to my carefree self in a second." Baylor laughed then reached out to squeeze my shoulder. "I'm just saying...remember to guard your heart. You only get one."

And with that, he left to join T.J., the two talking about how bad we were going to whoop up on this team and how they'd never want to have us back. I did my rounds, checked in with everyone, making sure they were in the right state of mind. We played with scouts in the stands all the time, but it never hurt to reassure the guys. They were here because we were champions. They came to scout *us*, not the other way around. The welfare of my team was paramount, and by the time we stepped out on the field, we were all rocking the winner's mindset.

But Baylor's words stuck with me.

Not because I was in any danger of getting my heart broken, though Baylor thought there was a good fifty-fifty chance. They stuck with me because instead of being fully focused on the game, like I always was, I was thinking about Honor watching in the stands, wondering if she was enjoying herself, waiting for the moment when we brought home this W, so I could speak to her again.

* * *

"So, his real name's James Alexander Malcom Mackenzie Fraser?" I said. "That's just crazy. Who has that many names?"

"I know," Chase said. "But Jamie's like the man. He's an outlaw from Scotland, who's loyal and brave, even though he's gone through all this terrible stuff."

"And he meets the love of his life because of some stones?" I asked, still not understanding.

"Yeah," Chase said, eyes bright. "But she has to travel through the stones first. It's time-travel and adventure and historical romance all rolled into one."

I shook my head still not really getting it.

Chase sighed. "Maybe you should just read the book."

Before I could pump him for more info about this guy Honor had been dreaming about, our teammates joined us, fresh from the showers as we left the locker room. The talk switched immediately from books and went straight to baseball.

"Man, I was on today," T.J. was saying. "Did you see my catch in the fourth to end the inning? It was a thing of beauty."

"You want to talk beauty," Mitch Snider said, "let's talk about my double or that perfect slide into Homeplate. That was on point."

"Yeah, and unnecessary," Chase mumbled from beside me.

It was true. Mitch had only slid into home because he could, not because he had to, trying to make it look more dramatic, hoping to catch the eye of one of the scouts no doubt. But he'd obviously forgotten about the errors he made in the second and fifth innings and how he'd struck out a few times before hitting that double. Snider only focused on the stuff that made him look good— which was why he had such a high opinion of himself.

"Those scouts would be crazy not to offer me a spot after this."

No one answered, but Snider didn't need any encouragement.

232

"The girls in stands sure were eating it up," he smirked.

"Yeah," Baylor said, unable to help himself. "It was a nice hit. Maybe you'd get a few more if you weren't so focused on hamming it up for the crowd."

T.J. rolled his eyes as Snider glared. "This coming from the guy known for pointing to left field before he bats like he's freaking Babe Ruth or something? You're one to talk."

"You do do that," T.J. muttered.

"I know," Baylor said with a shrug. "It's one of my many loveable quirks."

Parker Graves stepped in then. "Yeah, yeah, but can we talk about my man Chase here a second? If anyone's getting scouted it's this guy. That arm is fire."

Chase opened his mouth to respond, but Snider spoke over him.

"Are you kidding? After that slide into home?" he laughed. "Sorry man, but I do believe I stole the show."

Outwardly, I kept my face a mask, but mentally, I scoffed. If Snider thought his one measly hit was anything to my brother's stellar pitching, he really was delusional. Chase had only allowed two runs to score and five hits total the whole game.

"Everyone played great," I said. "Like Coach said, this win puts us in a good place going into to tomorrow's game. Which means our opponents will want to win even more since we schooled them today. But we're not gonna let that happen, right guys?"

They nodded.

"Rest up, eat well, and I'll see you for game two in the morning."

As my teammates dispersed, I saw Honor up in the stands. She was there with June—I'd noticed them during the pre-game warm-up and was glad Honor hadn't had to sit alone. June always came to our games. Home or away, she loved baseball and was one of our most devout fans. Though there were other girls, too, who weren't so in love with baseball who made it a point to be at nearly every game.

A group of them approached me before I could get to Honor.

"You're the catcher, right? Archer O'Brien?" one girl said, stepping into my path.

Fixing the frown on my face, I nodded. Honor and June were only a few feet away. My goal was to make this as quick as possible. "That's right."

"Your knees must hurt after squatting so long like that."

"Eh, you get used to it."

"It's really impressive." She looked me up and down, not trying to disguise the way she was checking me out while she twirled a lock of her red hair. "Your thighs must be so strong, and you'd have to be flexible to hold that pose for so long."

"I guess. If you'll excuse me, there's someone I—" But as I went to step around her, her friend put a hand on my chest.

"Oh Ashley," she said, meeting my eyes, "don't scare him off just yet. I wanted to speak to the captain, too."

I sighed to myself, but it wasn't as if this was new territory. The fans liked to talk to us after the games. It wasn't usually a hardship, but man, I really wanted to talk to my girl.

"Sorry Marguerite, I was just being nice," the redhead said.

"That's okay," Marguerite said then changed her focus back to me. "So, they say you and your brothers may play in the MLB someday. That true?"

I crossed my arms. "Not sure yet."

"You looked pretty good out there today," she said.

"Yeah, real good," another one of their friends piped up, causing a bout of giggles.

I raised a brow. "Thanks."

"Could you sign something for me?" she asked, holding up a marker she'd pulled from her purse.

"Sure," I said. It wasn't the first time a fan had asked for my autograph. "What did you want signed?"

"Just this hat"—I took the Wolves cap and pen and scribbled my signature quickly—"oh, and my shirt. Just here."

When I looked down, she was pointing to the area between her collarbone and her chest.

"It may be worth something," she said, staring at me as if it was a dare. "You know, if you get famous."

Staring past her, I could see Honor and June watching the whole thing, close enough to hear every word that'd been spoken. June was shaking her head while Honor just sat there slack-jawed. From personal experience and some of the fan stories I'd heard from the guys, this wasn't unusual, so I wasn't surprised. Honor, though...she looked like someone had just socked her in the gut.

Turning back, frown still in place, I said, "Sorry, only one autograph per fan."

Cheeks pink, Marguerite muttered her thanks, and she and her crew left soon after. I didn't like being a jerk, but you had to draw the line somewhere. Plus, they were keeping me from seeing my girl. Speaking of which...

I was about to walk towards her—when another obstacle suddenly blocked my way.

The two men who stood in front of me were wearing red shirts, khaki pants and red baseball caps with the Phillies stamp on them. Even without the clipboards in their hands, I would've known they were scouts from a mile away.

"Hey Archer," the first one said, holding out his

hand for me to shake. "I'm Jeff Perkins, and this is my associate Barkley Soledad. We're recruiters for the Phillies, and we just wanted to tell you good game, son."

"Thank you," I said after shaking both their hands. "I'm glad you enjoyed it."

"We did," Jeff said. The little bit of hair I could see beneath his cap was graying, but he was obviously the younger of the two men. Barkley was more wrinkled, shorter, and didn't seem to have any hair at all. "Your team played like a well-oiled machine out there. Though I hear that's the norm for you Wolves. Your wins and overall record proceeds you."

I shrugged. No need to brag. He was right. Our record spoke for itself.

"Are you interested in playing professional ball?" Barkley asked.

"Yes, sir," I said. "Though I think just about anyone on this team or any other would say the same."

"Good to know."

"I'm just going to get right to it." Jeff nodded. "You're a great player, and your catching skills are among the top in the nation, collegiate or professional. You're a hot commodity, Archer. We need leaders like you on our team. I've already talked it out with your Coach. Daisy O'Brien's not one to beat around the bush either. She told us you'd received other offers?"

"A few," I said.

"I hear it's more than a few," Barkley put in.

"If you want a tryout," Jeff went on, "we'd be more than happy to have you. Here's my card, so you can contact us at your convenience."

Taking the card, I looked it over. Nice cardstock, professional font, the same as all the other cards I'd gotten before. But I never took an offer for granted.

"Thank you, I appreciate you thinking of me," I said. "The Phillies are a great team. I'll definitely consider it."

"You do that," Jeff said with a smile. "And maybe try to convince that brother of yours with the arm to give us a try, too, when he's ready."

"I'll make sure he gets the message," I said.

After a few more compliments about me and my brothers, the men walked away, and I was finally able to move toward where I'd wanted to be this whole time. June had disappeared, but Honor was still there waiting in the stands. When I stopped in front of her, she stared at me as if she'd never seen me before. I had no idea what that look meant. But I could tell something was going on inside that brain of hers.

I just hoped it was something good.

16

Honor

Thank goodness for the scouts.

They'd just given me my story about Archer.

I mean, sure he'd answered several of my interview questions on the bus, but unlike Chase, it wasn't like I could use much of what he'd said— especially the parts referring to me. I'd been thinking I might have to interview him again, and my resistance was running low.

He did that to me.

But if I was looking for an angle, it had just played out in real time: the scouts, MLB plans, the girls. Archer O'Brien was in demand. He was a "hot commodity" like that one scout had said. The girls seemed to agree, one even asking for his autograph, though I thought it was obvious what she really wanted was a date. But who could blame her! And Archer had taken it all in stride as if this happened to him all time.

Maybe it did.

His future was bright. I wasn't much of a baseball fan, and even I'd known he was amazing. Archer played the game like he was born to do it. He was going places. He was destined for great things.

And God help me, but I wanted him.

It was the first time I'd admitted it to myself.

I, Honor Tierney, wanted Archer O'Brien for however long I could have him.

There was something freeing and terrifying about acknowledging that fact. I was glad June had gone to the bathroom. At least there was one less person to witness my moment of clarity and the uncertainty that followed.

Even as he stood there, looking at me, I couldn't find the words.

"Me and a few of the guys are going out for pizza later. You want to come?" he asked.

Did I? I wondered. What I really wanted was to figure out what to do about all of these crazy emotions.

Before I could answer, June came back followed by Chase, Dex and Baylor. Awesome. Maybe they could help mask how overwhelmed I felt. Archer was still looking at me as they sidled up next to us.

"Good news," June said, and it took me a second to realize she was speaking to me. "I figured out an answer to the room situation."

"You did?" I said faintly. "Oh, that's a relief."

She gave me a look but didn't ask any other questions for which I was grateful.

"What room situation?" Archer said.

I snapped out of it at the sound of his voice. "When I agreed to travel with the team, I didn't remember to book a room," I said. "Didn't even think about it really. Which was stupid, considering I knew this would be an overnight thing." I shrugged. "June and I were talking when suddenly I realized I had nowhere to stay."

"You can stay with me," Archer said quickly.

"Or me," Baylor said, smiling despite the scowl Archer directed at him.

"Or us," Chase said, elbowing Dex in the side. "We have room for her, right?"

Dex tilted his head, no doubt seeing the red sweeping over my cheeks if the grin on his face was any indication. "No arguments here," he said.

Archer looked like he was about to blow when another voice joined our little crew.

"Well, isn't it nice how all of you are so concerned for Honor's welfare," Coach O'Brien said, the sarcasm thick in her voice as she walked up, planting herself next to me. "But none of that will be necessary. Honor's going to be staying with me and June tonight."

A flash of something passed over Archer's face—disappointment maybe?—but it was gone a second later.

"Cool," he said, pushing his hands into the pockets of his jeans. "As long as she's covered. I was just concerned."

"Sure you were," Baylor mumbled after which Archer not-so-subtly elbowed him in the stomach. The resulting groan made Archer's lips tug up on one side.

"So," he said again, "pizza later?"

"I'm in," June said. "Would never turn down pizza. Yum."

"You kids have fun," Coach O'Brien said. "Me, Bear and the staff are going to a steak place not too far from the hotel. Had a whole bunch of five-star reviews online. I hope it's as good as everyone says."

And then all eyes were on me.

"Well," I said, wringing my hands, "I would come, but actually, I need to stay in and write."

"Are you sure?" June said. "Some of the other girls said they were planning to come, too, so it won't just be us and these guys." She hooked a thumb over her shoulder. "If that's what you're worried about. I totally get it. They can be…a lot."

Coach O'Brien nodded, but Baylor frowned. "Hey, I resent that, Junebug."

"You sure you can't come?" June said, ignoring him.

I nodded. "Yeah, I should really get these articles done. It's the reason I'm here after all."

I caught Archer's gaze then as he lifted a brow, and I heard what he didn't say just as surely as if he'd spoken aloud. His look said, *But that's not the only reason, right?* I tried to telegraph my response with my eyes. *Of course, it's not. I love being with you, spending time with you—so much more than I should— but right now, I just need to be alone to write and breathe.*

And, most of all, to think.

There would be a lot of thinking going on while the others were away. Of this, I was certain.

I wasn't sure he got all that, but he nodded a second later.

"No problem," he said.

June put a hand on my arm. "I'll bring you back a couple slices."

As we walked to the bus, I hung back, and Archer fell into step beside me.

Lowering his voice so only I could hear, he said, "You know, I could stay in, too. I don't have to go with the guys. They would understand."

I forced a laugh. "Oh no, please go. You just won, so you should celebrate."

"You sure?" he asked.

"Yes," I said. "I'm sure. You'll have more fun without me anyway."

He didn't say anything in response.

* * *

The hotel where we stayed was nice. The room I ended up in with Coach O'Brien and June had two beds and a big couch, the latter of which would be my bed for the night. I wasn't complaining. It was comfortable. My feet didn't hang off the end, the cushions were soft yet sturdy, and honestly, I was just happy not to be on the streets or sleeping on the bus. Coach O'Brien had mentioned before leaving for dinner with the rest of the staff that she'd always intended me to room with her when she'd invited me. June had even offered me the bed, but I declined. They were being so nice about everything, but it was clear they were in a groove, a pattern. I just wanted to be as undisruptive as possible.

And to get these freaking articles finished and sent off to Walter.

I'd decided to start with Archer.

He was the oldest, after all.

And the smartest.

And the most interesting.

And the funniest.

And the hottest.

I mean, those broad shoulders alone—

Gah, what the heck was wrong with me?

I mean, yeah, Archer was all of those things. It was true. Though he'd called his younger brother Finn a genius, I'd noticed Archer's quick wit, not just in conversation but on the field. And everything he did interested me, including how confident yet humble he was with such incredible talent. He had a great sense of humor, though he frowned a lot. And, as if it needed to be said again, he was a total stunner. From the steel gray eyes to his strong cheekbones, from those kissable lips to his rocking body, the guy ticked all of my boxes.

Despite this (or maybe because of it), I was having a hard time writing about him. The first time I'd tried the whole thing had gone wonky. It started as an article praising his baseball skills, outlining his many prospects, but before I knew it, the thing had somehow turned into an expose on what a kind, awesome and yes, gorgeous, human being he was. This in and of itself wasn't a problem. But goodness, if I was one of our *Howler* readers, I would've definitely gotten the wrong impression. It kind of sounded like I was falling for the guy.

And maybe I was.

But I could guard my heart.

Archer and I were an impossibility—which may have sounded bleak, but it was just the opposite. If we could never happen, if there couldn't be a real relationship between us and if I knew it, accepted it as a fact going in, I was free to pursue something with him.

And if I got hurt?

Well, maybe a little hurt was worth it.

Archer was going to be a professional baseball player. There was no doubt in my mind. That meant travel and fame and women throwing themselves at him. My future plans consisted of graduating, getting my CPA license and possibly freelancing on the side until I actually found my passion in life. The fact that we were so different, and our paths had crossed at all...it had to be fate.

Right?

I was just finishing up my second attempt at the Archer article—it turned out way better than the first, thank goodness—when my phone started ringing. I answered, and then suddenly Charlie's face filled the screen.

"Hey Honor," she said, "where are you? All I'm seeing is some crappy white ceiling."

With a laugh, I hit the save button on my computer and picked up my cell. "Sorry, I was just saving my work. Hey Charlie. How are you doing?"

"How am I?" she said, raising a brow. "I'm not the one on a trip with a bunch of hot athletes. Your day must've been ten times more interesting than mine, especially since you never texted me back. BTW, I'm still mad you didn't send me any hottie pics."

"I fell asleep on the bus." I shrugged, feeling my lips tug up as I thought about just whose shoulder I'd fallen asleep on. "Otherwise, I definitely would've sent you something."

"Hmm," she said suspiciously, "and what's that smile about?"

"Nothing."

"Oookay...and you seriously got no pics whatsoever?"

"I did get one," I said, biting my lip. "But it's not really what you asked for."

"Well, come on," she said. "Send it over."

Pulling up the surprise photo Archer had taken of the two of us, I hit send and waited for her reaction.

"Wow," Charlie said quietly. "You two are so stinking cute together. And the kiss on the forehead? Totally romantic."

"Whatever," I said, trying to laugh it off. "It was just a joke."

"Doesn't look that way to me."

A second later, I heard raised voices in the background. "What's that noise?" I asked.

Charlie rolled her eyes. "Emmy insisted on us watching this show called *Buffy the Vampire Slayer*. We've been binging it all day. It's about vampires, obviously, and all that stupid paranormal stuff." She raised her voice. "You know I despise silly, outdated TV shows."

"Oh shut your face," Emmy's voice said a second before she stepped up next to Charlie. Her words were harsh, but she was smiling. "Hey Honor." She waved to me. "What Charlie meant to say is *Buffy* will always be in style. It's timeless, and she's loving every *silly* second of it."

"I am not," Charlie said, but she was grinning, too.

A moment later, Rose appeared, carrying a big bowl of popcorn. "Seriously," she said, "just admit it, girl. You like the show. It's not a crime or anything." To me, she smiled and said, "Oh hi, Honor. Just so you know, Charlie's been worried about you all day, but we told her you'd be fine."

"I haven't been worried per se," Charlie muttered. "And I don't like *Buffy*. Not at all. Period."

"Not even Spike?" Rose said.

Charlie hesitated, and Emmy shot her a don't-even-try-to-lie grin. "Everybody loves Spike."

"Okay, okay," Charlie said finally and threw up her hands. "I like it a little. But only a little, and only because of Spike. Seriously Honor, you have to see this guy to understand. He's like sex on a stick."

"Ah, now I really wish I was there," I laughed and so did they. "He sounds amazing."

"You have no idea," Emmy said with a wink.

All of a sudden a new face entered the picture, and I had to do a double-take.

"Hey, are we watching more *Buffy* or what?" Finn said, standing just over Rose's shoulder. The youngest O'Brien brother—the one I knew the least—had another bowl filled with what looked like chips. "Hey, Honor, I didn't see you there."

"Hi Finn," I said in surprise.

"I hear we won today," he said. "Hope it was a good game."

"Yeah, the team played great."

"Awesome," he said. "Hey Rose, you want me to take that bowl into the living room? I was heading that way anyway."

"No, but thanks." Rose smiled at him, and I thought I saw a blush rise on Finn's cheeks. "I'll take it in myself. Talk to you later, Honor."

"Yeah, definitely," I said as the two walked away. Charlie and I exchanged a significant glance while the others weren't looking

"So, the game went well?" Emmy asked again. "I would've been there, but I have a project due Monday."

"It did," I said. "Your brothers killed it out there."

"Well, of course, they did," she said as if that was a given. "Is June there?"

I shook my head. "She went out for pizza with the team."

Emmy nodded. "Naturally. Well, tell her hi for me when you get a chance. It was good talking to you."

"You, too," I said, and then it was just me and Charlie again.

Her eyes were bright, but she didn't say

anything, forcing me to ask the question.

"Sooo..." I said, making sure to keep my voice low, "are you going tell me what the heck Finn is doing there?"

Charlie glanced over her shoulder then back to me, smiling like a kid in a candy store. "Well, I can't say for sure. Emmy decided on the *BtVS* marathon, ignoring my objections, and Rose found out she was off tonight, something about there being a water main break at the tattoo shop. But anyway, so Finn shows up all out of the blue, and he's been throwing Rose these puppy-dog glances that she's completely unaware of, of course."

"Of course," I said.

"It's been that way all night."

"Sounds like it would make a great reality show."

"Oh please," Charlie said. "Why watch other people living life instead of going and living it yourself? Speaking of which, tell me more about you and Archer. Have there been any new developments on that front? Besides the super cute picture. And remember, we're best friends, so I'll know if you're lying."

All of the thoughts I'd been having about Archer came tumbling out in a rush. I hadn't realized just how much I'd needed to tell someone, not just anyone but my best friend, until that moment. Charlie was my person. It had been that way since we were little. I could always count on her to give me good advice.

"Tell me if I have this right," she said after I was done. "You're really into Archer, and you've admitted to yourself that you want him."

"Very much," I said.

"But you don't think anything could happen between the two of you relationship-wise because you're too different, he's going places, you're not, yada, yada, yada."

I frowned at that but nodded.

"And this is a good thing you say since that means there's less chance of you getting attached and then heartbroken because you already know he'll leave?"

"That was my conclusion, yes."

Charlie tilted her head.

"So, what do you think?" I asked.

"Honor...are you crazy?" she said. "Listen, I can't tell you what to do here. That has to be your decision. But you have a soft heart, my friend. There is no way you won't get attached. If you ask me, you already are. And loathe as I am to have any kind of confidence in members of the opposite sex, Archer seems different. I'd say he's at least half-way in love with you already."

We talked some more, but Charlie wouldn't see things my way. I kept telling her that if I expected it, the abandonment, then there was very little risk involved. But she kept saying how he might want something real and for me to be open to that etc. I put it down to that picture. It was just Archer's idea of a joke, but it had addled her perception of things.

"Just don't stand in the way of your own happiness," she said before we hung up.

Afterward, I knocked out Chase's story. It was much easier than Archer's, took my mind off of things (at least for a while), and I needed the distraction. Badly. By the time I got the rough drafts for both stories finished, June had come home with the pizza she promised. There were three pieces with four kinds of cheese, and it was oh-so-good. We talked for a bit about her night, sounded like she and the guys had had a great time. But by 10:00 pm, all three of us, including Coach O'Brien, were in bed. The team had a curfew I hadn't known about.

I was nearly asleep when my phone buzzed.

With a frown, holding the phone close so the light wouldn't disturb Mrs. O'Brien or June, thinking it was probably Charlie, I opened the screen to see what was going on. But the text wasn't from her.

Archer: You were wrong.

Me: About what?

Archer: I would've definitely had more fun if I'd stayed with you.

My heart rate accelerated. How did he do that with such a simple sentence? I tried not to think about how much his next answer mattered.

Me: Why?

Archer: Is that a real question?

Me: umm yes...?

After about a minute, his answer came through.

Archer: Well, for one, I could've pumped you for more info about this Jamie guy. Fictional or not, it's always good to know the competition.

I laughed at that.

Archer: Two, if you'd been there, I could've stared at you instead of my brothers. A definite improvement. And three, between them and those girls from the game, I had a hard time concentrating.

Me: Oh. So, Marguerite and her friends were there?

Archer: Was that her name? I can't remember.

I rolled my eyes. Archer had just spent several hours with girls who doted on him, wanted his autograph, for goodness sakes, beautiful girls who by his own admission made it hard to concentrate. This shouldn't make me jealous, and I wasn't, not really. I just wished I'd gotten to spend that time with him as well.

Me: I'm sure it's hard to remember names when there are so many gorgeous girls around.

His response was instant.

Archer: It wasn't like that.

Me: I see.

Archer: I'm pretty sure you don't.

253

COOKIE O'GORMAN

There wasn't much I could say to that, so I waited instead.

Archer: Honor...come on. Like I said, it would've been more fun with you. My mind was on you the whole time. How was your night? How'd the writing go?

Me: It went well. Got done with two articles, and I did a lot of thinking.

Archer: Any thoughts about me?

Me: Maybe.

Archer: I hope they were good ones.

Me: They were.

Archer: Details?

Me: No way.

Archer: Okay, just tell me this. Was I wearing a kilt in any of these "thoughts"?

I laughed quietly.

Me: No, not this time.

Archer: Damn. Next question: Did I take off a kilt in any of them?

Me: Goodnight, Archer.

Archer: Goodnight, Honor. Sweet dreams. Hopefully of me.

As if he had willed it to happen, I did dream of Archer that night. And they were sweet (for the most part). But that bit of heat was in there, too, and there were no kilts this time. Just me and Archer, and it was more than enough. By the time I woke up the next day, I was even more confident in my

254

decision. I could hook up with Archer. No strings, no expectations, no heartbreak. Just fun with a guy I greatly esteemed and was attracted to. I was determined to see this through (if he still wanted me, of course).

No matter what happened after...

It would be worth it to have him just once.

17

Archer

Honor was acting strange.

After we won the second game against Covington, she hardly spoke to me, and then she'd opted to ride back to campus with June instead of taking the bus with the team. She had claimed it was to edit and work on her articles. She wanted to make sure they were print-ready before she sent them to her boss, but I still felt like something odd was going on.

It felt like she was avoiding me.

Though maybe I was just being paranoid. After all, it had only been a few days.

Wednesday was weights and conditioning for the team, so a bunch of the guys were in the gym. Usually, I led by example, one of the first to get in and get my reps done. But today I was dragging. Chase finished with his workout, and I was still at the half-way point.

He came up to me as I was doing my final set of bench presses.

"How's it going?" he said.

"Good," I replied, pushing out a breath as I lifted.

Chase raised a brow. "Any word from Honor?"

"No."

"And how are we feeling about that?"

"Fine." I laughed a bit breathlessly. Had it always been this hard to get through my circuit?

Chase made a hmm noise, but thankfully, he stopped with all the questions. After doing the last reps, I sat up, grabbed a drink while wiping the sweat from my forehead. Parker Graves came in a second later followed by Baylor, T.J. and Shawn.

"Y'all know how I was seeing that sorority girl, Claudia," Shawn said.

"Claudia," T.J. repeated. "She the one with the nice rack?"

Parker shook his head. "No man, that's Claudette. Claudia is the one with the fine apple booty."

"Ahh."

"Yeah, that's her." Shawn sighed. "Anyway, seemed like she was into me. We went to dinner. She let me kiss her. I even called her the next day like she asked me to. We went out again a few days after that. Been seeing or talking to her every day since. For weeks, it was all good, and then, radio silence."

My ears perked up at this.

"You hook up with her?" Baylor asked.

A shrug. "She may have given me a handy."

"Ewww," T.J. said, plugging his ears like a little kid. "TMI, my friend."

"Sorry."

"S'okay...but seriously, my last girl Vivi wouldn't do nothing like that. She said she was waiting for marriage."

The guys all groaned. Gossip wasn't something I was typically into, but I found myself paying way more attention to their conversation than I usually would.

Shawn still looked confused. "Well, Claudia's not waiting for marriage. We talked about it. Like I said, we've been talking or texting every day for a month."

"Sounds like maybe you scared her off," Parker said.

Shawn frowned. "What do you mean?"

"Well, girls don't like it if you're too attentive."

"It's true," Baylor said, sitting down at the leg press machine. "In my experience, that's how most girls are. They say call me tomorrow. But what they're really doing is testing you, seeing if you're

258

going to be chill or suffocating."

Chase was shaking his head, obviously listening, too, but Shawn seemed to be thinking hard.

"So, you're saying I should just ignore her?" he asked.

Baylor shrugged. "Yeah, let her come to you. Give it a couple more days, and if she texts, wait at least five minutes before responding. If not, move on to the next."

"Damn, Bay, that's cold," T.J. mumbled.

As they started their workout, I moved onto my next exercises. I thought about how I'd texted Honor every day since the weekend. On Monday, I'd asked if she wanted to hang out, but she was studying for an accounting test. Tuesday, she'd been writing a paper for another class. I'd definitely been the one to initiate almost all of our interactions so far. Was that the wrong move?

Chase narrowed his eyes. "I can't believe you'd listen to Baylor when it comes to advice about women."

I shook my head. "What? I didn't say anything."

"Yeah," he said, "but I can see what you're thinking."

Awesome, my brother was a mind reader now.

"If you want to talk to Honor, why don't you just call her?"

"Maybe, I don't want to talk to her," I said, though the words felt all wrong.

Pretending not to see Chase's look of disapproval, I made up my mind to let Honor take the lead. It was a hard thing to balance. I didn't want to scare her off. But I also didn't want to just let her go. That was why she needed to be the one to set this next part of our relationship in motion.

I pounded out my next series of triceps, lats and was just about to start my treadmill run when there was a knock at the door followed by someone clearing their throat.

My skin prickled, knowing it was her even before I turned.

Like something out of a dream, Honor was standing there dressed in jeans and a long-sleeve tee with her hair in a messy bun. There were at least nine guys from the team working out in here. We were all sweating bullets by now. And dang if she didn't look like a much needed breath of fresh air.

She looked over all of us, and I was sure my eyes were already doing that smiling thing she talked about, when she spoke not to me...but to Baylor.

Baylor of all people.

"Hi guys," she said, eyes glancing to me before she refocused on him. "Baylor, can I see you outside for a second?"

Rising smoothly from the bench, Baylor shot me a look, too. "Sure," he said. "It can't take too much time, though. I'm in the middle of my workout."

"Oh, it won't."

My eyes weren't smiling anymore. Here I was having decided to let Honor come to me—and instead, she shows up looking for my brother? This had to be a joke.

As Baylor went to join her in the hall, T.J. came up and gave my shoulder a pat.

"That's messed up," he said. When my eyes cut to him, he backed away slowly. "Hey, just trying to show support."

I knew it was true, but his sympathy wasn't appreciated. He was right about one thing, though. This was messed up. I grabbed some free weights— which just happened to be by the door—and got to work. If I happened to hear their conversation...well, that's what they got for leaving the door open.

I caught the tail end of what Honor was saying.

"...fans came up with most of them. Like I said, it's for your profile in *The Howler*."

Ah, so this was about Baylor's interview. I should've known. If I'd been thinking straight, I would've, but I was just so shocked when she wasn't here to see me.

"I typed it all up, so it would be easier. And less awkward," she added with a laugh. Her back was to me, but I could see Baylor's eyes as they skimmed down a sheet of paper in his hands. "I know you're busy now. Just turn it in when you're done. If you have any questions, let me know."

"Yeah," Baylor said. "I have a question. What do we do if the answer isn't on here?"

Honor tilted her head. "What do you mean?"

"Well, number five says something about boxers or briefs, but some days I go commando."

I rolled my eyes. Baylor was such an idiot sometimes.

"And the one before asks who I'm interested in," he said. "Is that about an actual person or my sexual preference? Because at one point, I thought I might be bi." Baylor nodded. "Yeah, there was this guy who I thought was pretty, but he actually ended up being a girl with really short hair. But I didn't know that when I talked to her, so...I'd say straight, but with an appreciation of all the sexes."

"Um well," Honor said. "In that case, I guess you just say...um that? If you're sure you're okay with me printing it?"

Baylor looked up at her. "Oh, I'm fine with people knowing. I'm sure Emmy and Archer already told you. I have no shame."

"Must be nice," Honor said.

"Most days it is," he said. "So, how are things going between you and my brother?"

I couldn't see her face, but it sounded like she was smiling when she said, "Good, I think."

"Not tired of him yet?"

"No way," she said which made my chest puff

up.

"You sure?" Baylor said, grinning down at her. "Because a second ago, you barely looked at him before your eyes went to me."

Honor sputtered. "I-I wasn't—"

"It's okay. I'm used to being ogled."

Her laugh came out in a burst. "Wow, you are so full of yourself."

"Can one really be full of oneself if it's true?" he asked as it was really some deep philosophical question.

"Yes, one can," Honor said. "And it isn't true because I wasn't ogling you."

Baylor shrugged. "It's okay if you were. I like it when pretty girls look at me."

Did he just...? My blood began to boil, but then Baylor shot me a look over Honor's shoulder. He'd known I was there all along, and I knew what was coming even before he said it.

"You know, if you're looking to have fun, maybe you should try me instead of Archer."

My eyes closed because now I knew exactly what he was doing—but Honor didn't. Despite the urge to knock him upside the head, I waited for her response.

After a moment, she said, "What? Is this a joke?"

"I'm just saying," Baylor went on, "a lot of girls want to bag an O'Brien. I'm definitely the easiest—not to mention the most good-looking. Plus, considering how you and Archer met, it would make sense. Party girls are more my scene than his."

Honor was motionless as Baylor took a step forward then leaned toward her.

"I'd be more than happy to show you a good time, Honor."

I barely suppressed my need to react, but before I could, Honor pushed him away.

"Ugh," she said, "that is so gross. I can't even... Does Archer know you do this, hit on the girls he's seeing? Because that is just wrong."

"So, you're not interested?" Baylor asked.

"No! For goodness sakes, I'm with your brother."

My heart filled at her words, and I noticed Baylor start to grin, but my girl wasn't done with him yet.

"And FYI, I'm not trying to 'bag an O'Brien.' I'm with Archer because I actually like him. A lot." Honor put her hands on her hips, jabbing a finger into Baylor's chest. "Which is more than I can say for you. He's twice the man you are. Maybe if you didn't have such a big head, you'd see that."

"Oh, no arguments here," Baylor said, laughing.

Honor poked him again. "How can you and Chase look so alike, huh? It's like there's two of you, but only one is a decent."

"Nah," he said. "There's only one of me."

"Well, thank goodness for that," she said. I was

about to step in when she lowered her voice. "And I don't know how you found out, but just because I went to that party looking to hook up with you and called out your name instead of Archer's, it doesn't mean anything. I didn't even know what you looked like."

I winced as Baylor bit back a smile. "Good to know," he said then met my eyes over her shoulder. "Congrats, she passed."

"Yeah, I heard," I said, walking out to join them.

Honor spun around and our gazes met. "Passed?" she said, sounding confused. "What's he talking about?"

"Nothing." My eyes drank her in from head to toe, the words she'd said just moments ago echoing in my ears. "Baylor has a bad habit of testing the women around us. He thinks he's so hot no one can resist him."

"That's because most of them can't," Baylor put in. He looked to Honor then, "but you did. Nicely done."

Honor let out a nervous laugh at that. "Wow, so, this was all some sort of messed up test?"

He gave her a nod. "One that you passed with flying colors."

"Oh," she said, wincing as her face got red. "I thought you were really hitting on me. Sorry Baylor, about yelling at you."

"It's okay." He threw her a wink. "I think I kind

265

of liked it."

"I liked it, too," I said under my breath, putting a hand on her waist.

"Okay," she squeaked. "Well, I really should let you guys get back to your workout. Just return the interview questions back to me as soon as you can."

"Will do," Baylor said.

She hesitated a moment but then stood on her tiptoes to kiss my cheek. "Talk to you later, Archer."

"Looking forward to it," I murmured.

Baylor and I both looked after her as she left, walking quickly with her head down. It looked like she might've been texting on her phone.

"I think you have a keeper," Baylor commented once she was out of earshot.

"I think you're right," I said. "And thanks. For that."

"No problem. What are brothers for?" he said, clasping my hand and clapping me on the back. "But if you think I'm going to be mature about this, you're sadly mistaken. My name? She called out my name while you two were hooking up? That's classic." He started laughing and didn't stop as he walked back into the weight room.

I knew he'd probably tell everyone, but I couldn't even be mad about it.

After everything Honor had just told him, how she'd put Baylor in his place, how could I be?

I was still looking down the hall at the place

where she had been when I felt my phone buzz. Pulling it out of my pocket I saw a new text.

Honor: I meant to ask. Do you want to come over tonight for a movie?

I didn't wait anywhere near five minutes to send her my response.

* * *

Honor was sitting inches away as we watched some sappy rom-com. If I were to move my arm, our shoulders would be pressed together. But, I reminded myself, I'd decided to let her make the first move.

Even if it killed me.

Being so close yet not touching was sweet torture. Ever since I knocked on her door, and she answered wearing a loose t-shirt and yoga pants, I'd been nothing but grateful. She'd let me in with a smile and led me back to her room. No one else was home. Apparently, Rose was at work, and the other girls had gone shopping, something about a night out they were planning. So, it was just me and Honor. Sitting next to each other on her bed, watching as the two characters on the screen tried to get it together. They were about to have their first kiss when I heard Honor sigh—and she finally rested her head on my shoulder.

Dear Lord, I thought, *I don't know what I did to deserve this, and I know I don't say it enough. But thank you.*

"For what?" Honor asked.

"Hmm," I said, wrapping my arm behind her and pulling her closer like I'd been dying to do this whole time.

"You just said thank you." She laughed. "I was wondering what I did to deserve it."

Had I spoken that thought aloud? Ah well. "Oh, I was just thinking. I'm glad you asked me over. It was a welcome surprise."

She sat up, putting some distance between us, and met my eyes. "I'm glad you came. I wasn't sure you'd be able to with your busy baseball schedule and everything."

"It's our bye week," I said. "Other than practice, the team has off."

"Oh, that's right. Also, sorry again for telling Baylor about...you know. I just assumed, since he's your brother, you'd talked about it."

"Never." I pushed a strand of hair that'd escaped behind her ear, watching her eyelashes flutter. "Whatever we do stays between us."

"You mean that?" Honor asked.

I nodded.

"Does it bother you when he does things like that? Baylor, I mean."

"Yeah." I sighed. "It does, but I know his heart's in the right place. That was just his way of looking out for me." Grinning, I added, "Plus, watching you tell him off was hilarious. I wouldn't trade that moment for anything."

She rolled her eyes. "It wasn't that funny."

"Hilarious," I repeated.

"Glad you enjoyed it. For a minute there, I thought he was serious."

"You know, it wouldn't have mattered if he was."

"I do know. You already volunteered as tribute after all," she said.

"That I did."

She looked down at her hands, twisting them together like she was nervous. Her voice though was strong when she said, "And if I wanted to try some things, romantically...are you still interested in the position?"

My heart began to pound. Waiting until our eyes connected, I nodded.

Her gaze dropped once more to her hands. "Are you sure? Because it's totally okay if you've changed your mind."

"I haven't changed my mind," I said, reaching out and tilting her chin up. "Just tell me what you want."

"Can I—"

"Yes." My answer was immediate.

Honor gave me a look. "But you didn't even let me finish. I could've asked for anything."

"Exactly. And I would give it to you."

She shivered, looked like she took a deep fortifying breath, then finally said in a whisper, "Can

269

I...touch you?"

As if I would ever deny her.

18

Honor

Archer closed his eyes.

I didn't know where I'd gotten the courage or the audacity to ask him that question. My thoughts had turned into a puddle as they so often did in his presence, Charlie's tips on seduction nowhere to be found. It was just me this time. Asking for what I wanted and hoping he wouldn't laugh or run away.

When his eyes opened again, they were an intense gray storm. But he didn't look amused or like he was about to run.

"You can touch me wherever, whenever, and for however long you want," he said, his deep voice rolling over me like a wave.

His words burrowed inside my chest, gave me

the courage to keep going.

Lifting his hand in both of mine, I placed a kiss on each of his knuckles and then his palm. "I love your hands," I murmured as he cupped my cheek. "How rough and strong they are. How good they feel against my skin."

I went to his jaw next and felt it flex as I ran my fingertips over it. "You chin, this neck...these shoulders." My hands smoothed across them. "Gah, they're beautiful. I feel like you could carry the weight of the world—and maybe you do sometimes."

Archer shivered beneath my hands as they moved lower.

Trailing my hand to the bottom of his shirt, pushing up on the material, I said, "Can you take this off?"

His shirt was on the floor before I could blink. Archer had tugged it up and off with just one hand.

I lifted a brow. "That was sexy."

"Honor," he said, but it was more of a plea than anything.

I wanted to give him everything he'd asked for in that one word and more. Skimming my palms along the ridges of his pecs down to his abs, I shook my head. That golden tan of his, the way his muscles rippled and tightened wherever I touched. Real people were not supposed to look like this.

"Your body is ridiculous." I sighed.

"Honor, please," he laughed—but stopped short a second later when I got to his waistband. My fingers hovered there a moment. Not to tease, but to seek permission.

"Wherever I want?" I asked.

Archer gave a tight nod.

I licked my lips then unbuttoned and unzipped his pants—thanking God when my hands didn't shake. My hand slowly slid below his belt, palming the hard length of him. The groan that followed was music to my ears.

"Is this okay?" I said, shifting my hand up, feeling him shake. "I've never done this before so—"

"It's perfect." Archer was breathing harder. "You're perfect."

Hardly, I thought but didn't say. I didn't want to take him out of this moment. His eyes were on my face, and he looked like he was fighting for calm. But that wouldn't do. I wanted to see him completely undone, to give him pleasure like he had me.

"I can't believe I'm touching you like this," I murmured.

Archer nodded, threaded his fingers into my hair. "Wherever and whenever you want." He dropped his lips to mine in a kiss I felt all the way to my toes. "That feels so good. God, Honor."

Hearing him say my name like that made my core tighten. It made me realize just how warm I

273

was, how much pleasure I was getting from the act. The feel of him, the knowledge that I could affect him this way, knowing it was me who was making him come apart like this. It was a heady thing.

My hand never lost its stroke. Up and down, I felt Archer shake on every upstroke, and there was an answering shake inside of me. His breaths were coming in fast pants now. Leaning in, I put my lips beside his ear.

"Let go," I said softly.

Archer met my gaze.

"It's okay. I want to watch."

Archer groaned again, and as if he'd needed permission, I watched as he came apart, his eyes closing but his hands still in my hair. I never released him, kept stroking until he was completely spent.

He surged up after, kissing me hard like the world was coming to an end. His lips were warm and demanding as they moved against mine, the feeling of his tongue a welcome invasion. I just held on for dear life.

When he leaned back an inch, I said, "So...it was good then?"

"Better than good, Honor," he said, his forehead pressed against mine. "I...you...thank you."

Inside my heart soared. It sounded like he was speechless, but the feeling in his words was obvious. He sounded euphoric.

"And now, it's your turn."

Looking up, I caught his hot gaze. "What? No, that's not why I did that. I wanted to."

"I know," he said, following me as I leaned backwards, a rare smile on his face. Archer almost looked...playful. "And there's nothing more I want right now "—he placed a kiss on my lips—"than to see you"—he rolled over, keeping me between his arms—"lose control"—he grinned as I gasped—"because of me."

As he stared down at me, I felt my courage rise again.

"Archer," I said, reaching up to place my hands on his forearms, "you can touch me wherever and whenever you want."

His eyes flared at the words, his words said back to him. As he leaned forward, I lifted my head to kiss him. Our mouths were hot against each other, the flame rekindling, but before it could get any farther, I heard the front door slam, and Charlie's voice said, "Honey, we're home!"

Archer and I broke apart, staring at each other.

Emmy's voice came next. "And we brought food. Yummy, yummy Chinese food."

"Come out here, and talk to us," Charlie called. "We have much to discuss."

Archer closed his eyes, shook his head, then looked at me.

"Raincheck?" I said.

275

"That's a promise," he replied and ran his thumb along my cheek before rolling away to stand. It was almost as good watching him put the shirt back on as it was seeing him take it off. Archer caught me staring and grinned again. "Don't worry. I keep my promises."

"I'm not," I said, which was true. I couldn't have done what we just did if I didn't trust him.

I stepped out of my bedroom first followed by Archer. We walked to the door side-by-side. Stopping there, Archer dropped down to give me a peck on the nose.

"I'll see you later," he said. Then to the other two occupants of the room who were entirely too quiet, "Emmy, Charlie, I hope you girls had fun."

"Not as much fun as you did," Emmy said, but he ignored that.

"Bye," he said again to me.

"Bye, Archer," I said back, and then he left, shutting the door behind him.

"Well then," Charlie said, studying my face as I turned around, "it appears we have more to discuss than I thought."

"Way more," I agreed.

I could feel myself smiling but couldn't seem to stop.

* * *

The girls were really great about the whole Archer thing. They didn't tease me too much (though there was definitely some teasing, especially considering the fact that I wouldn't tell them exactly what happened, leaving them to speculate wildly—which they did).

"Will you guys be having a summer wedding?" Charlie said. "I've always wanted to go to one on the beach."

I rolled my eyes.

"What? I could get a great tan, and obviously, since I'm going to be your maid of honor and all, I'd need to look good."

"I thought you said you always looked good," Emmy said.

"This is true." Charlie threw her a smile.

"Well then, there's no need to subject yourself to the sun's harsh rays. Also, a June wedding would be awful for Honor. She'd be so hot in her dress."

I sighed. "There's no wedding, and you guys are crazy."

Charlie gasped. "But I already started looking at venues." More soberly, she added, "Seriously though, Honor. As long as he makes you happy, I'm one hundred percent behind it."

Even Emmy seemed okay with me and Archer's relationship now.

"You're a cool chick," she had said at one point, "and he's old enough to make his own decisions. If you're both on the same page, who am I to stand in your way?"

But were we on the same page? I thought. It sure felt like we were the other night in my bedroom. I hoped we were.

With a sigh, I checked the time again.

It was Friday, and I was supposed to meet Dex at a bar called *Shake & Pour* for his interview. Coincidentally, it was the same bar I'd be meeting the girls at later. Charlie had planned everything. We were having a girls night out to celebrate Emmy's moving in. It was obvious Charlie and Rose had bonded with her while I was gone at the away game. I was glad of it, too. There was nothing so difficult as having to live with people you didn't like. We'd been lucky to find each other.

The bar had been Dex's idea. It'd just opened and was dead at this time of day. We were supposed to meet at 4:00 pm, right when the doors unlocked, but that had been ten minutes ago.

Dex strolled in at 15 after.

Dropping his bag to the floor, he took up the seat across from me, put his elbows on the table and just stared. At me. I guess, that was my cue.

"Hi Dex," I said. "So thanks for coming. I'm doing interviews of you and your brothers for the school paper."

He tipped his chin in a nod. "That's what Emmy said."

"Yeah, it was really great of her to call you and arrange all this," I said. "I've already done everyone else, but you were harder to track down. I guess I saved the best for last, huh?"

My joke fell on deaf ears because Dex didn't even crack a smile.

"Okay," I said after an awkward pause. Pulling out the sheet of paper, I passed it across the table to him. "Here are the questions. All you have to do is answer them, then turn them back into me, and we'll be good to go."

He glanced down at the sheet then back up to my face.

"There something wrong?" I asked.

"No," he said. "But why don't you just ask me the questions instead? That seems faster."

I smiled. "Well, some of them are kind of embarrassing, so I just thought—"

"For you or for me?" he cut in. "Because if it's you, to be honest, I don't really care. And if it's me, I don't embarrass that easily."

Taking in his hair, buzzed much shorter than the other O'Brien brothers, the silver earrings lining one ear, the tats which I could only see a hint of at his neck, the scar running along the side of his face, his ensemble of all black, and the overall badass vibes he was giving off? Yeah, I could tell self-consciousness was probably not something Dex O'Brien struggled with.

Still...

"But this way you can take your time, have some

privacy," I said.

The next thing I knew Dex had crumbled the sheet with my questions into a ball. I gasped as he tossed it over into the bin behind the bar. The scandalized look on my face seemed to amuse the heck out of him, the perpetual smirk he had because of his scar becoming more pronounced.

"I'm good with doing it now," he said.

His interview was definitely the shortest and strangest of them all. Short because he literally gave one-word answers to almost every question.

Question: What do you love about baseball?

Answer: Everything.

Question: Think you'll play professionally?

Answer: (a shrug) Maybe.

Question: Do you have a girlfriend?

Answer: Sometimes.

Question: Would you care to elaborate?

Answer: Not really.

It went like this the whole time, but like a good little reporter, I took down his answers without comment. At the end, I had a few specific ones just for him from the fans, so I went ahead and asked those, not expecting much.

"Can you tell me about your scar?" I asked.

Dex shrugged. "Got it in a fire. A board fell on me as I was running out."

"A fire?" I repeated.

"Yeah," he said. "I was just a kid. It was the

house we grew up in. Bad wiring in the kitchen or something."

"Did everyone get out okay?" I asked.

Dex nodded. "Emmy ran back in there to save the dog, but I ran in after her and pulled her out. It was all good."

"Wait," I said, putting my pen down. "So you ran in to save your sister and ended up scarred because of it? That's pretty brave."

"Nah," he said, "she was the brave one. She was only nine for God's sakes, and she just takes off, running into a burning house. She loved that pup like nothing else."

I thought he was downplaying his role, but now that he was actually answering in complete sentences, I was afraid to say something to stop the flow of words.

"So Emmy saved her? The dog, I mean?"

"Him," he said. "And yeah, she did."

"And you saved Emmy?"

"I guess."

I smiled at that. "I love it when the dog lives in the end. Don't you?"

Annnd apparently our bonding time was over because Dex crossed his arms. "Whatever," he said. "Is that all?"

"Yes," I said, packing up my pad and pen. "Thanks again for agreeing to meet with me."

He grunted. After a beat, he said, "So what's the

deal with you and Archer?"

Sitting back, I mirrored his crossed-arms position. "Deal?" I asked.

"Are you seeing him or what?"

I lifted a brow. "Yes."

"That means you like him, right?"

"Right."

"So, is it serious? The thing between you guys?"

"Maybe."

"Ah come on, what kind of answer is that?" he said.

"Yours." Dex looked confused, so I decided to clarify. "Not so nice is it? When you want info and the person you're trying to get it from is being all evasive and difficult."

As I continued to stare him down, his face suddenly cleared a small smile appearing.

"Ah honey," he said, "difficult is my middle name."

"I'll be sure to include that in the article," I said.

He gave a slow nod. "You're okay, Honor."

"You, too, Dex." I stood from the table and shook his hand. "Now, if you'll excuse me, I have to go home and change for girls night. Thanks again. It was definitely my hardest interview yet."

"My pleasure," he said, grinning as he ran a thumb over my knuckles, and I shook my head.

"You guys really are shameless aren't you?" I asked.

In answer, Dex shrugged and walked away, leaving me there staring at his back.

Difficult, I thought.

Yeah, that's an understatement.

19

Honor

"**A**lright, who told them we'd be here?" Glancing up, I looked over to where Charlie was glaring and froze.

"I thought we agreed not to tell Team Testosterone we were coming," she said. "That it would be more fun without Emmy's brothers tagging along. Rose?"

Rose held up her hands. "Hey, it wasn't me."

"Honor?" Charlie said. "Did you say something to Dex when you interviewed him today?"

Thinking back on it, I remembered the parting shot I delivered then winced. "I may have inadvertently revealed our plans for girls night." She groaned, and I hurried to add, "But I didn't tell him when it was or where we were going."

As we watched them enter, one after the other, Dex and the bartender did one of those hugs guys do where they hit each other on the back. They exchanged a few words, then I saw the guy tip his head in our direction.

"Just our luck," Charlie said on a sigh. "They have a guy on the inside. The bartender is a narc."

Five sets of gray eyes landed on our booth in the corner, and a moment later, the brothers started heading our way.

"And here they come," Rose murmured. "Damn, they look like an ad for Hot-Athletes-R-Us or something. Someone should give those guys a modeling contract. Or write a book series about them."

"Walter says they're like a boy band," I added.

"That works, too" she said.

It was sort of intimidating, seeing them in line, moving as a unit like that. My eyes snagged on Archer's as they drew closer. He was looking at me, too, and though I hadn't had any alcohol, my head felt a bit tipsy as he drew nearer. They stopped at our table, and surprisingly, Dex was the first to speak.

"Where's Emmy?" he said, looking around the bar.

Charlie gave him a look. "What are you, her babysitter? She's in the bathroom if you must know."

"She shouldn't be here at all," Archer said, still looking at me. "Our sister's underage."

Emmy and June walked up then and joined us.

"Hey guys," Emmy said with a smile, looking at her brothers. "You here for girls night? Because I must say, the look on all your faces is pretty freaking grim."

"What are you doing here?" Archer said.

Emmy's chin went up a fraction. "I'm here to celebrate my new living arrangement with my girls. Don't ruin it."

"Yeah," Charlie said, "we've got her back. You guys can scurry off and play with your balls and bats or whatever it is you do when you're not being mood killers."

Chase coughed a laugh.

"Junior," Baylor said and crossed his arms. "I'm disappointed. How'd you two even get in here?"

"Me? You're singling me out?" June said, shaking her head. "How did Finn get in? He's still in high school."

The youngest O'Brien brother shrugged. "Fake ID."

"Well, same for us."

Baylor held out a hand. "I'm going to need to confiscate those."

Emmy's eyes widened. "Jeez, Bay, stand down. I know for a fact you've been going to clubs since you were what, seventeen? Don't pull the protective

286

big brother act now."

"Sixteen," Baylor said. "But that's beside the point. You're not me, and you and June should go home."

"We're not even drinking," Emmy said, holding up the water bottle she'd been nursing all night. "I think you should leave, and let us get back to having a good, *sober* time."

"Hear, hear," Charlie said, clinking her glass on the table. She was drinking Ginger Ale as we'd all decided to be alcohol-free in solidarity.

Rose crossed her arms. "You gotta admit it's a bit hypocritical."

"Why don't we all just stay?" It was Chase who had spoken, and every eye shifted to him. "Seems like the best solution. Emmy gets to stay and be with her friends, and we get to relax and watch over her. It's a win-win."

There was some general grumbling, but no one could argue with his logic.

Archer nodded. "We stay. But if there's trouble, we're getting you out of here as fast as possible."

"If there's trouble," Emmy muttered, "it'll probably be because of you guys. But okay, as long as you don't try to stop me from having fun, I'm good."

As Archer and his brothers slid into the booth, the space seemed so much smaller than it had moments ago—which made sense. Not only were the O'Brien brothers big in number, they were all tall and broad-shouldered and took up a lot of space.

Charlie stood, grabbing Emmy and June. "Now that that drama's over, let's go dance."

Rose whooped, sliding out of the booth, too. "Honor, you coming?" she asked.

I nearly jumped out of my skin when Archer's hand landed on my thigh.

"I think I'll sit this one out," I said.

He leaned in as they walked away. "Good choice."

"Think I'll go dance, too. Just to keep an eye on them," Baylor said and was gone a minute later with Dex and Finn in tow.

I looked up at Archer as his fingers drew circles on my skin.

"Hi again," I said, a little breathlessly.

"Hi back," he said. "Did you enjoy your time with Dex?"

I shrugged. "He's a hard nut, but I think inside he may just be a big old softie."

Archer's lips jerked. "Not sure he'd like hearing that."

"Why not? You're like that, too."

"Oh, am I?"

"Yes," I said. We'd been leaning toward each other, but I didn't realize how close we were until I felt his warm breath caress my lips. Someone cleared their throat from across the table.

"Yeah," Chase said, standing up, looking anywhere but at us, "I'm just going to get something to drink."

I'd forgotten he was there, and as he hurried away, my cheeks reddened.

Looking out to the dance floor, I almost laughed when I spotted Charlie and the other girls. They were dancing alright, but every time some guy tried to push up on Emmy or June, Baylor would pull them back. Dex was doing the same the same thing for Charlie and Rose. Finn was kind of standing off to the side, but every few minutes the guys would rotate out. The look Charlie shot them whenever they pulled some handsy guy away from her was priceless. When Dex did it for the second time, she got all up in his face.

Archer laughed. "She looks pissed."

"Can you blame her? We just came here to dance and have fun."

"You want to go dance, Honor?" he asked.

I shook my head. "We've been here over an hour. I danced a lot already."

Archer tilted his head. "Something else you'd rather be doing?"

By the way he was looking at me, I got the feeling he knew exactly what I was thinking. That was further proven when Chase came back to the booth. As he sat, Archer stood and I slid out to stand next to him.

"Honor and I are going head out," he said, looking to me for confirmation. At my nod, he turned back to Chase. "Look after them. Call me if anyone needs anything."

"Will do," Chase said.

And just like that we left the bar. I texted Charlie to let her know I'd gone with Archer. It wasn't like I didn't trust Chase to tell her, but just in case, I didn't want her to worry. Her answering text was immediate and to the point.

Charlie: Have fun you little minx! Condoms are in my desk if you need them ;)

My cheeks burned as I put the phone away.

"Everything okay?" Archer asked, holding the passenger door of his car open for me. His eyes shined in the moonlight.

"Yeah," I said, "everything's good."

* * *

We didn't talk on the drive over. Maybe that was odd, but it didn't feel that way. I was comfortable, relaxed even. The tension, though, was thick inside that little space. Despite our flirting at the bar, it seemed like Archer was in his head, and I was definitely in mine.

He broke the silence once we were inside Magnolia House.

"Listen, Honor," he said. "If you want to watch a movie again or talk, I'm good with that. I don't have any expectations here. Just wanted to put that out there."

I walked him to my bedroom.

"Really," he said, "we don't have to—"

At the threshold, I turned and placed my fingers to his lips.

"Archer," I said, "do you remember the night we met?"

His eyes darkened as he nodded. I reached past him with my other hand to close and lock the door.

"Do you remember how much I wanted you? Even when I didn't know who you really were?"

I felt his breath exhale as I pulled my fingers away.

"I thought I was ready then. But I know I am now."

"Honor—" he said, but I spoke over him.

"Would you be willing to sleep with me?" His face showed recognition as I kept going. "I was hoping to have a one-night stand."

Archer shook his head, taking a step forward for each one that I took back, but his eyes stayed on me as he came closer. The look in them was the one I'd come to associate with him, that intense, unwavering focus.

Placing a hand on my cheek, his forehead softly meeting mine, he lowered his voice. "I would love to, Honor, but..." he trailed off.

"But what?" I asked.

After a deep breath, he said, "I don't think one

night would be enough. I know it won't be. There's so much more, *so* much more, I want to experience with you."

I smiled and spoke softly, my hands brushing the sides of his waist. "You feel that way now, but that could change."

I felt his skin brush mine as he shook his head. "Never enough."

"As long as you don't disappear after, I think I'll be okay."

"I won't," he said. It sounded like a promise.

Closing the distance between us, I kissed him. Archer O'Brien. The guy who had somehow worked his way into my heart, inch by inch, taking me completely by surprise and making his way past every one of my walls. It felt right. It felt like more than our lips meeting as his mouth moved in perfect harmony with mine. More than skin touching when his fingertips ran over my ribs as he lifted my shirt above my head and tossed it away. More than bodies pressing together as he laid atop me once we were both naked.

He stared down for a moment just taking me in beneath him.

Though his body was a thing of beauty, I couldn't take my eyes off his face. Didn't want to. Archer's eyes trailed slowly over my exposed skin, one hand following his progress. The feel of his rough hands awakened every cell inside me. But the look on his face was what made me feel cherished. His frown softened to something that looked like awe as I shivered.

"You're so beautiful," he said, meeting my eyes again. "So damn beautiful."

My hand ran over his neck and into his dark hair before pulling him in for another kiss. I felt ready. I needed him like I'd never needed anything or anyone else before.

"Archer," I breathed as his lips went to my neck...and then lower.

When his tongue flicked out to taste my breast, I thought I might explode.

"Archer," I said more urgently, trying to tug him back up. "I think I'm ready now."

He sucked one of my tight peaks into his mouth, and his eyes were smiling as I let out a surprised gasp. As his tongue moved over my flesh, he gave one last suck—then did the same to my other breast, giving it equal attention, before finally releasing me.

"There are so many things I want to do to this body, Honor," he said.

The deep sound of his voice made my legs quiver and then clench, the evidence of my arousal running onto my thighs.

"I've wanted to do this every day since I saw you. Every single day. So I'm going to take my time. If that's good with you?"

In a daze, I nodded, and he went back to giving

me more pleasure than I'd ever thought possible.

Archer used his fingers, hands, mouth, tongue, gah even a bit of teeth to bring me to a fever pitch. I could only try to hold on to those broad shoulders as he did things with his tongue that should've been illegal. It wasn't until after I was coming down from my high, feeling boneless, that he reached out to his pants to retrieve a condom.

My eyes traced his movements as he rolled it on. The action shouldn't have been sexy, but it was.

Getting back on the bed, Archer lined himself up at my entrance, looked into my eyes.

I could see the question there and nodded.

Yes, I still wanted this, wanted him. God, yes.

As he pressed into me, it hurt. It did. But he was so gentle I hardly felt the hint of pain that followed. Archer had prepared me so thoroughly, and I was so wet. But more to the point, I reveled in the look on his face, the way he was gazing down at me, the moment when he said my name as if it was a prayer. Then his lips met mine, and there was nothing but pleasure. So much pleasure my heart felt like it might burst right from my chest.

"Archer," I gasped as we crested and came down together.

The smile on his face, the way he pulled me closer as we lay next to each other, was something I would never forget.

He placed a kiss on my shoulder then said in a

rough voice, "I know it's late, but...do you want to go on a date with me tomorrow?"

"Yes, of course," I said, laughing as I did, hoping he couldn't hear the tears clogging my throat.

This had been so much more than I expected. *He* was more than I'd ever hoped for. And I didn't know if he meant it like this, but by asking me out, he'd reassured me. It was a signal he wanted this to continue. The question soothed and sent me soaring all at once.

And for me, it made all the difference.

As Archer's breath evened out against my back, holding me with an arm over my waist, I closed my eyes, certain of one undeniable fact.

I had fallen totally and completely in love with him.

20

Archer

Waking up had never felt so good.

The first thing I saw was Honor, wrapped in my arms. Her face was only inches away, little puffs of air hitting my chest as she breathed. Her soft mouth was parted just like it had been that day on the bus when she'd rested her head on my shoulder. I'd known then—before that even, if I was being honest.

She was the one for me.

Last night was amazing. Being with Honor...I couldn't remember ever feeling closer to another person, and I only hoped it had been as earth-shattering for her. I felt my lips twitch. It must've been good because she'd woken me up about an hour later, whispering, "Archer...I want you again.

Please?" A shiver went through me at the memory. As if I'd ever say no to her. The second time had been just as amazing as the first.

And if I had my way, I'd be her first, last and only.

After I kissed Honor one final time and said goodbye, I tried to be quiet while leaving the house. I was hoping to avoid any awkwardness with her roommates—especially Emmy—but the living room was empty. It looked like the girls weren't awake yet, which made sense since it was still early. They'd probably slept in after all that dancing at the bar.

I just hoped they and my brothers hadn't gotten into too much trouble.

With that thought, the first thing I did when I left was try to check my phone. But the screen was dark. The battery must've died. Frowning, I got into my car and hooked the phone up to the charger.

The screen lit up a second later with tons of missed calls and messages.

"What the—" I stopped, reading the last one I'd gotten from Dex.

Dex: Don't know where you are. But you should be here. Bad shit went down after you left.

Scrolling down I saw five more from Baylor.

Bay: Arch, something happened at the bar. Give me a call as soon as you can.

Bay: Arch, did you get my text?

Bay: Seriously, man, we're dying over here!

Please call me.

Bay: Emmy's tried to call you at least a dozen times, left messages. Archer, we're in deep. Why aren't you picking up?

Bay: WTF, man! Why the hell aren't you answering your phone? Chase is hurt and in the hospital! You should be here!

Finn had sent me an address, and I already had it plugged into my GPS and was speeding toward the hospital as I listened to Emmy's messages. Each one was a little more desperate than the last. It was clear she had been crying.

Hearing my phone ring, I picked up immediately.

"Archer," Emmy said, "are you okay?"

"Yeah," I said. "Are you? How is everyone?"

"We're fine," she sniffed. "It's just Chase. A fight broke out, and he got hurt. No one really knew what to do, and then we couldn't find you, and—"

"Don't worry. I'm on my way."

I pushed my car faster and sent up a prayer, both for my family and for God to get me to the hospital as quickly as possible. It took me under ten minutes. But the whole time I was tense with fear, terrified of what I'd find once I got there.

As I rushed through the hospital doors, my stomach dropped. The team was here and so was Bear. It had to be bad if they were all out here waiting like this.

"Where is he?" I asked.

"Third floor, room 255," Bear said, and his voice told me more than anything so far. The man's growl held a note of pity that I'd never heard in it before. "They'd only let family in."

I nodded then rode the elevator up to the right floor.

A nurse directed me to the correct room, but when I went in, the sight I saw stopped me dead in my tracks. It was like something out of a melodrama. Only this was my family. And that was my brother in that bed, attached to all those machines, with his arm in a cast that seemed too big for his body. His face was paler than usual—except for the bruises all up and down one side. There were a few scratches that looked fresh and raw, too, but as he looked up from the book he'd been reading, he smiled.

"Hey Archer," he said. "It's about time you got here."

"Past time," Baylor mumbled then stood up, putting a hand on my chest as I tried to walk past him. "I texted. Emmy called. Where the hell were you?"

I shoved my hands into my pockets. "My phone died."

Baylor just shook his head. "That's your excuse?"

"It's the truth," I grit out. "Now, will you move

so I can go check on my brother?"

"Chase needed you last night," he said. "We all did, and you were nowhere to be found. We needed you, Archer."

His words hit me like daggers. They sliced right through me until I slumped.

"I'm sorry," I said. "I didn't mean to let anyone down. You're right. I should've been there. I should've been."

Baylor studied me another moment before dropping his arm.

As I walked around him, Dex pulled me down to speak in my ear. "He's just feeling guilty," he said lowly.

Join the club, I thought.

"When the fight broke out, Baylor was in the bathroom, making out with some girl. He didn't even realize anything was wrong until after it was all done."

I nodded, walked past him, and then Emmy caught me up in a hug.

"It was awful, Archer," she said, and I squeezed her tight. "We were just out there dancing. Me, June, Charlie and Rose, and all of sudden these guys, like three of them, started going after this other smaller guy. Chase got caught in the middle."

"I was trying to calm things down," Chase put in. "But unfortunately, I overestimated my powers of persuasion."

"One of them picked up a barstool. He swung it so hard, Archer. It hit Chase in the arm, made him lose his footing, and when he went down, Chase clipped his head on a table. His head started bleeding," she said, the tears rolling down her face now. "It was so bad."

"I should've been there," I repeated, laying a kiss in her hair. "It won't happen again."

Finn was silent, standing next to Mom as she held Chase's hand.

Meeting her gaze, I noticed her eyes were red around the edges, and my heart clenched.

"I'm glad you're here, Archer," she said then reached out for me. "When no one could get ahold of you, I started imagining the worst. I'm just happy you're okay."

I took her hand, holding it tight. "How are you, Mom? I know you hate hospitals."

That was an understatement. Mom had loathed hospitals ever since we'd gone through that terrible time with Dad. With his cancer, he'd had to be in them nearly constantly. Some doctors and nurses were good. Others were not. The bad ones, the ones that were so heartless, so thoughtless that it bordered on cruel, were the ones who stuck out in my mind. I'd never forget those last few days, the horror they'd put my father through, the pain they'd caused us as a family. It made it even harder for me to see Mom having to sit here now, watching as one of her sons was in that hospital bed.

"I do hate them." She looked up at me. "But Chase needed help, so here we are."

I pulled her into a hug. "I'm here now, so if you need to go, you can."

She held me a moment too long, and I tried to give her all the strength I could.

"Maybe I will just pop out for a minute," she said, placing a hand on my cheek. "Just to use the bathroom and get some coffee."

"I'll go with you," Finn said, and I gave him a nod.

"Could you all go?" Chase said. "I want to talk to Archer for a second."

Once everyone was out of the room and the door had closed, his eyes met mine.

"God Chase," I said, stepping closer to the bed. "I'm so sorry I left you there, sorry this happened at all."

"Yeah, yeah," he said with a grin, "enough of all that. How did things go with Honor?"

I shook my head. "That's not important right now. What's important is you getting better."

"I beg to differ. You making love to a girl is far rarer than some bar fight."

"It should've been me," I said, speaking through the knot in my throat. "If I'd been there, none of this would've happened. I can't even look at you without feeling guilty."

302

"My face *is* a little banged up at the moment," he quipped.

"Just stop," I said. Running my hands through my hair, I gestured to him then winced. "Chase you're acting like you're okay, but nobody's buying it. This is serious."

His face lost all traces of the flippancy he'd shown before. "I know," he said.

"How long did the doctor say you have stay?"

"Only a couple days," he said. "They wanted to keep me in case I have a concussion. Did a scan and said one of the bones in my arm is broken and that the muscles in my shoulder were bruised. It's a clean break. They told me I should be glad it wasn't worse."

I cursed underneath my breath. "When does the cast come off?"

"A couple weeks," he said. "They'll scan it again then. If the bone heals right, I should start physical therapy a few weeks after that."

"And baseball?" I asked, voicing the thing I feared. "When will you be able to play again?"

"They said—" Chase cleared his throat and tried again. "They said, if I'm really lucky, and if I'm diligent about the PT, I should be able to get back out there in four to six months. If everything goes well."

I swallowed.

Chase was trying to hide it, but his lips were

trembling.

"And if it doesn't?" I whispered.

He just shook his head as I pulled him to me, careful of his damaged arm. Maybe it was the pitcher-catcher relationship, but I'd always felt a deep connection to Chase, could read him better than any of my other siblings. And right now, he was hurting, not just physically but in his soul. This was all my fault, I thought. I'd gone from having the best night of my life to watching my brother suffer what was possibly one of the biggest blows of his life. It was so unfair. This was the result of my selfishness. Chase was strong, but he'd needed me.

And I wasn't there.

The weight of that truth crushed me.

When everyone had returned, I excused myself into the hall and sent Honor a quick message saying I was sorry, but I'd have to cancel our date. She responded with, "That's cool. :) You want to reschedule?"

I didn't send my response until later that night, but I knew it was the right one.

Archer: Sorry. I don't want to hurt you, Honor, but my family needs me right now. I think we should take a break.

Honor: Got it, no problem. I hope everything's okay. I'll miss you.

I read her message over and over, holding onto those three last words, even as I knew I had to let her go.

21

Honor

Could a person literally die from a broken heart?
I didn't think so.

Otherwise, I would've been DOA a thousand times over.

It had been three weeks, and I still hadn't recovered from Archer's rejection. Forget broken. My heart was absolutely wrecked, the bits of it left in pieces on the floor nothing but dust now. It had hurt when I'd received his text weeks ago.

But it took a few days for the news to completely break me.

Weak and humiliating, the truth was it had taken that long for me to really get it. Though I'd never been stupid enough to put my faith in a man before, I'd given it to Archer easily enough. He'd taken more than just my virginity that night. I'd given him everything, my body, my love and my trust, too. Offered all of myself up on a silver platter...

...and he hadn't wanted me.

It probably would've been easier for me to take if I could hate him for it.

But the jerk hadn't even left me with that.

Charlie, Rose and Emmy had filled me in on all the details of what'd happened that night after we left the bar. How bad the fight had really been—which I knew because the whole thing ended up on the local news—how Chase was hurt and had to stay in the hospital, how no one had been able to reach Archer to tell him the news.

Because he'd been with me.

And now, here I was.

Alone, lying on my bed, still thinking about Archer O'Brien, wishing I could hate him.

But I really just hated myself for not being able to shake this off. I'd known better. I'd gone into this knowing full well that he'd never truly be mine. Archer was always meant for bigger, better things. It was my stupid fault for thinking, even for a minute, that I could have him for more than a night.

At my lowest, I'd even called my mom.

This was how that conversation went.

"Oh Honor," she said after I'd told her everything, spilled my guts in hopes that she'd actually be a real mother to me again. "I'm so sorry this happened."

"Thanks, Mom. I—"

"But you'd only known this Archer a few weeks. How could you possibly have fallen in love that quickly?"

I held the phone away from my ear a moment to check...and yep, it was still her.

"I mean, come on," she added. "What did you expect? From what you said, he's a superstar college athlete. Guys like that never settle down until much later in life. Take it from me. I know how it is."

"I know you do," I said grimly. That was why I had called in the first place, thinking we might be able to bond over shared heartache. How stupid of me.

"Well, at least, you're young," she said. "There will be other men. Speaking of, I have to go now. Dave's calling. Talk later."

"Bye, Mom."

And that was it.

Again, it was my bad for expecting anything different, but the way she'd brushed off my feelings still hurt. The sad part was that I didn't believe her words. Not for a second.

There will be other men?

Maybe for her, I thought. But definitely not for me.

Archer had ruined me just like I knew he would.

A knock on my door broke me out of my thoughts, but I didn't get up. Or say anything. It was probably Emmy with soup again...or Charlie with cake...or Rose with Chinese. My roommates seemed to think food could make me better. But like I'd told them before, I just wasn't hungry—or sick. Unless being heartsick was a real thing.

A second later, the door opened...revealing the last person on Earth I expected to see.

"Baylor?" My brow furrowed, and I sat up slowly. "What are you doing here?"

"Good question." He glanced around the room before his eyes settled on me. I must've looked pretty bad because the playboy winced. "Just here to help. Emmy said you guys were painting today."

I closed my eyes. "Oh yeah...I forgot about that."

"Did you forget to shower and eat, too?"

My eyes snapped open. "What?"

"That came out wrong. I was just thinking maybe you and my brother are coming down with the same thing." Baylor walked farther into the room and took a seat at my desk. His eyes pierced me. "Just so you know, Archer doesn't look any better than you do."

"Is that supposed to make me feel better?" I asked.

Because it didn't.

It really didn't.

He groaned. "Listen, I'm bad at this. But the

good twin is currently out of commission, and Archer's still swimming in guilt. So, I guess you're stuck with me."

Crossing my arms, I gave him my best glare. "I agree. You are bad at this." I sniffed, then added, "And what does Archer have to feel guilty about, anyway?"

"Well," Baylor said, "for one, he feels awful about how things ended with you—not that he told any of us the details. Archer keeps his pain all locked up, thinks he's fooling people. But I can see it. We all can."

I swallowed.

"And he feels guilty about Chase, too."

That made me sit up straighter. "But why? Even if he'd been there that night, things escalated so quickly."

"I know."

"The girls told me about it," I added. "They said those guys seemed like they were on something. The news said a gun was found in their car. If Chase hadn't stepped in, they might've killed someone. Why would Archer feel responsible for that? There was nothing he or any of you could do."

Baylor ran a hand through his hair. "I may have had something to do with that."

"How?"

He sighed. "I talked it over with Emmy, and she says I projected my own guilt onto Archer when he came to the hospital." Baylor cleared his throat. "She's usually right about these things. So, I admit it. I messed up, and I'm sorry about that."

"Archer makes his own decisions," I said. "You can't blame yourself."

"Actually, I can," he said. "Which is why I'm here now, asking you to give him another shot."

Tears filled my eyes, but I wouldn't let them fall. "I wasn't the one who broke it off in the first place."

Baylor nodded. "I know, Honor. But he's in love with you."

The wet drops fell fast against my cheeks.

"When he comes to you," he said, "I just wanted to make sure you'll hear him out. Don't worry. Archer's not like me. He's one of the good ones."

Getting myself under control, I took a deep breath then pushed away my tears and looked at him, really looked at him. Not the playboy, not the cocky athlete, but the guy underneath all that. "You're one of the good ones, too, Baylor O'Brien. Though you may not want anyone to know it."

His playful grin was back in an instant. "Oh? How so?"

"Well, you're here, singing your brother's praises, asking me to give him another go. There's just one problem," I said.

Baylor cocked his head and waited.

"Archer doesn't love me," I said with a shrug. "He's not coming back."

"We'll see about that."

The wink he sent me was full of confidence as he stood, but I only felt more tired. It was nice of Baylor to talk to me. But I couldn't allow it to give me hope. I'd already accepted the fact that Archer was an impossibility.

Now, I just had to work on the empty hole he'd left inside my chest.

22

Archer

"You look terrible," Chase said.

I shrugged. "Says the guy in the cast."

"Hey, don't use my injury against me, Archer. I'm just trying to understand why my once strong and stubborn brother is now moping around the house, looking like a kicked puppy, acting like he has nothing better to do than babysit me."

"Shut up," I mumbled half-heartedly.

Baylor and Dex walked through the door a moment later. Their shirts were covered in white and blue splatters, but I barely noticed.

"Where have you guys been?" Chase asked.

"At Emmy's," Baylor said, and my heart jumped, waiting to hear if he'd say more. "The girls were painting some shelves, so we decided to crash."

"Well, next time take this sad sack with you, so I can read in peace."

I shook my head. "Why would I want to go over there?"

"Why do girls like unicorns and guys like dragons?" Dex lifted his brows as we all looked to him. "What? I thought we were playing a game to see who could come up with dumbest question."

With an eyeroll, Chase said what I'd been dying to ask. "How was everyone?"

"Good," Baylor said as he got a glass from the kitchen and filled it with water. Dex followed behind him, grabbing a coke. "Well, except for that Honor chick."

I cut my eyes to him quickly. "What's wrong with her?"

"Why do you care?" Dex said. "I thought you said you didn't want to go over there."

"Can one of you idiots just answer the question?" I said.

It seemed like my heart was beating for the first time in three weeks. I hadn't gotten much sleep in nearly that amount of time. I'd just been coasting through the days, waking up, going to school, going to practice, coming home to see how Chase was doing and repeat. This was the first news I'd heard of Honor. She hadn't texted again, and Emmy was being so tight-lipped I couldn't get anything out of her. Not that I'd tried too hard. This was a bed of my own making, and I was currently drowning in it.

My frown only grew as Baylor bit back a grin. "Truth is she looks like she got hit by a truck."

"Or a train," Dex added.

"Yeah, or got ran over by a stampede of wild horses—which is basically the look you've been sporting these past couple weeks, Arch."

"Now, I wonder why that could be," Chase said.

"Guys," I said, "we've been over this. Yeah, I...feel a lot of things for Honor." Baylor snorted at this, but I kept going. "I'd probably lay down my life for that girl. But it doesn't matter. My family needs me more."

"My arm is healing," Chase said, "and there's nothing you can do to speed up the process. Why don't you just admit it? You miss her."

"I do miss her." My voice was losing its strength, but that seemed to be happening a lot recently. "All the time."

Baylor sat in the recliner across from me and Chase. "Then why don't you go and get her back?"

"What?"

"Why don't you get her back?" he repeated slowly. "It's the most obvious solution. So, you sent her a text telling her you guys needed to take a break. Well, guess what, Arch? Breaks end. You just need to stop your pity party and tell her how you feel."

That made my blood rise. "Pity party? I left

you for one night, and now Chase's arm is broken. I could've prevented it from happening."

"Really?" Dex said, leaned forward, putting his elbows on the counter of the kitchen. "Because Bay and I were there, and we couldn't stop it. Everything went from zero to sixty in the blink of an eye. I don't get your logic."

"Of course, you don't," I said. "I've been looking out for you guys all your lives."

"I know," Dex said.

I shook my head. "I don't think you do. Worrying about you guys is a full-time job. Chase was the one I didn't think I had to worry about and look what happened to him."

For once, Baylor wasn't smiling. His face only held concern. "You don't have to worry anymore, Arch. We're grown-up now."

"Yes, I do have to worry," I said, the words nearly a shout. I was trying to stay calm, but they just kept pushing. These past weeks without Honor had been a torment. I couldn't stop what came out of my mouth next if I wanted to. "None of you get it. You're my younger brothers. Emmy's my baby sister. It's my responsibility, my duty and privilege, to protect all of you and Mom. If Dad was here, he'd understand."

"But he's not here," Baylor said quietly. "And you're not him."

"I know that." I sighed.

Dex cocked his head. "And Dad wouldn't have blamed you for what happened. Or any of us. He would've blamed those idiots at the bar."

"You want to know what I think?" Chase said then kept going, not waiting for a response. "You're just mad at yourself because you forgot to be sad for once."

I opened my mouth to respond, but he cut me off with a look.

"No, Arch. It's true," he said. "Do you think Dad would want you to be miserable all the time? No. He wouldn't. He'd want you to find your happiness and live in it."

Dad always had a way with words, and Chase had inherited the quality from him.

"I just don't want to let any of you down," I said softly. "I don't want to let her down again."

"Well, why can't you save her, too?"

"What do you mean?"

"Honor," he said. "Why can't you save her? Like you said, you already do it for the rest of us—this one tiny incident excluded. You're there for Baylor when he's being an idiot, rescuing him from the girls and most of all himself."

Baylor scoffed. "I would argue that—if it wasn't so true."

"And what about Dex?" Chase held out a hand. "Every time he gets into a fight, who's there to bail him out? He would've probably already ended up in the hospital or prison if it wasn't for you."

"Accurate," Dex said.

"And you look out for me, Emmy, Finn, Mom and all the guys on the team the same way." Chase put his good hand on my shoulder. "What's one more person, Archer? One girl who made you the happiest we've all seen you be in years."

My mind was reeling with everything Chase had just said.

"A fine girl with a lickable little body," Baylor put in, and I scowled at him hard.

"Don't talk about her like that," I warned.

"Why not?" he said. "I thought you two were done."

My jaw clenched. "It's just a break."

"Well, maybe you should go get her back then, before someone else beats you to it."

"Maybe I will," I said.

"Ah, there he is." Baylor stood and cracked his back like he'd done some heavy lifting. "My work here is done."

Dex rolled his eyes at that. "Oh yeah, it was all you."

As the three of them kept ribbing each other, I was still thinking of all that was said—and what I was going to do about it.

The epiphany moment should've never taken this long to get here, but at least it had come.

It was time to get my girl.

I just hoped she'd take me back.

23

Honor

Charlie knocked and then entered my room without me saying a word.

"Honor." She sighed. "Your eyes are all splotchy again, and you're still wearing your paint clothes."

"Sorry," I said, sitting up.

"Don't apologize. It's Archer who owes us all an apology. I just wish you'd get angry already, so we can go key the guy's car or something."

Standing up and walking to the door, I met her there and forced a smile. "He's Emmy's brother, remember?"

"Whose idea do you think that was?" she said and threw her arms around me, pulling me in for an impromptu hug. "She thinks he's being a complete

idiot about this. I happen to agree. We're all on your room? What did he have to say?"
your side."

"But Chase—"

Charlie pulled away with an eyeroll. "That guy will probably be as good as new in a few months. I've seen people with worse injuries recover in my physical therapy classes. I don't know why everyone's acting like this is so dire."

I nodded. "I hope you're right. He really loves baseball."

"That whole crazy family does," she said. "By the way, was that the panty thief I saw coming out of your room? What did he have to say?"

"Nothing much," I mumbled, the lie sitting heavy on my tongue. I just didn't have the heart to rehash the whole conversation with Baylor so soon.

Rose came to the door then. "How's it going in here?"

"Good," I said. "That new paint is going to look awesome on your bookshelf when it dries."

She nodded. "Just trying to brighten up the room."

"The eggshell blue color is gorgeous," Charlie said. "A very happy color."

"And goodness knows, we could all use some more of that," Rose said, her eyes taking in my face. "It will be okay, Honor. I'm sure he'll come around eventually."

I'd opened my mouth to respond when there

was a ruckus at the front door. It sounded like Emmy was arguing with someone. The three of us exchanged a look and then dashed out into the living room.

I'll never forget the sight that met my eyes.

Emmy had Archer in a headlock, his body doubled over even more to adjust to her smaller size. I had no idea how she'd gotten him in that position. If I wasn't so sad, the whole thing would've been hilarious.

"I told you to call first," she said, squeezing him tight.

Archer's voice was muffled. "I tried to, but you didn't answer."

"That's because I'm so mad. You have to leave now. If Honor sees you, she's going to cry again, and I don't want that."

"Gah, Emmy," he said, "I'm here to make things right."

"I'm serious. You need to go before she sees you."

Charlie spoke then. "Well, too late for that."

Realizing there were other people in the room, Emmy backed off, and Archer straightened to his full height. He looked at her, frowning and rubbing his neck—until his eyes snagged on me.

"Hi," he said.

I nodded. "Hi."

We stood like that, quietly staring at each other,

with so much unspoken between us.

"Screw this," Charlie said a moment later and planted herself directly in front of Archer. "What are you even doing here?"

"I tried to get him to go," Emmy said, "but he refused. He says he's here to apologize to Honor."

"Then I better hear some groveling in the next five seconds, or I'll throw you out myself."

"I'm good with groveling," Archer said.

Charlie scoffed. "It's your choice, Honor. Do you want to hear what he has to say? Because you really don't have to listen. After disappearing on you, it's not like he's earned the right to be heard."

"I deserve that and worse." Archer looked over to meet my eyes, sounding pained. "But I just had to see you."

I held out my hands, self-conscious yet knowing there was nothing I could do about how I looked. "Well, here I am," I said.

His eyes were sad. "Yeah, and you're just as beautiful as ever."

"Maybe we should give them a minute," Rose commented.

"Okay," Charlie said, begrudgingly. "But if he hurts her again Emmy, you'll be minus one brother."

Emmy said nothing to that, but before the three of them left, I thought I heard her lean up to Archer and say, "Good luck."

They disappeared into one of the rooms. I

thought it was Charlie's, but to be honest, I wasn't paying that much attention. Archer's eyes were on mine, and now it was just me and him in the living room.

Just me and the man I was in love with.

Me...and the man who had broken my heart through a text.

Sighing, I sat down on the couch and gestured for him to do the same. "What do you want, Archer? Is everything okay with Chase?"

"It is," he said but opted to stay standing. The rejection stung but not half as much as his other one had, so I let it go. "But I'm not here for that. I came because I have to tell you something."

"What?" I asked.

He began pacing back and forth, and it was only then that I noticed how tired he looked. His clothes were disheveled, the dark circles under his eyes more pronounced, his hair messy as if he'd run his fingers through it one too many times. Archer looked almost as haggard as I felt inside.

"I know you probably don't want to see me," he said then stopped to meet my eyes.

He was so very wrong about that.

I'd wanted nothing more than to see him for the last three weeks.

But I didn't correct him.

"You have every right to be mad and probably never wanted to hear from me again."

324

Wrong again, I thought. I'd tried to be mad at Archer, on multiple occasions, but I'd failed every single time.

"I know I have no right whatsoever to be here right now, especially considering how I left." Archer stopped pacing and sat down next to me. "But I had to come see you. I had to tell you the truth even if you don't want to hear it."

"Oh?" I asked. "And what's that?"

"I love you," he said, and my breath caught in my chest. "I love you, Honor. I love how you read books, real books, and even carry them to parties. Sometimes leaving them behind by accident."

My eyes filled, but he kept going.

"I love the quirky clothes you wear, even when I don't know what they're about. I love the way you just blurt out exactly what you're feeling. I love how beautiful you are, inside and out."

His hand went to my cheek then slowly moved into my hair.

"I love your writing, too. The article you did about me was way too flattering by the way. You made me sound far more perfect than I am."

A small laugh escaped. "I wrote it before you sent me that text," I choked.

"I hate myself for sending that to you, for hurting you like that."

"S'okay. Your family needed you."

"No, it's not," he said, staring into my eyes. "And

they do need me, but you needed me, too. I didn't think I could be there for everyone, just thought I'd let you down over and over, but now, I know I was just being an idiot. I'll never forgive myself, Honor. But if you'd let me, I'll do my best to make it up to you. Every day from here on out. Please, will you give me a second chance?"

Archer's words were so sincere. The way he was looking at me as he waited for an answer made my whole body come alive. Still, it took me a minute to believe this was real. Before I could respond, he spoke again.

"Oh, I almost forgot. Before you answer," he said, looking a bit nervous, "I brought you something."

It was a testament to how distracting he was that I hadn't noticed the books. Archer lifted them, three in total, before gently placing the stack into my lap. My eyes moved over the hardbacks. I could tell they were old just from the look and heft of them. Opening the top one, I read the title page...and stared.

"*Jane Eyre,*" I murmured, "An Autobiography edited by Currer Bell..."

Out of my peripheral vision, I saw Archer nod, could feel his eyes on my face. "It was Charlotte Brontë's pen name. The book was originally published in three volumes."

I swallowed. "I know."

"It's a first edition," he added. "I thought you might like it."

My eyes met his then. "Like it? Archer, I love it. But this is way too much. I can't possibly accept."

"Yes, you can," he said simply.

"But...I...How did you even manage to get these?"

"My Aunt Genevieve collects rare books." He shrugged as if he hadn't just handed me a priceless piece of British literature. "She also lives about thirty minutes away and is a total romantic. When I told her how badly I'd messed up, that I needed them to try and get the girl I love back, she handed them over, kissed me on the cheek and wished me good luck."

The girl I love.

My heart felt too full to speak, but I forced out the words.

"So, she just gave them to you...to give to me?"

Seeing my expression, he nodded. "I've always been her favorite. At least that's what she says— though I think she says that to all of us, loves me and my siblings equally."

I closed the book as carefully as possible, cleared my throat. "Are you trying to bribe me with books?"

"I would never."

"Because that would be kind of unfair. You know how much I love them, especially Jane."

"I do." His eyes were cautious, but I could hear the smile in his voice. "That book brought us together. I was hoping it might do it again. So, will you give me another chance?"

After giving myself a moment, taking in a much-needed inhale and exhale, I gave him the only response in my heart.

"Of course, I will," I said. "How could I not?"

Archer closed his eyes in what looked like relief.

"Thank God," he said and pulled me to him for a long breathless kiss. His eyes searched mine as he leaned back a bit. "Not that I'm questioning it, and I probably shouldn't press my luck. But why? Why are you giving me a second chance? Was it my awesome groveling or the books?"

"Neither. It's just..." I shook my head. "I'd rather be with you, just breathing the same air as you, than anywhere with anyone else."

I heard his breath catch this time, but I'd only spoken the truth.

"And because I love you, too."

The smile that filled his usually frowning face was a stunner. Archer O'Brien was a lot of things: Captain to the Wolves baseball team, the oldest of six siblings, one of five brothers, a man who hardly ever smiled, a superstar athlete, the only person who made my heart feel like it was about to beat right out of my chest.

We may have started out as a mistake.

But he was the best mistake I'd ever made.

* * *

A c k n o w l e d g m e n t s

Archer and Honor—and all of the O'Briens—have been living in my head for a while now. I've always loved stories about families that stick together through thick and thin, who always have each other's backs. And I've also always loved sports romance! *The Best Mistake* is my take on both and my first New Adult romance. I wrote it just for fun, to feed my soul, but I hope it will touch readers' hearts as well :).

There are a lot of people to thank, so here we go!

To Susan Elizabeth Phillips (who will most likely never read this), thank you for the *Chicago Stars* and for introducing me to sports romance. I've loved the genre ever since.

To Julia Quinn (who will also never read this lol), thank you for the Bridgertons, one of my favorite fictional families of all time.

COOKIE O'GORMAN

To Mom, thank you for reading and saying you enjoy my books. You have no idea how much that pushes me to keep writing.

To Aunt Pat, thank you for being my best friend and for being as excited as I was when the idea for the O'Briens came all those years ago. I love you and miss you every day.

To Aunt Colleen, thank you for giving me that bag of romance books. I can't wait to read your book when it comes out.

To Sarah Hansen, thank you for this amazing cover! You rock!!!

To Stacey Blake, thank you for being SO awesome & making the book interior so pretty!

To whoever posted that pic of the Burgess brothers, thank you for the early inspiration!

To my literature teachers (and all teachers), thank you for all that you do. It really matters.

To my readers, thank you so much for your support! I'm so thankful for every encouraging message you've sent, every kind review, blog post and comment! Thank you for lifting my spirits and making the publishing journey a wonderful one!

330

And to YOU. Thank you so much for giving *The Best Mistake* a chance! My first New Adult sports romance, yay!!! If you're reading this, you're holding a piece of my heart in your hands. I hope it made you laugh/swoon/geek out lol. And I hope you enjoyed Archer and Honor's story as much as I enjoyed writing it <3. If you fell in love with Archer, Baylor, Chase, Dex, Emmy or Finn, please let me know lol! I love hearing from readers! And if you're that girl (or guy) who prefers paperbacks over parties, just know: You are not alone :).

About the Author

Cookie O'Gorman writes stories filled with humor and heart for the nerd in all of us. Fiery first kisses, snappy dialogue, smart girls, swoonworthy boys, and unbreakable friendships are featured in each of her books.

Cookie is a hopeless romantic, a Harry Potter aficionado, and a supporter of all things dork. Chocolate, Chinese food, and Asian dramas are her kryptonite. Above all, she believes that real life has enough sorrow and despair—which is why she always tries to give her characters a happy ending. She is the author of *Adorkable*, *Ninja Girl*, *The Unbelievable, Inconceivable, Unforeseeable Truth About Ethan Wilder* and *The Good Girl's Guide to*

Being Bad.   She is also the author of NA sports romance, *The Best Mistake*.

Whether it's about her books or just to fan-girl, Cookie would love to hear from you!

Website: http://cookieogorman.com

Twitter: http://www.twitter.com/CookieOwrites

Instagram:
https://www.instagram.com/cookieogorman

Facebook: www.facebook.com/cookieogorman

For the latest news on Cookie's books, access to fun, free content and monthly giveaways, subscribe to *The Cookie Jar* Newsletter!

Printed in Great Britain
by Amazon